I0764531

Jack o' Judgment

Books by Edgar Wallace —

Sanders of the River
Bones
Bosambo of the River
Bones in London
The Keepers of the King's Peace
The Council of Justice
The Duke in the Suburbs
The People of the River
Down under Donovan
Private Selby
The Admirable Carfew
The Man Who Bought London
The Just Men of Cordova
The Secret House
Kate, Plus Ten
Lieutenant Bones
The Adventures of Heine
Jack o' Judgment
The Daffodil Mystery
The Nine Bears
The Book of all Power
Mr. Justice Maxell
The Books of Bart
The Dark Eyes of London
Chick
Sandi, the King-Maker
The Three Oak Mystery
The Fellowship of the Frog
Blue Hand
Grey Timothy
A Debt Discharged
Those Folk of Bulboro
The Man Who Was Nobody
The Green Rust
The Fourth Plague
The River of Stars

Jack o' Judgment

Edgar Wallace

Ægypan Press

Special thanks to D. Alexander, Martin Pettit, and the Online Distributed Proofreading Team (which can be found at http://www.pgdp.net). Thanks also to The Internet Archive.

Jack o' Judgment
A publication of
ÆGYPAN PRESS

www.aegypan.com

Chapter I

THE KNAVE OF CLUBS

They picked up the young man called "Snow" Gregory from a Lambeth gutter, and he was dead before the policeman on point duty in Waterloo Road, who had heard the shots, came upon the scene.

He had been shot in his tracks on a night of snow and storm and none saw the murder.

When they got him to the mortuary and searched his clothes they found nothing except a little tin box of white powder which proved to be cocaine, and a playing card – the Jack of Clubs!

His associates had called him "Snow" Gregory because he was a doper, and cocaine is invariably referred to as "snow" by all its votaries. He was a gambler too, and he had been associated with Colonel Dan Boundary in certain of his business enterprises. That was all. The colonel knew nothing of the young man's antecedents except that he had been an Oxford man who had come down in the world. The colonel added a few particulars designed, as it might seem to the impartial observer, to prove that he, the colonel, had ever been an uplifting quantity. (This colonelcy was an honorary title which he held by custom rather than by law.)

There were people who said that "Snow" Gregory, in his more exalted moments, talked too much for the colonel's comfort, but people were very ready to talk unkindly of the colonel, whose wealth was an offence and a shame.

So they buried "Snow" Gregory, the unknown, and a jury of his fellow-countrymen returned a verdict of "Willful murder against some person or persons unknown."

And that was the end of a sordid tragedy, it seemed, until three months later there dawned upon Colonel Boundary's busy life a brand new and alarming factor.

One morning there arrived at his palatial flat in Albemarle Place a letter. This he opened because it was marked "Private and Personal." It was not a letter at all – as it proved – but a soiled and stained playing card, the Knave of Clubs.

He looked at the thing in perplexity, for the fate of his erstwhile assistant had long since passed from his mind. Then he saw writing on the margin of the card, and twisting it sideways read:

"JACK O' JUDGMENT"

Nothing more!

"Jack o' Judgment!"

The colonel screwed up his tired eyes as if to shut out a vision.

"Faugh!" he said in disgust and dropped the pasteboard into his waste-paper basket.

For he had seen a vision – a white face, unshaven and haggard, its lips parted in a little grin, the smile of "Snow" Gregory on the last time they had met.

Later came other cards and unpleasant, not to say disconcerting happenings, and the colonel, taking counsel with himself, determined to kill two birds with one stone.

It was a daring and audacious thing to have done, and none but Colonel Dan Boundary would have taken the risk. He knew better than anybody else that Stafford King had devoted the whole of his time for the past three years to smashing the Boundary Gang. He knew that this grave young man with the steady, grey eyes, who sat on the other side of the big Louis XV table in the ornate private office of the Spillsbury Syndicate, had won his way to the chief position in the Criminal Intelligence Department by sheer genius, and that he was, of all men, the most to be feared.

No greater contrast could be imagined than that which was presented between the two protagonists – the refined, almost æsthetic chief of police on the one hand, the big commanding figure of the redoubtable colonel on the other.

Boundary with his black hair parted in the center of his sleek head, his big weary eyes, his long, yellow walrus moustache, his double chin, his breadth and girth, his enormous hairy hands, now laid upon the table, might stand for force, brutal, remorseless, untiring. He stood for cunning too – the cunning of the stalking tiger.

Stafford was watching him with dispassionate interest. He may have been secretly amused at the man's sheer daring, but if he was, his inscrutable face displayed no such emotion.

"I dare say, Mr. King," said the colonel, in his slow, heavy way, "you think it is rather remarkable in all the circumstances that I should ask for you? I dare say," he went on, "my business associates will think the same, considering all the unpleasantness we have had."

Stafford King made no reply. He sat erect, alert and watchful.

"Give a dog a bad name and hang him," said the colonel sententiously. "For twenty years I've had to fight the unjust suspicions of my enemies. I've been libeled," he shook his head sorrowfully. "I don't suppose there's anybody been libeled more than me – and my business associates. I've had the police nosing – I mean investigating – into my affairs, and I'll be straight with you, Mr. Stafford King, and tell you that when it came to my ears and the ears of my business associates, that you had been put on the job of watching poor old Dan Boundary, I was glad."

"Is that intended as a compliment?" asked Stafford, with the faintest suspicion of a smile.

"Every way," said the colonel emphatically. "In the first place, Mr. King, I know that you are the straightest and most honest police official in England, and possibly in the world. All I want is justice. My life is an open book, which courts the fullest investigation."

He spread out his huge hands as though inviting an even closer inspection than had been afforded him hitherto.

Mr. Stafford King made no reply. He knew, very well he knew, the stories which had been told about the Boundary Gang. He knew a little and guessed a lot about its extraordinary ramifications. He was well aware, at any rate, that it was rich, and that this slow-speaking man could command millions. But he was far from desiring to endorse the colonel's inferred claim as to the purity of his business methods.

He leant a little forward.

"I am sure you didn't send for me to tell me all about your hard lot, colonel," he said, a little ironically.

The colonel shook his head.

"I wanted to get to know you," he said with fine frankness. "I've heard a lot about you, Mr. King. I am told you do nothing but specialize on the Boundary enterprises, and I tell you, sir, that you can't know too much about me, nor can I know too much about you."

He paused.

"But you're quite right when you say that I didn't ask you to come here – and a great honor it is for a big police chief to spare time to see me – to discuss the past. It is the present I want to talk to you about."

Stafford King nodded.

"I'm a law-abiding citizen," said the colonel unctuously, "and anything I can do to assist the law, why, I'm going to do it. I wrote you on this matter about a fortnight ago."

He opened a drawer and took out a large envelope embossed with a monogram of the Spillsbury Syndicate. This he opened and extracted a plain playing-card. It was a white-backed card of superfine texture, gilt-edged, and bore a familiar figure.

"The Knave of Clubs," said Stafford King lifting his eyes.

"The Jack of Clubs," said the colonel gravely; "that is its name I understand, for I am not a gambling man."

He did not bat a lid nor did Stafford King smile.

"I remember," said the detective chief, "you received one before. You wrote to my department about it."

The colonel nodded.

"Read what's written underneath."

King lifted the card nearer to his eyes. The writing was almost microscopic and read:

"Save crime, save worry, save all unpleasantness. Give back the property you stole from Spillsbury."

It was signed "Jack o' Judgment."

King put the card down and looked across at the colonel.

"What happened after the last card came?" he asked, "there was a burglary or something, wasn't there?"

"The last card," said the colonel, clearing his throat, "contained a diabolical and unfounded charge that I and my business associates had robbed Mr. George Fetter, the Manchester merchant, of £60,000 by means of card tricks – a low practice of which I would not be guilty nor would any of my business associates. My friends and myself knowing nothing of any card game, we of course refused to pay Mr. Fetter, and I am sure Mr. Fetter would be the last person who would ask us to do so. As a matter of fact, he did give us bills for £60,000, but that was in relation to a sale of property. I cannot imagine that Mr. Fetter would ever take money from us or that he knew of this business – I hope not, because he seems a very respectable – gentleman."

The detective looked at the card again.

"What is this story of the Spillsbury deal?" he asked.

"What is that story of the Spillsbury deal?" said the colonel.

He had a trick of repeating questions – it was a trick which frequently gave him a very necessary breathing space.

"Why, there's nothing to it. I bought the motor works in Coventry. I admit it was a good bargain. There's no law against making a profit. You know what business is."

The detective knew what business was. But Spillsbury was young and wild, and his wildness assumed an unpleasant character. It was the kind of wildness which people do not talk about – at least, not nice people. He had inherited a considerable fortune, and the control of four factories, the best of which was the one under discussion.

"I know Spillsbury," said the detective, "and I happen to know Spillsbury's works. I also know that he sold you a property worth £300,000 in the open market for a sum which was grossly inadequate – £30,000, was it not?"

"£35,000," corrected the colonel. "There's no law against making a bargain," he repeated.

"You've been very fortunate with your bargains."

Stafford King rose and picked up his hat.

"You bought Transome's Hotel from young Mrs. Rachemeyer for a sum which was less than a twentieth of its worth. You bought Lord Bethon's slate quarries for £12,000 – their value in the open market was at least £100,000. For the past fifteen years you have been acquiring property at an amazing rate – and at an amazing price."

The colonel smiled.

"You're paying me a great compliment, Mr. Stafford King," he said with a touch of sarcasm, "and I will never forget it. But don't let us get away from the object of your coming. I am reporting to you, as a police officer, that I have been threatened by a blackguard, a thief, and very likely a murderer. I will not be responsible for any action I may take – Jack o' Judgment indeed!" he growled.

"Have you ever seen him?" asked Stafford.

The colonel frowned.

"He's alive, ain't he?" he growled. "If I'd seen him, do you think he'd be writing me letters? It is your job to pinch him. If you people down at Scotland Yard spent less time poking into the affairs of honest business men –"

Stafford King was smiling now, frankly and undisguisedly. His grey eyes were creased with silent laughter.

"Colonel, you have *some* nerve!" he said admiringly, and with no other word he left the room.

Chapter II

JACK O' JUDGMENT — HIS CARD

The wrong side of a stage door was the outside on a night such as this was. The rain was bucketing down and a chill northwester howled up the narrow passage leading from the main street to the tiny entry.

But the outside, and the darkest corner of the *cul-de-sac* whence the stage door of the Orpheum Music Hall was reached, satisfied Stafford King. He drew further into the shadow at sight of the figure which picked a finicking way along the passage and paused only at the open doorway to furl his umbrella.

Pinto Silva, immaculately attired with a white rose in the buttonhole of his faultless dress-jacket, had no doubt in his mind as to which was the most desirable side of the stage door. He passed in, nodding carelessly to the doorkeeper.

"A rotten night, Joe," he said. "Miss White hasn't gone yet, has she?"

"No, sir," said the man obsequiously, "she's only just left the stage a few minutes. Shall I tell her you're here, sir?"

Pinto shook his head.

He was a good-looking man of thirty-five. There were some who would go further and describe him as handsome, though his peculiar style of good looks might not be to everybody's taste. The olive complexion, the black eyes, the well-curled moustache and the effeminate chin had their attractions, and Pinto Silva admitted modestly in his reminiscent moments that there were women who had raved about him.

"Miss White is in No. 6," said the doorkeeper. "Shall I send somebody along to tell her you're here?"

"You needn't trouble," said the other, "she won't be long now."

The girl, hurrying along the corridor, fastening her coat as she came, stopped dead at the sight of him and a look of annoyance came to her face. She was tall for a girl, perfectly proportioned and something more than pretty.

Pinto lifted his hat with a smile.

"I've just been in front, Miss White. An excellent performance!"

"Thank you," she said simply. "I did not see you."

He nodded.

There was a complacency in his nod which irritated her. It almost seemed to infer that she was not speaking the truth and that he was humoring her in her deception.

"You're quite comfortable?" he asked.

"Quite," she replied politely.

She was obviously anxious to end the interview, and at a loss as to how she could.

"Dressing room comfortable, everybody respectful and all that sort of thing?" he asked. "Just say the word, if they give you trouble or cheek, and I'll have them kicked out whoever they are, from the manager downwards."

"Oh, thank you," she said hurriedly, "everybody is most polite and nice." She held out her hand. "I am afraid I must go now. A – a friend is waiting for me."

"One minute, Miss White." He licked his lips, and there was an unaccustomed embarrassment in his manner. "Maybe you'll come along one night after the show and have a little supper. You know I'm very keen on you and all that sort of thing."

"I know you're very keen on me and all that sort of thing," said Maisie White, a note of irony in her voice, "but unfortunately I'm not very keen on supper and all that sort of thing."

She smiled and again held out her hand.

"I'll say good night now."

"Do you know, Maisie –" he began.

"Good night," she said and brushed past him.

He looked after her as she disappeared into the darkness, a little frown gathering on his forehead, then with a shrug of his shoulders he walked slowly back to the doorkeeper's office.

"Send somebody to get my car," he snapped.

He waited impatiently, chewing his cigar, till the dripping figure of the doorkeeper reappeared with the information that the car was at the end of the passage. He put up his umbrella and walked through the pelting rain to where his limousine stood.

Pinto Silva was angry, and his anger was of the hateful, smoldering type which grew in strength from moment to moment and from hour to hour. How dare she treat him like this? She, who owed her engagement to his influence, and whose fortune and future were in his hands. He would speak to the colonel and the colonel could speak to her father. He had had enough of this.

He recognized with a start that he was afraid of the girl. It was incredible, but it was true. He had never felt that way to a woman before, but there was something in her eyes, a cold disdain which cowed even as it maddened him.

The car drew up before a block of buildings in a deserted West End thoroughfare. He flashed on the electric light and saw that the hour was a little after eleven. The last thing in the world he wanted was to take part in a conference that night. But if he wanted anything less, it was to cross the colonel at this moment of crisis.

He walked through the dark vestibule and entered an automatic lift, which carried him to the third floor. Here, the landing and the corridor were illuminated by one small electric lamp sufficient to light him to the heavy walnut doors which led to the office of the Spillsbury Syndicate. He opened the door with a latchkey and found himself in a big lobby, carpeted and furnished in good style.

A man was sitting before a radiator, a paper pad upon his knees, and he was making notes with a pencil. He looked up startled as the other entered and nodded. It was Olaf Hanson, the colonel's clerk – and Olaf, with his flat expressionless face, and his stiff upstanding hair, always reminded Pinto of a Struwwelpeter which had been cropped.

"Hullo, Hanson, is the colonel inside?"

The man nodded.

"They're waiting for you," he said.

His voice was hard and unsympathetic, and his thin lips snapped out every syllable.

"Aren't you coming in?" asked Pinto in surprise, his hand upon the door.

The man called Hanson shook his head.

"I've got to go to the colonel's flat," he said, "to get some papers. Besides, they don't want me."

He smiled quickly and wanly. It was a grimace rather than an expression of amusement and Pinto eyed him narrowly. He had, however, the good sense to ask no further questions. Turning the handle of the door, he walked into the large, ornate apartment.

In the center of the room was a big table and the chairs at its sides were, for the most part, filled.

He dropped into a seat on the colonel's right and nodded to the others at the table. Most of the principals were there – "Swell" Crewe, Jackson, Cresswell, and at the farther end of the table, Lollie Marsh with her baby face and her permanent expression of open-mouthed wonder.

"Where's White?" he asked.

The colonel was reading a letter and did not immediately reply. Presently he took off his pince-nez and put them into his pocket.

"Where's White?" he repeated. "White isn't here. No, White isn't here," he repeated significantly.

"What's wrong?" asked Pinto quickly.

The colonel scratched his chin and looked up to the ceiling.

"I'm settling up this Spillsbury business," he said. "White isn't in it."

"Why not?" asked Pinto.

"He never was in it," said the colonel evasively. "It was not the kind of business that White would like to be in. I guess he's getting religious or something, or maybe it's that daughter of his."

The eyelids of Pinto Silva narrowed at the reference to Maisie White and he was on the point of remarking that he had just left her, but changed his mind.

"Does she know anything about – about her father?" he asked.

The colonel smiled.

"Why, no – unless you've told her."

"I'm not on those terms," said Pinto savagely. "I'm getting tired of that girl's airs and graces, colonel, after what we've done for her!"

"You'll get tireder, Pinto," said a voice from the end of the table and he turned round to meet the laughing eyes of Lollie Marsh.

"What do you mean?" he asked.

"I've been out taking a look at her today," she said, and the colonel scowled at her.

"You were out taking a look at something else if I remember rightly," he said quietly. "I told you to get after Stafford King."

"And I got after him," she said, "and after the girl too."

"What do you mean?"

"That's a bit of news for you, isn't it?" She was delighted to drop the bombshell: "you can't shadow Stafford King without crossing the tracks of Maisie White."

The colonel uttered an exclamation.

"What do you mean?" he asked again.

"Didn't you know they were acquainted? Didn't you know that Stafford King goes down to Horsham to see her, and takes her to dinner twice a week?"

They looked at one another in consternation. Maisie White was the daughter of a man who, next to the colonel, had been the most daring member of the gang, who had organized more coups than any other man, save its leader. The news that the daughter of Solomon White was meeting the Chief of the Criminal Intelligence Department, was incredible and stunning.

"So that's it, is it?" said the colonel, licking his dry lips. "That's why Solomon White's fed up with the life and wants to break away."

He turned to Pinto Silva, whose face was set and hard.

"I thought you were keen on that girl, Pinto," he said coarsely. "We left the way open to you. What do you know about it?"

"Nothing," said the man shortly. "I don't believe it."

"Don't believe it," broke in the girl. "Listen! There was a matinée at the Orpheum today and King went there. I followed him in and got a seat next to him and tried to get friendly. But he had only eyes for the girl on the stage, and I might as well have been the paper on the wall for all the notice he took of me. After her turn, he went out and waited for her at the stage door. They went to Roymoyers for tea. I went back to the theater and saw her dresser. She is the woman I recommended when Pinto put her on the stage."

"What sort of work is Maisie doing?" asked the saturnine Crewe.

"Male impersonations," said the girl. "Say! she looks dandy in a man's kit! She's the best male impersonator I've ever seen. Why, when she talks –"

"Never mind about that," interrupted the colonel, "what did you discover?"

"I discovered that Stafford King comes regularly to the theater, that he takes her to dinner and that he visits the house at Horsham."

"Solly never told me that – the swine!" rapped the colonel, "he's going to double-cross us, that fellow."

"I don't believe it."

It was Crewe that spoke. "Swell" Crewe, whose boast it was that he had a suit for every day in the year.

"I know Solomon and I've known him for years," he said. "I know him as well as you, colonel. As far as we are concerned, Solly is straight. I'm not denying the possibility that he wants to break away, but that's only natural. He's a man with a daughter, and he's made his pile, but I'll stake my life that he'll never double-cross us."

"Double-cross us?" the colonel had recovered his wonted equanimity. "What has he to 'double-cross'?" he demanded almost jovially. "We have a straightforward business! I am not aware that any of us are guilty of dishonest actions. Double-cross! Bah!"

He brought his big hand down with a thump on the table, and they knew from experience that this was the gavel of the chairman that ended all discussions.

"Now, gentlemen," said the colonel, "let us get to business. Ask Hanson to come in – he's got the figures. It is the last lot of figures of ours that he'll ever handle," he added.

Somebody went to the door of the anteroom and called the secretary, but there was no reply.

"He's gone out."

"Gone out?" said the colonel and bent his brows. "Who told him to go out? Never mind, he'll be back in a minute. Shut the door."

He lifted a deed-box from the floor at his feet, placed it on the table, opened it with a key attached to his watch-chain and removed a bundle of documents.

"We're going to settle the Spillsbury business tonight," he said. "Spillsbury looks like squealing."

"Where is he?" asked Pinto.

"In an inebriates' home," said the colonel grimly; "it seems there are some trustees to his father's estate who are likely to question the legality of the transfers. But I've had the best legal opinion in London and there is no doubt that our position is safe. The only thing we've got to do tonight is to make absolutely sure that all those fool letters he wrote to Lollie have been destroyed."

"You've got them?" said the girl quickly.

"I had them?" said the colonel, "and I burned them all except one when the transfer was completed. And the question is, gentlemen," he said, "shall we burn the last?"

He took from the bundle before him an envelope and held it up.

"I kept this in case there was anything coming, but if he's in a booze home, why, he's not going to be influenced by the threat of publishing a slushy letter to a girl. I guess his trustees are not going to be very much influenced either. On the other hand, if this letter were found among business documents, it would look pretty bad for us."

"Found by whom?" asked Pinto.

"By the police," said the colonel calmly.

"Police?"

The colonel nodded.

"They're getting after us, but you needn't be alarmed," he said. "King is working to get a case, and he is not above applying for a search warrant. But I'm not scared of the police so much." His voice slowed and he spoke with greater emphasis. "I guess there are enough court cards in the Boundary pack to beat that combination. It's the Jack –"

"The Jack – ha! ha! ha!"

It was a shrill bubble of laughter which cut into his speech and the colonel leapt to his feet, his hand dropping to his hip-pocket. The door had opened and closed so silently that none had heard it, and a figure stood confronting them.

It was clad from head to foot in a long coat of black silk, which shimmered in the half-light of the electrolier. The hands were gloved, the head covered with a soft slouch hat and the face hidden behind a white silk handkerchief.

The colonel's hand was in his hip-pocket when he thought better and raised both hands in the air. There was something peculiarly businesslike in the long-barreled revolver which the intruder held, in spite of the silver-plating and the gold inlay along the chased barrel.

"Everybody's hands in the air," said the Jack shrilly, "right up to the beautiful sky! Yours too, Lollie. Stand away from the table, everybody, and back to the wall. For the Jack o' Judgment is amongst you and life is full of amazing possibilities!"

They backed from the table, peering helplessly at the two unwinking eyes which showed through the holes in the handkerchief.

"Back to the wall, my pretties," chuckled the Thing. "I'm going to make you laugh and you'll want some support. I'm going to make you rock with joy and merriment!"

The figure had moved to the table, and all the time it spoke its nimble fingers were turning over the piles of documents which the colonel had disgorged from the dispatch box.

"I'm going to tell you a comical tale about a gang of blackmailers."

"You're a liar," said the colonel hoarsely.

"About a gang of blackmailers," said the Jack with shrill laughter, "fellows who didn't work like common blackmailers, nor demand money. Oh, no! not naughty blackmailers! They got the fools and the vicious in their power and made them sell things for hundreds of pounds that were worth thousands. And they were such a wonderful crowd! They were such wonderfully amusing fellows. There was Dan Boundary who started life by robbing his dead mother, there was 'Swell' Crewe, who was once a gentleman and is now a thief!"

"Damn you!" said Crewe, lurching forward, but the gun swung round on him and he stopped.

"There was Lollie who would sell her own child –"

"I have no child," half-screamed the girl.

"Think again, Lollie darling – dear little soul!"

He stopped. The envelope that his fingers had been seeking was found. He slipped it beneath the black silk cloak and in two bounds was at the door.

"Send for the police," he mocked. "Send for the police, Dan! Get Stafford King, the eminent chief. Tell him I called! My card!"

With a dexterous flip of his fingers he sent a little pasteboard planing across the room. In an instant the door opened and closed upon the intruder and he was gone.

For a second there was silence, and then, with a little sob, Lollie Marsh collapsed in a heap on the floor. Colonel Dan Boundary looked from one white face to the other.

"There's a hundred thousand pounds for any one of you who gets that fellow," he said, breathing hard, "whether it is man or woman."

Chapter III

THE DECOY

Colonel Boundary, sitting at his desk the morning after, pushed a bell. It was answered by the thickset Olaf. He was dressed, as usual, in black from head to foot and the colonel eyed him thoughtfully.

"Hanson," he said, "has Miss Marsh come?"

"Yes, she has come," said the other resentfully.

"Tell her I want her," said the colonel and then as the man was leaving the room: "Where did you get to last night when I wanted you?"

"I was out," said the man shortly. "I get some time for myself, I suppose?"

The colonel nodded slowly.

"Sure you do, Hanson."

His tone was mild, and that spelt danger to Hanson, had he known it. This was the third sign of rebellion which the man had shown in the past week.

"What's happened to your temper this morning, Hanson?" he asked.

"Everything," exploded the man and in his agitation his foreign origin was betrayed by his accent. "You tell me I shall haf plenty money, thousands of pounds! You say I go to my brother in America. Where is dot money? I go in March, I go in May, I go in July, still I am here!"

"My good friend," said the colonel, "you're too impatient. This is not a moment I can allow you to go away. You're getting nervous, that's what's the matter with you. Perhaps I'll let you have a holiday next week."

"Nervous!" roared the man. "Yes, I am. All the time I feel eyes on me! When I walk in the street, every man I meet is a policeman. When I go to bed, I hear nothing but footsteps creeping in the passage outside my room."

"Old Jack, eh?" said the colonel, eyeing him narrowly.

Hanson shivered.

He had seen the Jack o' Judgment once. A figure in gossamer silk who had stood beside the bed in which the Scandinavian lay and had talked wisdom whilst Olaf quaked in a muck sweat of fear.

The colonel did not know this. He was under the impression that the appearance of the previous night had constituted the first of this mysterious menace.

So he nodded again.

"Send Miss Marsh to me," he said.

Hanson would have got on his nerves if he had nerves. The man, at any rate, was becoming an intolerable nuisance. The colonel marked him down as one of the problems calling for early solution.

The secretary had not been gone more than a few seconds before the door opened again and the girl came in. She was tall, pretty in a doll-like way, with an aura of golden hair about her small head. She might have been more than pretty but for her eyes, which were too light a shade of blue to be beautiful. She was expensively gowned and walked with the easy swing of one whose position was assured.

"Good morning, Lollie," said the colonel. "Did you see him again?"

She nodded.

"I got a pretty good view of him," she said.

"Did he see you?"

She smiled.

"I don't think so," she said; "besides, what does it matter if he did?"

"Was the girl with him?"

She shook her head.

"Well?" asked the colonel after a pause. "Can you do anything with him?"

She pursed her lips.

If she had expected the colonel to refer to their terrifying experience of the night before, she was to be disappointed. The hard eyes of the man compelled her to keep to the matter under discussion.

"He looks pretty hard," said the girl. "He is not the man to fall for that heart-to-heart stuff."

"What do you mean?" asked the colonel.

"Just that," said the girl with a shrug. "I can't imagine his picking me up and taking me to dinner and pouring out the secrets of his young heart at the second bottle."

"Neither can I," said the colonel thoughtfully. "You're a pretty clever girl, Lollie, and I'm going to make it worth your while to get close to that fellow. He's the one man in Scotland Yard that we want to put out of business. Not that we've anything to be afraid of," he added vaguely, "but he's just interfering with –"

He paused for a word.

"With business," said the girl. "Oh, come off it, colonel! Just tell me how far you want me to go."

"You've got to go to the limit," said the other decidedly. "You've got to put him as wrong as you can. He must be compromised up to his neck."

"What about my young reputation?" asked the girl with a grimace.

"If you lose it, we'll buy you another," said the colonel dryly, "and I reckon it's about time you had another one, Lollie."

The girl fingered her chin thoughtfully.

"It is not going to be easy," she said again. "It isn't going to be like young Spillsbury – Pinto Silva could have done that job without help – or Solomon White even."

"You can shut up about Spillsbury," growled the colonel. "I've told you to forget everything that has ever happened in our business! And I've told you a hundred times not to mention Pinto or any of the other men in this business! You can do as you're told! And take that look off your face!"

He rose with extraordinary agility and leant over, glowering at the girl.

"You've been getting a bit too fresh lately, Lollie, and giving yourself airs! You don't try any of that grand lady stuff with me, d'ye hear?"

There was nothing suave in the colonel's manner, nothing slow or ponderous or courtly. He spoke rapidly and harshly and revealed the brute that many suspected but few knew.

"I've no more respect for women than I have for men, understand! If you ever get gay with me, I'll take your neck in my hand like that," he clenched his two fists together with a horribly suggestive motion and the frightened girl watched him, fascinated. "I'll break you as if you were a bit of china! I'll tear you as if you were a rag! You needn't think you'll ever get away from me – I'll follow you to the ends of the earth.

You're paid like a queen and treated like a queen and you play straight – there was a man called 'Snow' Gregory once –"

The trembling girl was on her feet now, her face ashen white.

"I'm sorry, colonel," she faltered. "I didn't intend giving you offence. I – I –"

She was on the verge of tears when the colonel, with a quick gesture, motioned her back to the chair. His rage subsided as suddenly as it had risen.

"Now do as you're told, Lollie," he said calmly. "Get after that young fellow and don't come back to me until you've got him."

She nodded, not trusting herself to speak, and almost tiptoed from his dread presence.

At the door he stopped her.

"As to Maisie," he said, "why, you can leave Maisie to me."

Chapter IV

THE MISSING HANSON

Colonel Dan Boundary descended slowly from the Ford taxi-cab which had brought him up from Horsham station and surveyed without emotion the domicile of his partner. It was Colonel Boundary's boast that he was in the act of lathering his face on the tenth floor of a Californian hotel when the earthquake began, and that he finished his shaving operations, took his bath and dressed himself before the earth had ceased to tremble.

"I shall want you again, so you had better wait," he said to the driver and passed through the wooden gates toward Rose Lodge.

He stopped halfway up the path, having now a better view of the house. It was a red brick villa, the home of a well-to-do man. The trim lawn with its border of rose trees, the little fountain playing over the rockery, the quality of the garden furniture within view and the general air of comfort which pervaded the place, suggested the home of a prosperous City man, one of those happy creatures who have never troubled to get themselves in line for millions, but have lived happily between the four and five figure mark.

Colonel Boundary grunted and continued his walk. A trim maid opened the door to him and by her blank look it was evident that he was not a frequent visitor.

"Boundary – just say Boundary," said the colonel in a deep voice which carried to the remotest part of the house.

He was shown to the drawing room and again found much that interested him. He felt no twinge of pity at the thought that Solomon White would very soon exchange this almost luxury for the bleak discomfort of a prison cell, and not even the sight of the girl who came through the door to greet him brought him a qualm.

"You want to see my father, colonel?" she asked.

Her tone was cold but polite. The colonel had never been a great favorite of Maisie White's, and now it required a considerable effort on her part to hide her deep aversion.

"Do I want to see your father?" said Colonel Boundary. "Why, yes, I think I do and I want to see you too, and I'd just as soon see you first, before I speak to Solly."

She sat down, a model of patient politeness, her hands folded on her lap. In the light of day she was pretty, straight of back, graceful as to figure and the clear grey eyes which met his faded blue, were very understanding.

"Miss White," he said, "we have been very good to you."

"We?" repeated the girl.

"We," nodded the colonel. "I speak for myself and my business associates. If Solomon had ever told you the truth you would know that you owe all your education, your beautiful home," he waved his hand, "to myself and my business associates." His tongue rolled round the last two words. They were favorites of his.

She nodded her head slightly.

"I was under the impression that I owed it to my father," she said, with a hint of irony in her voice, "for I suppose that he earned all he has."

"You suppose that he earned all that he has?" repeated the colonel. "Well, very likely you are right. He has earned more than he has got but pay-day is near at hand."

There was no mistaking the menace in his tone, but the girl made no comment. She knew that there had been trouble. She knew that her father had for days been locked in his study and had scarcely spoken a word to anybody.

"I saw you the other night," said the colonel, changing the direction of his attack. "I saw you at the Orpheum. Pinto Silva came with me. We were in the stage box."

"I saw you," said the girl quietly.

"A very good performance, considering you're a kid," said Boundary; "in fact, Pinto says you're the best mimic he has ever seen on the stage –" He paused – "Pinto got you your contracts."

She nodded.

"I am very grateful to Mr. Silva," she said.

"You have all the world before you, my girl," said Boundary in his slow, ponderous way, "a beautiful and bright future, plenty of money, pearls, diamonds," he waved his hand with a vague gesture, "and Pinto, who is the most valuable of my business associates, is very fond of you."

The girl sighed helplessly.

"I thought that matter had been finished and done with, colonel," she said. "I don't know how people in your world would regard such an offer, but in my world they would look upon it as an insult."

"And what the devil is your world?" asked the colonel, without any sign of irritation.

She rose to her feet.

"The clean, decent world," she said calmly, "the law-abiding world. The world that regards such arrangements as you suggest as infamous. It is not only the fact that Mr. Silva is already married –"

The colonel raised his hand.

"Pinto talks very seriously of getting a divorce," he said solemnly, "and when a gentleman like Pinto Silva gives his word, that ought to be sufficient for any girl. And now you have come to mention law-abiding worlds," he went on slowly, "I would like to speak of one of the law-abiders."

She knew what was coming and was silent.

"There's a young gentleman named Stafford King hanging round you." He saw her face flush but went on, "Mr. Stafford King is a policeman."

"He is an official of the Criminal Intelligence Department," said the girl, "but I don't think you would call him a policeman, would you, colonel?"

"All policemen are policemen to me," said Boundary, "and Mr. Stafford King is one of the worst of the policemen from my point of view, because he's trying to trump up a cock-and-bull story about me and get me into very serious trouble."

"I know Mr. King is connected with a great number of unpleasant cases," said the girl coolly. "It would be a coincidence if he was in a case which interested you."

"It would be a coincidence, would it?" said the colonel, nodding his huge head. "Perhaps it is a coincidence that my clerk, Hanson, has disappeared and has been seen in the company of your friend, eh? It is a coincidence that King is working on the Spillsbury case – the one case that Solly knows nothing about – eh?"

She faced him, puzzled and apprehensive.

"Where does all this lead?" she asked.

"It leads to trouble for Solly, that's all," said the colonel. "He's trying to put me away and put his business associates away, and he has got to go through the mill unless –"

"Unless what?" she asked.

"Pinto's a merciful man, I'm a merciful man. We don't want to make trouble with former business associates, but trouble there is going to be, believe me."

"What kind of trouble?" asked the girl. "If you mean that your so-called business association with my father will cease, I shall be happier. My father can earn his living and I have my stage work."

"You have your stage work," the colonel did not smile but his tone betrayed his amusement, "and your father can earn his living, eh? He can earn his living in Portland Jail," he said, raising his voice.

"For the matter of that, so can you, colonel."

The colonel turned his head slowly and surveyed the spare figure in the doorway.

"Oh, you heard me, did you, Solly," he said not unpleasantly.

"I heard you," said Solomon White, his lean face a shade whiter than the girl had ever seen it and his breathing was a little labored.

"If you are thinking of jailing me," said White, "why, I think we shall make up a pretty jolly party."

"Meaning me?" said the colonel, raising his eyebrows.

"You amongst others. Pinto Silva, 'Swell' Crewe and Selby, to name a few."

Colonel Boundary permitted himself to chuckle.

"On what charge?" he asked, "tell me that, Solly? The cleverest men in Scotland Yard have been laying for me for years and they haven't got away with it. Maybe they have your assistance and that dog Hanson –"

"That's a lie," interrupted White, "so far as I am concerned – I know nothing about Hanson."

"Hanson," said the colonel slowly, "is a thief. He bolted with £300 of mine, as I've reported to the police."

"I see," said White with a little smile of contempt, "got your charge in first, eh, colonel – discredit the witness. And what have you framed for me?"

"Nothing," said the colonel, "except this. I've just had from the bank a check for £4,000 drawn in your favor on our joint account and purporting to be signed by Silva and myself."

"As it happens," said White, "it was signed by you fellows in my presence."

The colonel shook his head.

"Obdurate to the last, brazening it out to the end – why not make a frank confession to an old business associate, Solly? I came here to see you about that check."

"That's the game, is it?" said White. "You are going to charge me with forgery, and suppose I spill it?"

"Spill what?" asked the colonel innocently. "If by 'spill' you mean make a statement to the police derogatory to myself and my business associates, what can you tell? I can bring a dozen witnesses to prove that both Pinto and I were in Brighton the morning that check was signed."

"You came up by car at night," said White harshly. "We arranged to meet outside Guildford to split the loot."

"Loot?" said Colonel Boundary, puzzled. "I don't understand you."

"I'll put it plainer," said White, his eyes like smoldering fire: "a year ago you got young Balston the shipowner to put fifty thousand pounds into a fake company."

He heard Maisie gasp, but went on.

"How you did it I'm not going to tell before the girl, but it was blackmail which you and Pinto engineered. He paid his last installment – the four thousand pounds was my share."

Colonel Boundary rose and looked at his watch.

"I have a taxi-cab waiting, and with a taxi-cab time is money. If you are going to bring in the name of an innocent young man, who will certainly deny that he had any connection with myself and my business associates, that is a matter for your own conscience. I tell you I know nothing about this check. I have made your daughter an offer."

"I can guess what it is," interrupted White, "and I can tell you this, Boundary, that if you are going to sell me, I'll be even with you, if I wait twenty years! If you imagine I am going to let my daughter into that filthy gang –" His voice broke, and it was some time before he could recover himself. "Do your worst. But I'll have you, Boundary! I don't doubt that you'll get a conviction, and you know the things that I can't talk about, and I'll have to take my medicine, but you are not going to escape."

"Wait, colonel." It was the girl who spoke in so low a voice that he would not have heard her, but that he was expecting her to speak. "Do you mean that you will – prosecute my father?"

"With law-abiding people," said the colonel profoundly, "the demands of justice come first. I must do my duty to the state, but if you should change your mind –"

"She won't change her mind," roared White.

With one stride he had passed between the colonel and the door. Only for a second he stood, and then he fell back.

"Do your worst," he said huskily, and Colonel Boundary passed out, pocketing the revolver which had come from nowhere into his hand, and presently they heard the purr of the departing motor.

He came to Horsham station in a thoughtful frame of mind. He was still thinking profoundly when he reached Victoria.

Then, as he stepped on the platform, a hand was laid on his arm, and he turned to meet the smiling face of Stafford King.

"Hullo," said the colonel, and something within him went cold.

"Sorry to break in on your reverie, colonel," said Stafford King, "but I've a warrant for your arrest."

"What is the charge?" asked the colonel, his face grey.

"Blackmail and conspiracy," said King, and saw with amazement the look of relief in the other's eyes.

Then:

"Boundary," he said between his teeth, "you thought I wanted you for 'Snow' Gregory!"

The colonel said nothing.

Chapter V

IN THE MAGISTRATE'S COURT

Never before in history had the dingy little street, in which North Lambeth Police Court stands, witnessed such scenes as were presented on that memorable 4th of December, when counsel for the Crown opened the case against Colonel Dan Boundary.

Long before the building was open the precincts of the court were besieged by people anxious to secure one of the very few seats which were available for the public. By nine o'clock it became necessary to summon a special force of police to clear a way for the numerous motorcars which came bowling from every point of the compass and which were afterwards parked in the narrow side streets, to the intense amazement and interest of the curious denizens of the unsavory neighborhood in which the court is located.

Admission was by ticket. Even the reporters, those favored servants of democracy, had need to produce a printed pass before the scrutinizing policeman at the door allowed them to enter. Every available seat had been allotted. Even the magistrate's sacristy had been invaded, and chairs stood three-deep to left and right of him.

There were some who came out of sheer morbid curiosity, in order that they might boast that they were present when this remarkable case was heard. There were others who came, inwardly quaking at the revelations which were promised or hinted at in the daily Press, for the influence which the Boundary gang exercised was wide and far-reaching.

A young man stood upon the congested pavement, watching with evident impatience the arrival of belated cars. The magistrate had already come and had disappeared behind the slate-colored gates which led to the courtyard. Stafford saw fashionably-dressed women and (with a smile) worried-looking men who were figures in the political and social world, and presently he involuntarily stepped forward into the roadway as though to meet the electric limousine which came noiselessly to the main entrance.

The solitary occupant of the car was a man of sixty – a grey-haired gentleman of medium height, dressed with scrupulous care, and wearing on his clean-shaven face a perpetual smile, as though life were an amusement which never palled.

Stafford King took the extended hand with a little twinkle in his eye.

"I was afraid we shouldn't be able to keep your place for you, Sir Stanley," he said.

Sir Stanley Belcom, First Commissioner of Criminal Intelligence, accentuated his smile.

"Well, Stafford," he drawled, "I've come to see the culminating triumph of your official career."

Stafford King made a little grimace.

"I hope so," he said dryly.

"I hope so, too," said the baronet, "yet – I'll tell you frankly, Stafford, I have a feeling that the ordinary processes of the law are inadequate to trap this organization. The law has too wide a mesh to deal with the terror which this man exercises. Such men are the only justification of lynch law, the quick, sharp justice which is administered without subtlety and without quibble."

Stafford looked at the other and made no attempt to hide his astonishment.

"You believe in – the Jack o' Judgment?" he asked.

Sir Stanley shot a swift glance at him.

"That is the bugbear of the gang, isn't it?"

"So Hanson says," replied the other. "I verily believe that Hanson is more afraid of that mysterious person than he is of Boundary himself."

The Attorney-General had begun his opening speech when the two men made their way into the crowded court and found their seats at the end of the solicitors table.

In the dock sat Colonel Boundary, the least concerned of all that assembly. The colonel was leaning forward, his arms resting on the rails, his chin on the back of his hairy hand, his eyes glued upon the grey-haired lawyer who was dispassionately opening the case.

"The contention of the Crown," the Attorney-General was saying, "is that Colonel Boundary is at the head of a huge blackmailing organization, and that in the course of the past twenty years, by such means as I shall suggest and as the principal witness for the Crown will tell you, he has built up his criminal practice until he now controls the most complex and the most iniquitous organization that has been known in the long and sordid history of crime.

"Your Worship will doubtless hear," he went on, "of a bizarre and fantastic figure which flits through the pages of this story, a mysterious somebody who is called the 'Jack.' But I shall ask your Worship, as I shall ask the jury, when this case reaches, as it must reach ultimately, the Central Criminal Court, to disregard this apparition, which displayed no part in bringing Boundary to justice.

"The contention of the Crown is, as I say, that Boundary, by means of terrorization and blackmail, through the medium and assistance of his creatures, has from time to time secured a hold over rich and foolish men and women, and from these has acquired the enormous wealth which is now his and his associates'. As to these latter, their prosecution depends very largely upon the fate of Boundary. There are, I believe, some of them in court at this moment, and though they are not arrested, it will be no news to them to learn that they are under police observation."

"Swell" Crewe, sitting at the back of the court, shifted uneasily and, turning his head, he met the careless gaze of the tall, military-looking man who had "detective" written all over him.

There had been a pause in the Attorney-General's speech whilst he examined, shortsightedly, the notes before him.

"In the presentation of this case, your Worship," he went on, "the Crown is in somewhat of a dilemma. We have secured one important and, I think, convincing witness – a man who has been closely associated with the prisoner, a Scandinavian named Hanson, who, considering himself badly treated by this gang, has been for a long time secretly getting together evidence of an incriminating character. As to his object we need not inquire. There is a possibility suggested by my learned friend, the counsel for the defense, that Hanson intended blackmailing the blackmailers, and presenting such a weight of evidence against Boundary that he could do no less than pay handsomely for his confederate's silence. That is as may be. The main fact is that Hanson has accumulated this documentary evidence, and that that documentary evidence is in existence in certain secret hiding places in this country, which will be revealed in the course of his examination.

"We are at this disadvantage, that Hanson has not yet made anything but the most scanty of statements. Fearing for his life, since this gang will stick at nothing, he has been closely guarded by the police from the moment he made his preliminary statement. Every effort which has been made to induce him to commit his revelations to writing has been in vain, and we are compelled to take what is practically his affidavit in open court."

"Do I understand," interrupted the magistrate, in that weary tone which is the prerogative of magistrates, "that you are not as yet in possession of the evidence on which I am to be asked to commit the prisoner to the Old Bailey?"

"That is so, your Worship," said the counsel. "All we could procure from Hanson was the bald affidavit which was necessary to secure the man's arrest."

"So that if anything happened to your witness, there would be no case for the Crown?"

The Attorney-General nodded.

"Those are exactly the circumstances, your Worship," he said, "and that is why we have been careful to keep our witness in security. The man is in a highly nervous condition, and we have been obliged to humor him. But I do not think your Worship need have any apprehension as to the evidence which will be produced today, or that there will not be sufficient to justify a committal."

"I see," said the magistrate.

Sir Stanley turned to Stafford and whispered:

"Rather a queer proceeding."

Stafford nodded.

"It is the only thing we could do," he said. "Hanson refused to speak until he was in court – until, as he said, he saw Boundary under arrest."

"Does Boundary know this?"

"I suppose so," replied Stafford with a little smile, "he knows everything. He has a whole army of spies. Sir Stanley, you don't know how big this organization is. He has roped in everybody. He has Members of Parliament, he has the best lawyers in London, and two of the big detective agencies are engaged exclusively on his work."

Sir Stanley pursed his lips thoughtfully and turned his attention to the prosecuting counsel. The address was not a long one, and presently the Attorney-General sat down, to be followed by a leading member of the Bar, retained for the defense. Presently he too had finished, and again the Attorney-General rose.

"Call Olaf Hanson," he said, and there was a stir of excitement.

The door leading to the cells opened, and two tall detectives came through, and two others followed. In the midst of the four walked the short, grey-faced man, in whose hands was the fate, and indeed the life, of Colonel Dan Boundary.

He did not as much as glance at the dock, but hurried across the floor of the court and was ushered to the witness stand, his four guardians disposing themselves behind and before him. The man seemed on the point of crumbling. His fear-full eyes ranged the court, always avoiding the gross figure in the railed dock. The lips of the witness were white and trembling. The hands which clutched the front of the box for support twitched spasmodically.

"Your name is Olaf Hanson?" asked the Attorney-General soothingly.

The witness tried to speak but his lips emitted no sound. He nodded.

"You are a native of Christiania?"

Again Hanson nodded.

"You must speak out," said Counsel kindly, "and you need have no fear. How long have you known Colonel Boundary?"

This time Hanson found his voice.

"For ten years," he said huskily.

An usher came forward from the press at the back of the court with a glass of water and handed it to the witness, who drank eagerly. Counsel waited until he had drained the glass before he spoke again.

"You have in your possession certain documentary evidence convicting Colonel Boundary of certain malpractices?"

"Yes," said the witness.

"You have promised the police that you will reveal in court where those documents have been stored?"

"Yes," said Hanson again.

"Will you tell the court now, in order that the police may lose as little time as possible, where you have hidden that evidence?"

Colonel Boundary was showing the first signs of interest he had evinced in the proceedings. He leaned forward, his head craned round as though endeavoring to catch the eye of the witness.

Hanson was speaking, and speaking with difficulty.

"I haf – put those papers," – he stopped and swayed – "I haf put those papers –" he began again, and then, without a second's warning, he fell limply forward.

"I am afraid he has fainted," said the magistrate.

Detectives were crowding round the witness, and had lifted him from the witness stand. One said something hurriedly, and Stafford King left his seat. He was bending over the prostrate figure, tearing open the collar from his throat, and presently was joined by the police surgeon, who was in court. There was a little whispered consultation, and then Stafford King straightened himself up and his face was pale and hard.

"I regret to inform your Worship," he said, "that the witness is dead."

Chapter VI

STAFFORD KING RESIGNS

A week later, Stafford King came into the office of the First Commissioner of the Criminal Intelligence Department, and Sir Stanley looked up with a kindly but pitying look in his eye.

"Well, Stafford," he said gently, "sit down, won't you. What has happened?"

Stafford King shrugged his shoulders.

"Boundary is discharged," he said shortly.

Sir Stanley nodded.

"It was inevitable," he said, "I suppose there's no hope of connecting him and his gang with the death of Hanson?"

"Not a ghost of a hope, I am afraid," said Stafford, shaking his head. "Hanson was undoubtedly murdered, and the poison which killed him was in the glass of water which the usher brought. I've been examining the usher again today, and all he can remember is that he saw somebody pushing through the crowd at the back of the court, who handed the glass over the heads of the people. Nobody seems to have seen the man who passed it. That was the method by which the gang got rid of their traitor."

"Clever," said Sir Stanley, putting his fingertips together. "They knew just the condition of mind in which Hanson would be when he came into court. They had the dope ready, and they knew that the detectives would allow the usher to bring the man water, when they would not allow anybody else to approach him. This is a pretty bad business, Stafford."

"I realize that," said the young chief. "Of course, I shall resign. There's nothing else to do. I thought we had him this time, especially with the evidence we had in relation to the Spillsbury case."

"You mean the letter which Spillsbury wrote to the woman Marsh? How did that come, by the way?"

"It reached Scotland Yard by post."

"Do you know who sent it?"

"There was no covering note at all," replied Stafford. "It was in a plain envelope with a typewritten address and was sent to me personally. The letter, of course, was valueless by itself."

"Have you made any search to discover the documents which Hanson spoke about?"

"We have searched everywhere," said the other a little wearily, "but it is a pretty hopeless business looking through London for a handful of documents. Anyway, friend Boundary is free."

The other was watching him closely.

"It is a bitter disappointment to you, my young friend," he said; "you've been working on the case for years. I fear you'll never have another such chance of putting Boundary in the dock. He's got a lot of public sympathy, too. Your thorough-paced rascal who escapes from the hands of the police has always a large following amongst the public, and I doubt whether the Home Secretary will sanction any further proceedings, unless we have most convincing proof. What's this?"

Stafford had laid a letter on the table.

"My resignation," said that young man grimly.

The First Commissioner took up the envelope and tore it in four pieces.

"It is not accepted," he said cheerfully; "you did your best, and you're no more responsible than I am. If you resign, I ought to resign, and so ought every officer who has been on this game. A few years ago I took exactly the same step – offered my resignation over a purely private and personal matter, and it was not accepted. I have been glad since, and so will you be. Go on with your work and give Boundary a rest for awhile."

Stafford was looking down at him abstractedly.

"Do you think we shall ever catch the fellow, sir?"

Sir Stanley smiled.

"Frankly, I don't," he admitted. "As I said before, the only danger I see to Boundary is this mysterious individual who apparently crops up now and again in his daily life, and who, I suspect, was the person who sent you the Spillsbury letter – the Jack o' Judgment, doesn't he call himself? Do you know what I think?" he asked quietly. "I think that if you found the 'Jack,' if you ran him to earth, stripped him of his mystic guise, you would discover somebody who has a greater grudge against Boundary than the police."

Stafford smiled.

"We can't run about after phantoms, sir," he said, with a touch of asperity in his voice.

The chief looked at him curiously.

"I hear you do quite a lot of running about," he said carelessly, as he began to arrange the papers on his table. "By the way, how is Miss White?"

Stafford flushed.

"She was very well when I saw her last night," he said stiffly; "she is leaving the stage."

"And her father?"

Stafford was silent for a second.

"He left his home a week before the case came into court and has not been seen since," he said.

The chief nodded.

"Whilst White is away and until he turns up I should keep a watchful eye on his daughter," he said.

"What do you mean, sir?" asked Stafford.

"I'm just making a suggestion," said the other. "Think it over."

Stafford thought it over on his way to meet the girl, who was waiting for him on a sunny seat in Temple Gardens, for the day was fine and even warm, and, two hours before luncheon, the place was comparatively empty of people.

She saw the trouble in his face and rose to meet him, and for a moment forgot her own distress of mind, her doubts and fears. Evidently she knew the reason for his attendance at Scotland Yard, and something of the interview which he had had.

"I offered my resignation," he replied, in answer to her unspoken question, "and Sir Stanley refused it."

"I think he was just," she said. "Why, it would be simply monstrous if your career were spoilt through no fault of your own."

He laughed.

"Don't let us talk about me," he said. "What have you done?"

"I've canceled all my contracts; I have other work to do."

"How are –" He hesitated, but she knew just what he meant, and patted his arm gratefully.

"Thank you, I have all the money I want," she said. "Father left me quite a respectable balance. I am closing the house at Horsham and storing the furniture, and shall keep just sufficient to fill a little flat I have taken in Bloomsbury."

"But what are you going to do?" he asked curiously.

She shook her head.

"Oh, there are lots of things that a girl can do," she said vaguely, "besides going on the stage."

"But isn't it a sacrifice? Didn't you love your work?"

She hesitated.

"I thought I did at first," she said. "You see, I was always a very good mimic. When I was quite a little girl I could imitate the colonel. Listen!"

Suddenly to his amazement he heard the drawling growl of Dan Boundary. She laughed with glee at his amazement, but the smile vanished and she sighed.

"I want you to tell me one thing, Mr. King –"

"Stafford – you promised me," he began.

She reddened.

"I hardly like calling you by your Christian name but it sounds so like a surname that perhaps it won't be so bad."

"What do you want to ask?" he demanded.

She was silent for a moment, then she said:

"How far was my father implicated in this terrible business?"

"In the gang?"

She nodded.

He was in a dilemma. Solomon White was implicated as deeply as any save the colonel. In his younger days he had been the genius who was responsible for the organization and had been for years the colonel's right-hand man until the more subtle villainy of Pinto Silva, that Portuguese adventurer, had ousted him, and, if the truth be told, until the sight of his girl growing to womanhood had brought qualms to the heart of this man, who, whatever his faults, loved the girl dearly.

"You don't answer me," she said, "but I think I am answered by your silence. Was my father – a bad man?"

"I would not judge your father," he said. "I can tell you this, that for the past few years he has played a very small part in the affairs of the gang. But what are you going to do?"

"How persistent you are!" she laughed. "Why, there are so many things I am going to do that I haven't time to tell you. For one thing, I am going to work to undo some of the mischief which the gang have wrought. I am going to make such reparation as I can," she said, her lips trembling, "for the evil deeds my father has committed."

"You have a mission, eh?" he said with a little smile.

"Don't laugh at me," she pleaded. "I feel it here." She put her hand on her heart. "There's something which tells me that, even if my father built up this gang, as you told me once he did – ah! you had forgotten that."

Stafford King had indeed forgotten the statement.

"Yes?" he said. "You intend to pull it down?"

She nodded.

"I feel, too, that I am at bay. I am the daughter of Solomon White, and Solomon White is regarded by the colonel as a traitor. Do you think they will leave me alone? Don't you think they are going to watch me day and night and get me in their power just as soon as they can? Think of the lever that would be, the lever to force my father back to them!"

"Oh, you'll be watched all right," he said easily, and remembered the commissioner's warning. "In fact, you're being watched now. Do you mind?"

"Now?" she asked in surprise.

He nodded towards a lady who sat a dozen yards away and whose face was carefully shaded by a parasol.

"Who is she?" asked the girl curiously.

"A young person called Lollie Marsh," laughed Stafford. "At present she has a mission too, which is to entangle me into a compromising position."

The girl looked towards the spy with a new interest and a new resentment.

"She has been trailing me for weeks," he went on, "and it would be embarrassing to tell you the number of times we have been literally thrown into one another's arms. Poor girl!" he said, with mock concern, "she must be bored with sitting there so long. Let us take a stroll."

If he expected Lollie to follow, he was to be disappointed She stayed on watching the disappearing figures, without attempting to rise, and waiting until they were out of sight, she walked out on to the Embankment and hailed a passing taxi. She seemed quite satisfied in her mind that the plan she had evolved for the trapping of Stafford King could not fail to succeed.

Chapter VII

THE COLONEL CONDUCTS HIS BUSINESS

A merry little dinner party was assembled that night in a luxurious flat in Albemarle House. It was a bachelor party, and consisted of three

– the colonel, resplendent in evening dress, "Swell" Crewe and a middle-aged man whose antique dress coat and none too spotless linen certainly did not advertise their owner's prosperity. Yet this man with the stubbly moustache and the bald head could write his check for seven figures, being Mr. Thomas Crotin, of the firm of Crotin and Principle, whose swollen mills occupy a respectable acreage in Huddersfield and Dewsbury.

"You're Colonel Boundary, are you?" he said admiringly, and for about the seventh time since the meal started.

The colonel nodded with a good-humored twinkle in his eye.

"Well, fancy that!" said Mr. Crotin. "I'll have something to talk about when I go back to Yorkshire. It is lucky I met your friend, Captain Crewe, at our club in Huddersfield."

There was something more than luck in that meeting, as the colonel well knew.

"I read about the trial and all," said the Yorkshireman; "I must say it looked very black against you, colonel."

The colonel smiled again and lifted a bottle towards the other.

"Nay, nay!" said the spinner. "I'll have nowt more. I've got as much as I can carry, and I know when I've had enough."

The colonel replaced the bottle by his side.

"So you read of the trial, did you?"

"I did and all," said the other, "and I said to my missus: 'Yon's a clever fellow, I'd like to meet him.'"

"You have an admiration for the criminal classes, eh?" said the colonel good-humoredly.

"Well, I'm not saying you're a criminal," said the other, taking his host literally, "but being a J.P. and on the bench of magistrates, I naturally take an interest in these cases. You never know what you can learn."

"And what did your lady wife say?" asked Boundary.

The Yorkshireman smiled broadly.

"Well, she doesn't take any interest in these things. She's a proper London lady, my wife. She was in a high position when I married."

"Five years ago," said Boundary, "you married the daughter of Lord Westsevern. It cost you a hundred thousand pounds to pay the old man's debts."

The Yorkshireman stared at him.

"How did you know that?" he asked.

"You're nominated for Parliament, too, aren't you. And you're to be Mayor of Little Thornhill?"

Mr. Crotin laughed uproariously.

"Well, you've got me properly taped," he said admiringly, and the colonel agreed with a gesture.

"So you're interested in the criminal classes?"

Mr. Crotin waved a protesting hand.

"I'm not saying you're a member of the criminal classes, colonel," he said. "My friend Crewe here wouldn't think I would be so rude. Of course, I know the charge was all wrong."

"That's where you're mistaken," interrupted the colonel calmly; "it was all right."

"Eh?"

The man stared.

"The charge was perfectly sound," said the colonel, playing with his fruit knife; "for twenty years I have been making money by buying businesses at about a twentieth of their value and selling them again."

"But how –" began the other.

"Wait, I'll tell you. I've got men working for me all over the country, agents and sub-agents, who are constantly on the look-out for scandal. Housekeepers, servants, valets – you know the sort of people who get hold of information."

Mr. Crotin was speechless.

"Sooner or later I find a very incriminating fact which concerns a gentleman of property. I prefer those scandals which verge on the criminal," the colonel went on.

The outraged Mr. Crotin was rolling his serviette.

"Where are you going? What are you going to do? The night's young," said the colonel innocently.

"I'm going," said Mr. Crotin, very red of face. "A joke's a joke, and when friend Crewe introduced me to you, I hadn't any idea that you were that kind of man. You don't suppose that I'm going to sit here in your society – me with my high connections – after what you've said?"

"Why not?" asked the colonel; "after all, business is business, and as I'm making an offer to you for the Riverborne Mill –"

"The Riverborne Mill?" roared the spinner. "Ah! that's a joke of yours! You'll buy no Riverborne Mill of me, sitha!"

"On the contrary, I shall buy the Riverborne Mill from you. In fact, I have all the papers and transfers ready for you to sign."

"Oh, you have, have you?" said the man grimly. "And what might you be offering me for the Riverborne?"

"I'm offering you thirty thousand pounds cash," said the colonel, and his bearer was stricken speechless.

"Thirty thousand pounds cash!" he said after awhile. "Why, man, that property is worth two hundred thousand pounds."

"I thought it was worth a little more," said the colonel carelessly.

"You're a fool or a madman," said the angry Yorkshireman. "It isn't my mill, it is a limited company."

"But you hold the majority of the shares – ninety-five percent, I think," said the colonel. "Those are the shares which you will transfer to me at the price I suggest."

"I'll see you damned first," roared Crotin, bringing his hand down smash on the table.

"Sit down again for one moment." The colonel's voice was gentle but insistent. "Do you know Maggie Delman?"

Suddenly Crotin's face went white.

"She was one of your father's mill-girls when you were little more than a boy," the colonel proceeded, "and you were rather in love with her, and one Easter you went away together to Blackpool. Do you remember?"

Still Crotin did not speak.

"You married the young lady and the marriage was kept secret because you were afraid of your father, and as the years went on and the girl was content with the little home you had made for her and the allowance you gave her, there seemed to be no need to admit your marriage, especially as there were no children. Then you began to take part in local politics and to accumulate ambitions. You dared not divorce your wife and you thought there was no necessity for it. You had a chance of improving yourself socially by marrying the daughter of an English lord, and you jumped at it."

"You've got to prove that," he said huskily.

The man found his voice.

"I can prove it all right. Oh, no, your wife hasn't betrayed you – your real wife, I mean. You've betrayed yourself by insisting on paying her by telegraphic money orders. We heard of these mysterious payments but suspected nothing beyond a vulgar love affair. Then one night, whilst your placid and complacent wife was in a cinema, one of my people searched her box and came upon the certificate of marriage. Would you like to see it?"

"I've nothing to say," said Crotin thickly. "You've got me, mister. So that is how you do it!"

"That is how I do it," said the colonel. "I believe in being frank with people like you. Here are the transfers. You see the place for your signature marked with a pencil."

Suddenly Crotin leaped at him in a blind fury, but the colonel gripped him by the throat with a hand like a steel vice, and shook him as a dog would shake a rat. And the gentle tone in his voice changed as quickly.

"Sit down and sign!" snarled Boundary. "If you play that game, I'll break your damned neck! Come any of those tricks with me and I'll smash you. Give him the pen, Crewe."

"I'll see you in jail for this," said the white-faced man shakily.

"That's about the place you will see me, if you don't sign, and it is the inside of that jail you'll be to see me."

The man rose up unsteadily, flinging down the pen as he did so.

"You'll suffer for this," he said between his teeth.

"Not unduly," said the colonel.

There was a tap at the door and the colonel swung round.

"Who's that?" he asked.

"Can I come in?" said a voice.

Crewe was frowning.

"Who is it?" asked the colonel.

The door opened slowly. A gloved hand, and then a white, hooded face, slipped through the narrow entry.

"Jack o' Judgment! Poor old Jack o' Judgment come to make a call," chuckled the hateful voice. "Down, dog; down!" He flourished the long-barreled revolver theatrically, then turned with a chuckle of laughter to the gaping Mr. Crotin.

"Poor Jacob!" he crooned, "he has sold his birthright for a mess of pottage! Don't touch that paper, Crewe, or you die the death!"

His hand leapt out and snatched the transfer, which he thrust into the hand of the wool-spinner.

"Get out and go home, my poor sheep," he said, "back to the blankets! Do you think they'd be satisfied with one mill? They'd come for a mill every year and they'd never leave you till you were dead or broke. Go to the police, my poor lamb, and tell them your sad story. Go to the admirable Mr. Stafford King – he'll fall on your neck. You won't, I see you won't!"

The laughter rose again, and then swiftly with one arm he swung back the merchant and stood in silence till the door of the flat slammed.

The colonel found his voice.

"I don't know who you are," he said, breathing heavily, "but I'll make a bargain with you. I've offered a hundred thousand pounds to anybody who gets you. I'll offer you the same amount to leave me alone."

"Make it a hundred thousand millions!" said Jack o' Judgment in his curious, squeaky voice, "give me the moon and an apple, and I'm yours!"

He was gone before they could realize he had passed through the door, and he had left the flat before either moved.

"Quick! The window!" said the colonel.

The window commanded a view of the front entrance of Albemarle House, and the entry was well lighted. They reached the window in time to see the Yorkshireman emerge with unsteady steps and stride into the night. They waited for their visitor to follow. A minute, two minutes passed, and then somebody walked down the steps to the light. It was a woman, and as she turned her face the colonel gasped.

"Maisie White!" he said in a wondering voice. "What the devil is she doing here?"

Chapter VIII

THE LISTENER AT THE DOOR

Maisie White had taken up her abode in a modest flat in Doughty Street, Bloomsbury. The building had been originally intended for a dwelling house, but its enterprising owner had fitted a kitchenette and a bathroom to every floor and had made each suite self-contained.

She found the one bedroom and a sitting room quite sufficient for her needs. Since the day of her father's departure she had not heard from him, and she had resolutely refused to worry. What was Solomon White's association with the Boundary gang, she could only guess. She knew it had been an important one, but her fears on his behalf had less to do with the action the police might take against him than with Boundary's sinister threat.

She had other reasons for leaving the stage than she had told Stafford King. On the stage she was a marked woman and her movements could be followed for at least three hours in the day, and she was anxious for more anonymity. She was conscious of two facts as she opened the outer door that night to let herself into the hallway, and hurried up to her apartments. The first was that she had been followed home, and that impression was the more important of the two. She did not switch on the light when she entered her room, but bolting the door behind her, she moved swiftly to the window and raised it noiselessly. Looking out, she saw two men on the opposite side of the street, standing together in consultation. It was too dark to recognize them, but she thought that one figure was Pinto Silva.

She was not frightened, but nevertheless she looked thoughtfully at the telephone, and her hand was on the receiver before she changed her mind. After all, they would know where she lived and an inquiry at her agents or even at the theater would tell them to where her letters had been readdressed. She hesitated a moment, then pulled down the blinds and switched on the light.

Outside the two men saw the light flash up and watched her shadow cross the blind.

"It is Maisie all right," said Pinto. "Now tell me what happened."

In a few words Crewe described the scene which he had witnessed in the Albemarle flat.

"Impossible!" said Pinto; "are you suggesting that Maisie is Jack o' Judgment?"

Crewe shrugged.

"I know nothing about it," he said; "there are the facts."

Pinto looked up at the light again.

"I'm going across to see her," he said, and Crewe made a grimace.

"Is that wise?" he asked; "she doesn't know we have followed her home. Won't she be suspicious?"

Pinto shrugged.

"She's a pretty clever girl that," he said, "and if she doesn't know we're outside, there's nothing of Solomon White in her composition."

He crossed the road and struck a match to discover which was her bell. He guessed right the first time. Maisie heard the tinkle and knew what it portended. She had not started to disrobe, and after a few moments' hesitation she went down the stairs and opened the door.

"It is rather a late hour to call on you," said Pinto pleasantly, "but we saw you going away from Albemarle Place, and could not overtake you."

There was a question in his voice, though he did not give it actual words.

"It is rather late for small talk," she said coolly. "Is there any reason for your call?"

"Well, Miss White, there were several things I wanted to talk to you about," said Pinto, taken aback by her calm. "Have you heard from your father?"

"Don't you think," she said, "it would be better if you came at a more conventional hour? I don't feel inclined to gossip on the doorstep and I'm afraid I can't ask you in."

"The colonel is worrying," Pinto hastened to explain. "You see, Solly's one of his best friends."

The girl laughed softly.

"I know," she said. "I heard the colonel talking to my father at Horsham," she added meaningly.

"You've got to make allowances for the colonel," urged Pinto; "he lost his temper, but he's feeling all right now. Couldn't you persuade your father to communicate with us – with him?"

She shook her head.

"I am not in a position to communicate with my father," she replied quietly. "I am just as ignorant of his whereabouts as you are. If anybody is anxious it is surely myself, Mr. Silva."

"And another point," Silva went on, so that there should be no gap in the conversation, "why did you give up your theatrical engagements, Maisie? I took a lot of trouble to get them for you, and it is stupid to jeopardize your career. I have plenty of influence, but managers will not stand that kind of treatment, and when you go back –"

"I am not going back," she said. "Really, Mr. Silva, you must excuse me tonight. I am very tired after a hard day's work –" she checked herself.

"What are you doing now, Maisie?" asked Silva curiously.

"I have no wish to prolong this conversation," said the girl, "but there is one thing I should like to say, and that is that I would prefer you to call me Miss White."

"All right, all right," said Silva genially, "and what were you doing at the flat tonight, Mai – Miss White?"

"Good night," said the girl and closed the door in his face.

He cursed angrily in the dark and raised his hand to rap on the panel of the door, but thought better of it and, turning, walked back to the interested Crewe, who stood in the shadow of a lamp-post watching the scene.

"Well?" asked Crewe.

"Confound the girl, she won't talk," grumbled Silva. "I'd give something to break that pride of hers, Crewe. By Jove, I'll do it one of these days," he added between his teeth.

Crewe laughed.

"There's no sense in going off the deep end because a girl turns you down," he said. "What did she say about the flat? And what did she say about her visit to Albemarle Place?"

"She said nothing," said the other shortly. "Come along, let's go back to the colonel."

On the return journey he declined to be drawn into any kind of conversation, and Crewe, after one or two attempts to procure enlightenment as to the result of the interview, relapsed into silence.

They found the colonel waiting for them, and to all appearances the colonel was undisturbed by the happenings of the evening.

"Well?" he asked.

"She admits she was here," said Pinto.

"What was she doing?"

"You'd better ask her yourself," said the other with some asperity. "I tell you, colonel, I can't handle that woman."

"Nobody ever thought you could," said the colonel. "Did she give you any idea as to what her business was?"

Pinto shook his head and the colonel paced the big room thoughtfully, his big hands in his pockets.

"Here's a situation," he said. "There's some outsider who's following every movement we make, who knew that boob from Huddersfield was coming, and who knew what our business was. That somebody was this infernal Jack o' Judgment, but who is Jack o' Judgment, hey?"

He looked round fiercely.

"I'll tell you who he is," he went on, speaking slowly "He's somebody who knows our gang as well as we know it ourselves, somebody who has been on the inside, somebody who has access, or who has had access, to our working methods. In fact," he said using his pet phrase, "a business associate."

"Rubbish!" said Pinto.

This polished man of Portugal, who had come into the gang very late in the day, was one of the few people who were privileged to offer blunt opposition to the leader of the Boundary Gang.

"You might as well say it is I, or that it is Crewe, or Dempsey, or Selby –"

"Or White," said the colonel slowly; "don't forget White."

They stared at him.

"What do you mean?" asked Crewe with a frown.

White had been a favorite of his.

"How could it be White?"

"Why shouldn't it be White?" said the colonel. "When did Jack o' Judgment make his first appearance? I'll tell you. About the time we started getting busy framing up something against White. Did we ever see him when White was with us – no! Isn't it obviously somebody who has been a business associate and knows our little ways? Why, of course it is. Tell me somebody else?

"You don't suggest it is 'Snow' Gregory, anyway?" he added sarcastically.

Crewe shivered and half-closed his eyes.

"For heaven's sake don't mention 'Snow' Gregory," he said irritably.

"Why shouldn't I?" snarled the colonel. "He's worth money and life and liberty to us, Crewe. He's an awful example that keeps some of our business associates on the straight path. Not," he added with elaborate care, "not that we were in any way responsible for his untimely end. But he died – providentially. A doper's bad enough, but a doper who talks and boasts and tells me, as he told me in this very room, just where he'd put me, is a mighty dangerous man, Crewe."

"Did he do that?" asked Crewe with interest.

The colonel nodded.

"In this very room where you're standing," he said impressively, "at the end of that table he stood, all lit up with 'coco' and he told me things about our organization that I thought nobody knew but myself. That's the worst of drugs," he said, shaking his head reprovingly; "you never know how clever they'll make a man, and they made 'Snow' a bit too clever. I'm not saying that I regretted his death – far from it. I don't know how he got mixed up in the affair –"

"Oh, shut up!" growled Pinto; "why go on acting before us? We were all in it."

"Hush!" said the colonel with a glance at the door.

There was a silence. All eyes were fixed on the door.

"Did you hear anything?" asked the colonel under his breath.

His face was a shade paler than they had ever remembered seeing it.

"It is nothing," said Pinto; "that fellow's got on your nerves."

The colonel walked to the sideboard and poured out a generous portion of whisky and drank it at a gulp.

"Lots of things are getting on my nerves," he said, "but nothing gets on my nerves so much as losing money. Crewe, we've got to go after that Yorkshireman again – at least somebody has got to go after him."

"And that somebody is not going to be me," said Crewe quietly. "I did my part of the business. Let Pinto have a cut."

Pinto Silva shook his head.

"We'll drop him," he said decisively, and for the first time Crewe realized how dominating a factor Pinto had become in the government of the band.

"We'll drop him –"

Suddenly he stopped and craned his head round.

It was he who had heard something near the door, and now with noiseless steps he tiptoed across the room to the door, and gripping the handle, opened it suddenly. A gun had appeared in his hand, but he did not use it. Instead, he darted through the open doorway and they heard the sound of a struggle. Presently he came back, dragging by the collar a man.

"Got him!" he said triumphantly, and hurled his captive into the nearest chair.

Chapter IX

THE COLONEL EMPLOYS A DETECTIVE

Their prisoner was a stranger. He was a lean, furtive-looking man of thirty-five, below middle height, respectably dressed, and at first glance, the colonel, whose hobby was distinguishing at a look the social standing of humanity, was unable to place him.

Crewe locked thc door.

"Now then," said the colonel, "what the devil were you doing listening at my door? Was that his game, Mr. Silva?"

"That was his game," said the other, brushing his hands.

"What have you got to say before I send for the police?" asked the colonel virtuously. "What have you got to say for yourself? Sneaking about a gentleman's flat, listening at keyholes!"

The man, who had been roughly handled, had risen and was putting his collar straight. If he had been taken aback by the sudden onslaught, he was completely self-possessed now.

"If you want to send for the police, you'd better start right away," he said; "you've got a telephone, haven't you? Perhaps I'll have a job for the policeman, too. You've no right to assault me, my friend," he said, addressing Pinto resentfully.

"What were you doing?" asked the colonel.

"Find out," said the man sharply.

The colonel stroked his long moustache, and his manner underwent a change.

"Now look here, old man," he said almost jovially; "we're all friends here, and we don't want any trouble. I daresay you've made a mistake, and my friend has made a mistake. Have a whisky and soda?"

The man grinned crooked.

"Not me, thank you," he said emphatically; "if I remember rightly, there was a young gentleman who took a glass of water in North Lambeth Police Court the other day, and –"

The colonel's eyes narrowed.

"Well, sit down and be sociable. If you're suggesting that I'm going to poison you, you're also suggesting that you know something which I don't want you to tell. Or that you have discovered one of those terrible secrets that the newspapers are all writing about. Now be a sensible man; have a drink."

The man hesitated.

"You have a drink of whisky out of the same bottle, and I'll join you."

"Help yourself," said the colonel good-naturedly. "Give me any glass you like."

The man went to the sideboard, poured out two pegs and sent the soda-water sizzling into the long glasses.

"Here's yours and here's mine," he said; "good luck!"

He drank the whisky off, after he had seen the colonel drink his, and wiped his mouth with a gaudy handkerchief.

"I'm taking it for granted," said the colonel, "that we've made no mistake and that you were listening at our door. Now we want no unpleasantness, and we'll talk about this matter as sensible human beings and man to man."

"That's the way to talk," said the other, smacking his lips.

"You've been sent here to watch me."

"I may have and I may not have," said the other.

Pinto shifted impatiently, but the colonel stopped him with a look.

"Now let me see what you are," mused the colonel, still wearing that benevolent smile of his. "You're not an ordinary tradesman. You've got a look of the book canvasser about you. I have it – you're a private detective!"

The man smirked.

"Perhaps I am," said he, "and," he added, "perhaps I'm not."

The colonel slapped him on the shoulder.

"Of course you are," he said confidently; "we don't see shrewd-looking fellows like you every day. You're a split!"

"Not official," said the man quickly.

He had all the English private detective's fear of posing as the genuine article.

"Now look here," said the colonel, "I'm going to be perfectly straight with you, and you've got to be straight with me. That's fair, isn't it?"

"Quite fair," said the man; "if I've been misconducting myself in any manner –"

"Don't mention it," said the colonel politely, "my friend here will apologize for handling you roughly, I'm sure; won't you, Mr. Silva?"

"Sure!" said the other, without any great heartiness.

He was tired of this conversation and was anxious to know where it was leading.

"You're not in the private detective business for your health," said the colonel, and the man shook his head.

"I bet you're working for a firm that's paying you about three pounds a week and your miserable expenses – a perfect dog's life."

"You're quite right there," said the man, and he spoke with the earnestness of the ill-used wage-earner, "it is a dog's life; out in all kinds of weather, all hours of the day and night, and never so much as 'thank you' for any work you do. Why, we get no credit at all, sir. If we go into the witness-box, the lawyers treat us like dirt."

"I absolutely agree with you," said the colonel, shaking his head. "I think the private detective business in this country isn't appreciated as it ought to be. And it is very curious we should have met you," he went on; "only this evening I was saying to my friends here, that we ought to get a good man to look after our interests. You've heard about me, I'm sure, Mr. –"

"Snakit," said the other; "here's my card."

He produced a card from his waistcoat pocket, and the colonel read it.

"Mr. Horace Snakit," he said, "of Dooby and Somes. Now what do you say to coming into our service?"

The man blinked.

"I've got a good job –" he began inconsistently.

"I'll give you a better – six pounds a week, regular expenses and an allowance for dressing."

"It's a bet!" said Mr. Snakit promptly.

"Well, you can consider yourself engaged right away. Now, Mr. Snakit, as frankness is the basis of our intercourse, you will tell me straight away whether you were engaged in watching me?"

"I'll admit that, sir," said the man readily. "I had a job to watch you and to discover if you knew the whereabouts of a certain person."

"Who engaged you?"

"Well –" the man hesitated. "I don't know whether it isn't betraying the confidence of a client," he waited for some encouragement to pursue the path of rectitude and honor, but received none. "Well, I'll tell you candidly, our firm has been engaged by a young lady. She brought me here tonight –"

"Miss White, eh?" said the colonel quickly.

"Miss White it was, sir," said Snakit.

"So that was why she was here? She wanted to show you –"

"Just where your rooms were, sir," said the man. "She also wanted to show me the back stairs by which I could get out of the building if I wanted to."

"What were your general instructions?"

"Just to watch you, sir, and if I had an opportunity when you were out, of sneaking in and nosing round."

"I see," said the colonel. "Crewe, just take Mr. Snakit downstairs and tell him where to report. Fix up his pay – you know," he gave a significant sideways jerk of his head, and Crewe escorted the gratified little detective from the apartment.

When the door had closed, the colonel turned on Silva.

"Pinto," he said and there was a rumble in his voice which betrayed his anger, "that girl is dangerous. She may or may not know where her father is – this detective business may be a blind. Probably Snakit was sent here knowing that he would be captured and spill the beans."

"That struck me, too," said Pinto.

"She's dangerous," repeated the colonel.

He resumed his promenade up and down the room.

"She's an active worker and she's working against us. Now, I'm going to settle with Miss White," he said gratingly. "I'm going to settle with her for good and all. I don't care what she knows, but she probably knows too much. She's hand in glove with the police and maybe she's working with her father. You'll get Phillopolis here tomorrow morning –"

The other's eyes opened.

"Phillopolis?" he almost gasped. "Good heavens! You're not going to –"

The colonel faced him squarely.

"You've had your chance with the girl and you've missed it," he said. "You've tried your fancy method of courting and you've fallen down."

"But I'm not going to stand for Phillopolis," said the other, with tense face. "I tell you I like the girl. There's going to be none of that –"

"Oh, there isn't, isn't there?" said the colonel in his silkiest tone.

Then suddenly he leaned forward across the table and his face was the face of a devil.

"There's only one Boundary Gang, Pinto, and this is it," he said between his clenched white teeth, "and there's only one Dan Boundary and that's me. Do you get me, Pinto? You can go a long way with me if I happen to be going that way. But you stand in the road and you're going to get what's coming. I've been good to you, Pinto. I've stood your interference because it amused me. But you come up against me, really up against me, and by the Lord Harry! you'll know it. Did you get that?"

"I've got it" said Pinto sullenly.

Chapter X

THE GREEK PHILLOPOLIS

The upbuilding of the Boundary gang had neither been an accident, nor was it exactly designed on the lines which it ultimately followed.

The main structure was Boundary himself, with his extraordinary financial genius, his plausibility, his lightning exploitation of every advantage which offered. Outwardly he was the head of three trading corporations which complied with the laws, paid small but respectable dividends and cloaked other operations which never appeared in the official records of the companies.

The sidelines of the gang came through force of circumstances. Men – good, bad and indifferent – were drawn into the orbit of its activities, as extraordinary circumstances arose or dire necessities dictated. Throughout the length and breadth of Britain, through France, Italy, and in the days before the war, and even during the war, in Germany, in Russia and in the United States, were men who, if they could not be described as agents, were at least ready tools.

He had a finger in every unsavory pie. The bank robber discharged from jail did not ask Colonel Boundary to finance him in the purchase of a new kit of tools – an up-to date burglar's kit costs something over two hundred pounds – but there were people who would lend the money, which eventually came out of the colonel's pocket. Some of the businesses he financed were on the border line of respectability. Some into which his money was sunk were frankly infamous. But it was a popular fiction that he knew nothing of these. Or, if he did know, that he was financing or at the back of a scoundrel, it was insisted that that scoundrel was engaged in (so far as the colonel knew) legitimate enterprise.

Paul Phillopolis was a small Greek merchant, who had an office in Mincing Court – a tiny room at the top of four flights of stairs. On the glass panel of its door was the announcement: "General Exporter."

Mr. Phillopolis spent three or four hours at his office daily and for the rest of the time, particularly towards the evening, was to be found in a *brasserie* in Soho. He was a dark little man, with fierce mustachios and a set of perfect white teeth which he displayed readily, for he was easily amused. His most intimate acquaintances knew him to be an exporter of Greek produce to South America, and he was, in the large sense of the word, eminently respectable.

Occasionally he would be seen away from his customary haunt, discussing with a compatriot some very urgent business, which few knew about. For there were ships which cleared from the Greek ports, carrying cargoes to the order of Mr. Phillopolis, which did not appear in any bill of lading. Dazed-looking Armenian girls, girls from South Russia, from Greece, from Smyrna, en route to a promised land, looked forward to the realization of those wonderful visions which the Greek agent had so carefully sketched.

In half a dozen South American towns the proprietors of as many dance halls would look over the new importations approvingly and remit their bank drafts to the merchant of Mincing Court. It was a profitable business, particularly in pre-war days.

The colonel departed from his usual practice and met the Greek himself, the place of meeting being a small hotel in Aldgate. Whatever other pretences the colonel made, he did not attempt to continue the fiction that he was ignorant of the Greek's trade.

"Paul," he said after the first greetings were over, "I've been a good friend to you."

"You have indeed, colonel," said the man gratefully.

He spoke English with a very slight accent, for he had been born and educated in London.

"If ever I can render you a service –"

"You can," said the colonel, "but it is not going to be easy."

The Greek eyed him curiously.

"Easy or hard," he said, "I'll go through with it."

The colonel nodded.

"How is the business in South America?" he asked suddenly.

The Greek spread out his hands in deprecation.

"The war!" he said tragically, "you can imagine what it has been like. All those girls waiting for music hall engagements and impossible to ship them owing to the fleets. I must have lost thousands of pounds."

"The demand hasn't slackened off, eh?" asked the colonel, and the Greek smiled.

"South America is full of money. They have millions – billions. Almost every other man is a millionaire. The music halls have patrons but no talent."

The colonel smiled grimly.

"There's a girl in London of exceptional ability," he said. "She has appeared in a music hall here, and she's as beautiful as a dream."

"English?" asked the Greek eagerly.

"Irish, which is better," said the other; "as pretty as a picture, I tell you. The men will rave about her."

The Greek looked puzzled.

"Does she want to go?" he asked.

The colonel snarled round at him:

"Do you think I should come and ask you to book her passage if she wanted to go?" he demanded. "Of course she doesn't want to go, and she doesn't know she's going. But I want her out of the way, you understand?"

Mr. Phillopolis pulled a long face.

"To take her from England?"

"From London," said the colonel.

The Greek shook his head.

"It is impossible," he said; "passports are required and unless she was willing to go it would be impossible to take her. You can't kidnap a girl and rush her out of the country except in storybooks, colonel."

Boundary interrupted him impatiently.

"Don't you think I know that?" he asked; "your job is, when she's in a fit state of mind, to take her across and put her somewhere where she's not coming back for a long time. Do you understand?"

"I understand that part of it very well," said the Greek.

"I'm not to be mixed up in it," said Boundary. "The only thing I can promise you is that she'll go quietly. I'll have her passports fixed. She'll be traveling for her health – you understand? When you get to South America I want you to take her into the interior of the country. You're not to leave her in the music halls in one of the coast towns where English and American tourists are likely to see her."

"But how are you going to –"

"That's my business," said the colonel. "You understand what you have to do. I'll send you the date you leave and I'll pay her passage and yours. For any out-of-pocket expenses you can send the bill to me, you understand?"

Obviously it was not a job to the liking of Phillopolis, but he had good reason to fear the colonel and acquiesced with a nod. Boundary went back to where he had left Pinto and found the Portuguese biting his fingernails – a favorite spare-time occupation of his.

"Did you fix it?" he asked in a low voice.

"Of course, I fixed it," said the colonel sharply.

"I'm not going to have anything to do with it," said the other, and the colonel smiled.

"Maybe you'll change your mind," he said significantly.

There was a knock at the door and the colonel himself answered it. He took the card from the servant's hand and read:

"MR. STAFFORD KING,
"Criminal Intelligence Department"

He looked from the card to Pinto, then
"Show him in."

Chapter XI

THE COLONEL AT SCOTLAND YARD

The two men had not met since they had parted at the door of the North Lambeth Police Court, and there was in Colonel Boundary's smile something of forgiveness and gentle reproach.

"Well, Mr. King," he said, "come in, come in, won't you?"

He offered his hand to the other, but Stafford apparently did not see it.

"No malice, I trust, Mr. King?" said the colonel genially. "You know my friend Mr. Silva? A business associate of mine, a director of several of my companies."

"I know him all right," said Stafford and added, "I hope to know him better."

Pinto recognized the underlying sense of the words, but not a muscle of his face moved. For Stafford King the hatred with which he regarded the law lost its personal character. This man was something more than a thief-taker and a tracker of criminals. Pinto chose to regard him as the close friend of Maisie White, and as such, his rival.

"And to what are we indebted for this visit?" asked the bland colonel.

"The chief wants to see you."

"The chief?"

"Sir Stanley Belcom. Being the chief of our department I should have thought you had heard of him."

"Sir Stanley Belcom," repeated the other; "why, of course, I know Sir Stanley by repute. May I ask what he wants to see me about? And how is my young friend – er – Miss White?" asked the colonel.

"When I saw her last," replied Stafford steadily, "she was looking pretty well, so far as I could tell."

"Indeed!" said the colonel politely. "I have a considerable interest in the welfare of Miss White. May I ask when you saw her?

"Last night," replied Stafford. "She was standing at the door of her apartments in Doughty Street, having a little talk with your friend," he nodded to Pinto, and Pinto started; "also," said the cheerful Stafford, "another mutual friend of ours, Mr. Crewe, was within hailing distance, unless I am greatly mistaken."

"So you were watching, eh?" burst out Pinto "I thought after the lesson you had a couple of weeks ago, you'd have –"

"Let me carry on this conversation, if you don't mind," said the colonel, and the fury in his eyes silenced the Portuguese.

"We have agreed to let bygones be bygones, Mr. King, and I am sure it is only his excessive zeal on my behalf that induced our friend to be so indiscreet as to refer to the unpleasant happenings – which we will allow to pass from our memories."

So the girl was being watched. That made things rather more difficult than he had imagined. Nevertheless, he anticipated no supreme obstacle to the actual abduction. His plans had been made that morning, when he saw in the columns of the daily newspaper a four-line advertisement which, to a large extent, had cleared away the greatest of his difficulties.

"And if Mr. King is looking after our young friend, Maisie White, the daughter of one of our dearest business associates – why, I'm glad," he went on heartily. "London, Mr. King, is a place full of danger for young girls, particularly those who are deprived of the loving care of a parent, and one of the chief attractions, if I may be allowed to say so, which the police have for me, is the knowledge that they are the protectors of the unprotected, the guardians of the unguarded."

He made a little bow, and for all his amusement Stafford gravely acknowledged the handsome compliment which the most notorious scoundrel in London had paid the Metropolitan Police Force.

"When am I to see your chief?"

"You can come along with me now, if you like, or you can go tomorrow morning at ten o'clock," said Stafford.

The colonel scratched his chin.

"Of course, I understand that this summons is in the nature of a friendly –" he stopped questioningly.

"Oh, certainly," said Stafford, his eyes twinkling, "it isn't the customary 'come-along-o'-me' demand. I think the chief wants to meet you, to discover just the kind of person you are. You will like him, I think, colonel. He is the sort of man who takes a tremendous interest in – er –"

"In crime?" said the colonel gently.

"I was trying to think of a nice word to put in its place," admitted Stafford; "at any rate, he is interested in you."

"There is no time like the present," said the colonel. "Pinto, will you find my hat?"

On the way to Scotland Yard they chatted on general subjects till Stafford asked:

"Have you had another visitation from your friend?"

"The Jack o' Judgment?" asked the colonel. "Yes, we met him the other night. He's rather amusing. By the way, have you had complaints from anywhere else?"

Stafford shook his head.

"No, he seems to have specialized on you, colonel. You have certainly the monopoly of his attentions."

"What is going to happen supposing he makes an appearance when I happen to have a lethal weapon ready?" asked the colonel. "I have never killed a person in my life, and I hope the sad experience will not be mine. But from the police point of view, how do I stand suppose – there is an accident?"

Stafford shrugged his shoulders.

"That is his look out," he said. "If you are threatened, I dare say a jury of your fellow countrymen will decide that you acted in self-defense."

"He came the other night," the colonel said reminiscently, "when we were fixing up a particularly difficult – er – business negotiation."

"Bad luck!" said Stafford. "I suppose the mug was scared?"

"The what?" asked the puzzled colonel.

"The mug," said Stafford. "You may not have heard the expression. It means 'can' – 'fool' – 'dupe.'"

The colonel drew a long breath.

"You still bear malice, I see, Mr. King," he said sadly.

He entered the portals of Scotland Yard without so much as a tremor, passed up the broad stairs and along the unlovely corridors, till he came to the double doors which marked the First Commissioner's private office. Stafford disappeared for a moment and presently returned with the news that the First Commissioner would not be able to see his visitor for half an hour. Stafford apologized but the colonel was affability itself and kept up a running conversation until a beckoning secretary notified them that the great man was disengaged.

It was King who ushered the colonel into his presence. Sir Stanley was writing at a big desk and looked up as the colonel entered.

"Sit down, colonel," he said, nodding his head to a chair on the opposite side of the desk. "You needn't wait, King. There are one or two things I want to speak to the colonel about."

When the door had closed behind the detective, Sir Stanley leaned back in his chair. Their eyes met, the grey and the faded blue, and for the space of a few seconds they stared. Sir Stanley Belcom was the first to drop his eyes.

"I've sent for you, colonel," he said, "because I think you might give me a great deal of information, if you're willing."

"Command me," said the colonel grandly.

"It is on the matter of a murder which was committed in London a few months ago," said the commissioner quietly and for a moment Colonel Boundary did not speak.

"I presume you are referring to the 'Snow' Gregory murder?" he said at last.

"Exactly," nodded the commissioner. "We have had an inquiry from America as to the identity of this young man. Now, you knew him better than anybody else in London, colonel. Can you tell me, was he an American?"

"Emphatically not," said the colonel with a little sigh, as though he were relieved at the turn the conversation was taking. "I came to know him through – er – circumstances, and exactly what they were I cannot for the moment remember. I had a lot to do with him. He did odd jobs for me."

"Was he well educated?" asked the commissioner.

"Yes, I should say he was," said the colonel slowly. "There was a story that he had been to Oxford, and that's very likely true. He spoke like a college man."

"Do you know if he had any relations in England?"

The commissioner eyed the other straightly and the colonel hesitated. How much does this man know? he wondered, and decided that he could do no harm if he told all the truth.

"He had no relations in England," he said, "but he had a father who was abroad."

"Ah, now we're getting at some facts," said the commissioner and drew a slip of paper towards him. "What was the father's name?"

The colonel shook his head.

"That I can't tell you, sir," he said. "I should like to oblige you but I have no more idea of what his name was than the man in the moon. I believe he was in India, because letters from India used to come to Gregory."

"Was Gregory his name?"

"His Christian name, I think," said the colonel after a moment's thought. "He went wrong at college and was sent down. Then he went to Paris and started to study art, and he got in trouble there, too. That's as much as he ever told me."

"He had no brothers?" asked the commissioner.

"None," said the colonel emphatically. "I am certain of that, because he once thanked God that he was the only child."

"I see," the commissioner nodded; "you have formed no theory as to why he met his death or how?"

"No theory at all," said the colonel, but corrected himself. "Of course, I've had ideas and opinions, but none of them has ever worked out. So far as I know, he had no enemies, although he was a quick-tempered chap, especially when he was recovering from a dose of 'coco,' and would quarrel with his own grandmother."

"You've no idea why he was in London? Apparently he did not live here."

The colonel shrugged his massive shoulders.

"No, I couldn't tell you anything about that, sir," he said.

"He was not an American?" asked the commissioner again.

"I could swear to that," answered the colonel.

There was a pause and he waited.

"There's another matter." The commissioner spoke slowly. "I understand that you are being bothered by a mysterious individual who calls himself the Knave of Judgment."

"Jack o' Judgment," corrected the colonel with a contemptuous smile. "Those sort of monkey tricks don't bother me, I can assure you."

"I have my theories about the Jack o' Judgment," said the commissioner. "I have been looking up the circumstances of the murder, and I seem to remember that on the body was found a playing card."

"That's right," said the colonel, who had remembered the fact himself many times, "the Jack of Clubs."

"Do you know what that Jack of Clubs signified?" asked the commissioner, but the colonel could honestly say that he did not. Its presence on the body had frequently puzzled him and he had never found a solution.

"There is a certain type of ruffian to be found, particularly in Paris, who affects this sort of theatrical trade-mark – did you know that?" asked the commissioner.

The colonel was suddenly stricken to silence. He did not know this fact, in spite of his extraordinary knowledge of the criminal world.

"These men have their totems and their sign manuals," said the commissioner. "For example, the apache Flequier, who was executed at Nantes the other day, invariably left a domino – the double-six – near his victim."

This was news to the colonel too.

"I've been giving a great deal of thought and time to this case," said the commissioner, "and I was hoping that perhaps you could help me.

The most workable theory that I can suggest is that this unfortunate man was destroyed by a French criminal of the class which I have indicated, the bullying apache type, which is so common in France. Why the murder was committed," the commissioner fingered his paper-knife carelessly, "what led to it and who committed it, and more especially who instigated the crime, are matters which seem to me to defy detection. Do you agree?"

"I quite agree," said the colonel, licking his dry lips.

"Now I suggest to you," said the commissioner, "that your Jack o' Judgment, whoever he is, is some relation to the dead man."

He spoke slowly and emphatically and the colonel did not raise his eyes from the desk.

"It is not my business to make life any easier for you," the commissioner was saying, "or to assist you in any way. But as the Jack o' Judgment seems to me to be engaged in a wholly illegal practice, and as I, in my capacity, must suppress illegal practices, I make you a present of this suggestion."

"That the Jack o' Judgment is related to 'Snow' Gregory?" asked the colonel huskily.

"That is my suggestion," said the commissioner.

"And you think –"

The commissioner raised his shoulders.

"I think he is your greatest danger, colonel," he said, "far greater than the police, far greater than the clever minds which are planning to bring you to the dock and possibly," he added, "to the gallows."

Ordinarily the colonel would have protested at the suggestion in the speech, protested laughingly or with dignity, but now he was stricken dumb, both by the seriousness of the commissioner's voice and by the consciousness of a new and a more terrible danger than any that had confronted him. He rose, realizing that the interview was ended.

"I am greatly obliged to you, Sir Stanley," he said clearing his throat. "It is good of you to warn me, but I'd not like you to think that I am engaged in any dishonest –"

"We'll let that matter stand over for discussion until another time," said the commissioner dryly, as Stafford King came into the room. "You might show the colonel the way to the street. Otherwise he will be getting himself entangled in some of our detention rooms. Good morning, Colonel Boundary. Don't forget."

"I'm not likely to," said the colonel.

He recovered his poise quickly enough and by the time he was in the street he was back in his old mood. But he had had a shock. That sunny afternoon was filled with shadows. The booming bells of Big Ben tolled

"Jack o' Judgment," the very wheels of the taxi droned the words. And Colonel Boundary came back to Albemarle Place for the first time in his life with his confidence in Colonel Boundary shaken.

There was nobody in save the one manservant he kept by the day, and he passed into the dining room overlooking the street. He had work to do and it had to be done quickly. In one of the walls was set a stout safe, and this he opened, taking from it a steel box which he carried to the table. There was a fire laid on the hearth and to this he put a match though the day was warm enough. Then he proceeded to unlock the box. Apparently it was empty, but, taking out his scarf-pin, he inserted the point in a tiny hole, which would have escaped casual observation, and pressed.

Half the steel bottom of the box leapt up, disclosing a shallow cavity beneath. The colonel stared. There had been two letters put in there, letters which he had put away against the moment when it might be necessary to bring a recalcitrant agent to heel. They had gone. He slid his fingers beneath the half of the bottom which had not opened and felt a card. He drew this out and looked at it, licking his lips the while.

For the space of a minute he stared and stared at the Knave of Clubs he held in his hand. A Knave of Clubs signed with a flourish across its face: "Jack o' Judgment." Then he flung the card into the fire and, walking to the sideboard, splashed whisky into a tumbler with a hand that shook.

Chapter XII

BUYING A NURSING HOME

The building in which Colonel Boundary had his beautiful home was of a type not uncommonly met with in the West End of London. The street floor was taken up entirely with shops, the first floor with offices and the remainder of the building was practically given over to the colonel. One by one he had ousted every tenant from the building, and practically the whole of the fourteen sets of apartments which constituted the residential portion of the building was held by him in one name or another. Some he had obtained by the payment of heavy premiums, some he had secured when the lease of the former tenant had lapsed, some he had gathered in by sub-hiring. He had tried to buy the building, since it served his purpose well, but came against a deed of trust and the Court of Chancery, and had wisely refrained from going any further into a matter which must bring him vis-à-vis with a Master in Chancery, with all the publicity which such a transaction entailed.

Nor had he been successful in acquiring any of the premises on the first floor. They were held by three very old established businesses – an estate agent, a firm of land surveyors and the offices of a valuer. He missed his opportunity, at any rate, of securing the business of Lee and Hol, the surveyors, and did not know it was in the market until after it had been transferred to a new owner. But they were quiet, sober tenants, who closed their offices between five and six every night and did not open them until between nine or ten on the following morning, and their very respectability gave him a certain privacy.

The new proprietor of Lee and Hol was a short-sighted, elderly man of no great conversational power, and apparently of no fixed purpose in life except to say "no" to the very handsome offers which the colonel's agents made when they discovered there was a chance of re-purchasing the business. Boundary had personally inspected all the offices. He had found an excuse to visit them several times, duly noted the arrangement of the furniture, the sizes of the staffs and the general character of the business which was being carried on. This was a necessary precaution because these offices were immediately under his own flat. But just now they had a special value, because it was a practice during the daytime for the three firms to employ a commissionaire, who occupied a little glass-partitioned office on the landing and attended impartially to the needs of all three tenants to the best of his ability.

Boundary descended the stairs and found the elderly man in his office, leisurely and laboriously affixing stamps to a pile of letters. He called him from his task.

"Judson," he said, "have you seen anybody go up to my rooms this afternoon?"

The man thought.

"No, sir, I haven't," he replied.

"Have you been here all the time?"

"Yes, since one o'clock I have been in my office," said the commissionaire. "None of our young gentlemen wanted anything."

"You didn't go out to go to the post?"

"No, sir," said the man. "I've not stirred from this office except for one minute when I went into Mr. Lee's office to get these letters."

"And you've seen nobody go upstairs?"

"Not since Mr. Silva came down, sir. He came down after you, if you remember."

"Nobody's been up?" insisted the other.

"Not a soul. Your servant came down before you, sir."

"That's true," said the colonel remembering that he had sent the man on a special journey to Huddersfield with a letter to the bigamous Mr. Crotin. "You haven't seen a lady go up at all?" he asked suddenly.

"Nobody has gone up them stairs," said the commissionaire emphatically. "I hope you haven't lost anything, sir?"

The colonel shook his head.

"No, I haven't lost anything. Rather, I've found something," he said grimly.

He slipped half-a crown into the man's hand.

"You needn't mention the fact that I've been making inquiries," he said and went slowly up the stairs again.

The card had been put there that day. He would swear it. The ink on the card had not had time to darken and when he made a further search of his room, this view was confirmed by the appearance of his blotting-pad. The card had been dried there, and the pen, which had been left on the table, was still damp.

The colonel passed into his bedroom and took off his coat and vest. He searched his drawer and found what looked to be like a pair of braces made of light fabric. These he slipped over his shoulder, adjusting them so that beneath his left arm hung a canvas holster. From another drawer he took an automatic pistol, pulled the magazine from the butt and examined it before he returned it, and forced a cartridge into the breach by drawing back the cover. This he carefully oiled, and then, pressing up the safety catch, he slipped the pistol into the holster and resumed his coat and vest.

It was a long time since the colonel had carried a gun under his arm, but his old efficiency was unimpaired. He practiced before a mirror and was satisfied with his celerity. He loaded a spare magazine, and dropped it into the capacious pocket of his waistcoat. Then, putting the remainder of the cartridges away tidily, he closed the box, shut the drawer and went back to his room. If all the commissioner had hinted were true, if this mysterious visitor was laying for him because of the 'Snow' Gregory affair, he should have what was coming to him.

The colonel was no coward and if this eerie experience had got a little on his nerves, it was not to be wondered at. He drew up a chair to the table, sitting in such a position that he could see the door, took a pencil and a sheet of paper and began to write rapidly.

The man's knowledge was encyclopædic. Not once did he pause or refer to a catalogue, and he was still writing when Crewe came in. The colonel looked up.

"You're the man I want," he said.

He handed the other three sheets of paper, closely covered with writing.

"What's this?" asked Crewe and read:

"Twenty-three iron bedsteads, twenty-three mattresses, twenty-three –"

"Why, what's all this, colonel?"

"You can go down to Tottenham Court Road and you can order all that furniture to be taken into No. 3, Washburn Avenue."

"Are you furnishing a children's orphanage or something?" asked the other in surprise.

"I am furnishing a nursing home, to be exact," said the colonel slowly. "I bought it this morning, and I'm going to furnish it tomorrow. Send Lollie Marsh to me. Tell her I want her to get three women of the right sort to take charge of a mental case which is coming to my nursing home. By the way, you had better telegraph to old Boyton, or better still, go in a cab and get him. He'll probably be drunk but he's still on the medical register and he's the man I want. Take him straight away to Washburn Avenue, and don't forget that it's his nursing home and not mine. My name doesn't occur in this matter and you'd better get a dummy to do the buying for you from the furniture people."

"Who is the mental case?" asked the other.

"Maisie White," snapped the colonel, and Crewe stared.

"Mad?" he said incredulously. "Is Maisie mad?"

"She may not be at present," said Boundary, "but –"

He did not finish his sentence, and Crewe, who was once a gentleman and was now a thief, swallowed something – but he had swallowed too much to choke at the threat to a girl in whom he had not the slightest interest.

Chapter XIII

THE LOVE OF STAFFORD KING

Maisie White had no illusions. When the report came to her that the detective she had employed had passed his services over to the man he was engaged to watch, she knew that the full force of the Boundary Gang would be employed to her extinction. Strangely enough, she did not appear to be disturbed, as she confessed to Stafford King. They were lunching together at the Hotel Palatine and the detective was unusually thoughtful.

"Why don't you go out of London?" he asked.

"I must go on with my work," she said.

"What is your work?" he asked.

"I have told you once," she replied. "I am trying to disentangle my father from disgrace. I am working to put him apart when the day of reckoning comes."

"You've not heard from him?" he asked.

She shook her head, and her eyes filled with tears.

"He has been a good father to me," she said, "the kindest and best of daddies. It is dreadful to think –" her lips quivered and she could go no further.

Nor could Stafford King make matters any easier for her. He knew better than she the depth of Solomon White's commitments. If the gang ever smashed, and if by good fortune the law ever took its course, there was no hope for Solomon White's escape from his share of the responsibility.

"Why do you think your father went away?" he asked, to turn the subject to a new aspect.

She did not reply instantly.

"I think he was scared," she said after a while. "I was shocked when I discovered how much in awe of the colonel he stood. He was just terrified at the threat, and yet I know he would have given his life to protect me from harm. I think it was just I that spurred him on to make the plans he did."

Stafford King agreed with a gesture.

"Now what are we going to do about you?" he asked, half-humorously, half-seriously. "I cannot let you go wandering loose about London – I'm scared to death as it is."

She smiled at him.

"You had better lock me up," she said flippantly and he nodded in the same spirit.

"I know a little house in St. John's Wood that would serve us beautifully as a prison," he said. "It has ten rooms and two admirable bathrooms. There is central heating and a large shady garden, and if you will only let me take you before a Justice of the Peace, or even a commonplace clergyman –"

She shook her head.

"That isn't prison," she said quietly and put her hand over the table.

He caught it in his and held it tight.

"Maisie," he said, "you know I love you. I love you more dearly than anything in the world."

She did not speak.

"As my wife," he went on, "you would be safe and I should be happy. I just want you all the time."

Gently she disengaged her hand, shaking her head with a little smile.

"What would that mean, Stafford?" she said. "You know you are deceiving me when you agree that my father –" again her voice shook – "no, no," she said, "it would ruin your career to have the daughter of a convict for your wife. I realize very well what it will mean, for I know – I know – I know!"

"What do you know?" he asked in a low voice.

"I know that all my work will be in vain. But I must go on with it. I must, or I shall go mad. I know nothing on earth can clear my father, but I'm not going to tell you that again. I just want to think there is a possibility that some miracle will happen, that all the evidence which even I have against him will be explained away."

He took her unresisting hand in his, and under the cover of the tablecloth held it tight.

"That is why I wanted to leave the service," he said, and she looked at him quickly.

"Because you thought that it would mean ruin?"

He smiled.

"No, not that. It would hurt you, that is all. Of course, if such a thing happened I would be obliged to resign."

"And you'd never forgive yourself."

"I wanted to anticipate such a happening, and, darling, you've got to face the future without any other illusions."

She winced at the word "other" but he went on, unnoticing:

"Boundary is a tiger. If he thinks there is reason to fear you, he will never let up on you till he has you in his grip. I tell you this," he said earnestly, "that for all the power of the police, for all their organization and the backing which the law gives them, they may be helpless against this man if he has marked you down for punishment."

"I'm not afraid," she said quietly.

"But I am," said he. "I'm so afraid, that I'm sick with apprehension sometimes."

"Poor Stafford!" she said softly, and there was a look in her eyes which compensated him for much. "But you mustn't worry, dear. Truly, truly, you mustn't worry. I'm quite capable of looking after myself."

"And that's the greatest of all your illusions," he said, half-laughingly and half-irritably. "You're just the meekest little mouse that ever came under the paw of a cat."

She shook her head smilingly.

"But I tell you I'm speaking seriously," he went on. "I'll do my best to look after you. I'll have a man watching you day and night."

"But you mustn't," she protested. "There's no immediate cause for worry."

He saw her to the door of the restaurant and showed her into the taxi-cab which came at his whistle, and she leant out of the window and waved her hand in farewell as she drove off.

Two men stood on the opposite side of the road and watched her depart.

"That's the girl," said Crewe.

Chapter XIV

THE TAKING OF MAISIE WHITE

A week passed without anything exceptional happening, and Maisie White had ceased even to harbor doubts as to her own safety – doubts which had been present, in spite of the courageous showing she had made before Stafford King. Undeterred by her previous experience, she had made arrangements with another and a more responsible detective agency and had chosen a new watcher, though she had small hopes of obtaining results. She knew his task was one of almost insuperable difficulty, and she was frank in exposing to him what those difficulties were. Still, there was a faint chance that he might discover something, and moreover she had another purpose to serve.

She had seen Pinto Silva once. He had called, and she had noticed with surprise that the debonair, self-confident man she had known, whose air of conscious superiority had been so annoying to her, had undergone a considerable change. He was ill-at-ease, almost incoherent at moments, and it was a long time before she could discover his business.

This time she received him in her tiny sitting room, for Pinto was somehow less alarming to her than he had been. Perhaps she was conscious that at the corner of the street stood a quietly dressed man doing nothing particular, who was relieved at the eighth hour by an even less obtrusive-looking gentleman from Scotland Yard.

She waited for Pinto to disclose his business, and the Portuguese was apparently in no hurry to do so. Presently he blurted it out.

"Look here, Maisie," he said, "you've got things all wrong. Things are going to be very rotten for you unless – unless –" he floundered.

"Unless what?" she asked.

"Unless you make up with me," he said in a low voice. "I'm not so bad, Maisie, and I'll treat you fair. I've always been in love with you –"

"Stop," she said quietly. "I dare say it is a great honor for a girl that any man should be in love with her, but it takes away a little of the compliment when the man is already married."

"That's nothing," he said eagerly. "I can divorce her by the laws of my country. Maisie, she hates me and I hate her."

"In those circumstances," she smiled, "I wonder you wait until you fall in love again before you get divorced. No, Mr. Silva, that story doesn't convince me. If you were single or divorced, or if you were ever so eligible, I would not marry you."

"Why not?" he demanded truculently. "I've got money."

"So have I," she said, "of a sort."

"My money's as clean as yours, if it is Solomon White's money."

She nodded.

"I'm well aware of that, too," she said. "It is Gang money, isn't it – loot money. I don't see what good I shall get out of exchanging mine for yours, anyway. It is just as dirty. The money doesn't come into it at all, Mr. Silva, it is just liking people well enough – for marriage. And I don't like you that way."

"You don't like me at all," he growled.

"You're very nearly right," she smiled.

"You're a fool, you're a fool!" he stormed, "you don't know what's coming to you. You don't know."

"Perhaps I do," she said. "Perhaps I can guess. But whatever is coming to me, as you put it, I prefer that to marrying you."

He started back as though she had struck him across the face, and he turned livid.

"You won't say that when –"

He checked himself and without another word left the room, and she heard his heavy feet blundering down the stairs.

And then she met him again. It was two nights after. She met him in a horrible dream. She dreamt he was flying after her, that they were both birds, she a pigeon and he a hawk; and as she made her last desperate struggle to escape, she heard his hateful voice in her ear:

"Maisie, Maisie, it is your last chance, your last chance!"

She had gone to bed at ten o'clock that night, and it seemed that she had hardly fallen asleep before the vision came. She struggled to sit up in bed, she tried to speak, but a big hand was over her mouth.

Then it was true, it was no dream. He was in the room, his hand upon her mouth, his voice in her ear. The room was in darkness. There was no sound save the sound of his heavy breathing and his voice.

"They'll be up here in five minutes," he whispered. "I can save you from hell! I can save you, Maisie! Will you have me?"

She summoned all the strength at her command to shake her head.

"Then keep quiet!"

There was a note of savagery in his voice which made her turn sick.

For a second she filled her lungs to scream, but at that instant a mass of cotton-wool was thrust over her face, and she began to breathe in a sickly sweet vapor. Somebody else was in the room now. They were holding her feet. The voice in her ear said:

"Breathe. Take a deep breath!"

She sobbed and writhed in an agony of mind, but all the time she was breathing, she was drawing into her lungs the chloroform with which the wool was saturated.

At two o'clock in the morning a uniformed constable, patrolling his beat, saw an ambulance drawn up outside a house in Doughty Street. He crossed the road to make inquiries.

"A case of scarlet fever," said the driver.

"You don't say," said the sympathetic constable.

The door opened and two men walked out, carrying a figure in a blanket. The policeman stood by and saw the "patient" laid upon a stretcher and the back of the ambulance closed. Then he continued his walk to the corner of the street, where he found, huddled up in a doorway, the unconscious figure of a Scotland Yard detective, whose observation had been interrupted by a well-directed blow from a life preserver.

Chapter XV

THE COMMISSIONER HAS A THEORY

"To all stations. Stop Ambulance Motor No. LKO 9943. Arrest and detain driver and any person found therein. Warn all garages and report. – COMMISSIONER."

This order flashed from station to station throughout the night, and before the dawn, nine thousand policemen were on the look-out for the motor ambulance.

"There's a chance, of course," said Stafford, "but it is a poor chance."

He was looking white and heavy-eyed.

"I don't know, sir," said Southwick, his subordinate. "There's always a chance that a crook will do the obviously wrong thing. I suppose you've no theory as to where they have gone?"

"Not out of town – of that I'm certain," said King, "that is why the quest is so hopeless. Why, they'll have got to their destination hours before the message went out!"

They were standing in the girl's bedroom, which still reeked with chloroform, and all the clues were piled together on the table. There were not many. There was a pad of cotton-wool, a half-empty bottle of chloroform, bearing the label of a well-known wholesaler, and one of a pair of old wash-leather gloves, which had evidently been worn by somebody in his desire to avoid leaving fingerprints.

"We've not much to go on there," said Stafford disconsolately; "the chloroform may have been sold years ago. Any chemist would have supplied the cotton-wool, and as for the glove" – he picked it up and looked at it carefully, then he carried it to the light.

Old as it was, it was of good shape and quality, and when new had probably been supplied to order by a first-class glove-maker.

"There's nothing here," said Stafford again, and threw the glove back on the table.

A policeman came into the room and saluted.

"I've cycled over from the Yard, sir. We have had a message asking you to go at once to Sir Stanley Belcom's private house."

"How did Sir Stanley know about this affair?" asked Stafford listlessly.

"He telephoned through, sir, about five o'clock this morning. He often makes an early inquiry."

Stafford looked round. There was nothing more that he could do. He passed down the stairs into the street and jumped on to the motorcycle which had brought him to the scene.

Sir Stanley Belcom lived in Cavendish Place, and Stafford had been a frequent visitor to the house. Sir Stanley was a childless widower, who was wont to complain that he kept up his huge establishment in order to justify the employment of his huge staff of servants. Stafford suspected him of being something of a sybarite. His dinners were famous, his cellar was one of the best in London and because of his acquaintances and friendships in the artistic sets, he was something of a dabbler in the arts he patronized.

The door was opened and an uncomfortable-looking butler was waiting on the step to receive Stafford.

"You'll find Sir Stanley in the library, sir," he said.

Despite his sorrow, Stafford could not help smiling at this attempt on the part of an English servant to offer the conventional greeting in spite of the hour.

"I'm afraid we've got you up early, Perkins," he said.

"Not at all, sir."

The man's stout face creased in a smile.

"Sir Stanley's a rare gentleman for getting up in the middle of the night and ordering a meal."

Stafford found his grey-haired chief, arrayed in a flowered silk dressing gown, balancing bread on an electric toaster.

"Bad news, eh, Stafford?" he said. "Sit down and have some coffee. The girl is gone?"

Stafford nodded.

"And our unfortunate detective-constable, who was sent to watch, is halfway to the mortuary, I presume?"

"Not so bad as that, sir," said Stafford, "but he's got a pretty bad crack. He's recovered consciousness but remembers nothing that happened."

Sir Stanley nodded.

"Very scientifically done," he said admiringly. "This, of course, is the work of the Boundary Gang."

"I wish –" began Stafford between his teeth.

"Save your breath, my friend," smiled Sir Stanley; "wishing will do nothing. You could arrest every known member of the gang, and they'd have twenty alibis ready, and jolly good alibis too. It is years since the colonel staged an outrage of this kind and his right hand has not lost its cunning. Look at the organization of it! The men get into the house without attracting the attention of your watcher. Then, at the exact second that the ambulance is due, along comes their 'cosher,' knocks down the policeman on duty. I don't suppose the thing took more than ten minutes. Everything was timed. They must have known the hour the policeman on the beat passed along the street."

Sir Stanley poured out the coffee with his own hands, and relapsed back into his armchair.

"Why do you think they did it?"

"They were afraid of her, sir," said Stafford.

Sir Stanley laughed softly.

"I can't imagine Boundary being afraid of a girl."

"She was Solly White's daughter," said Stafford.

"Even then I can't understand it," replied the chief, "unless – by Jove! Of course."

He hit his knee a smack and Stafford waited.

"Probably they've got some other game on, but I'll tell you one of the ideas of taking that girl – it is to bring back Solomon White. He disappeared, didn't he?"

Stafford nodded.

"That's the game – to bring back Solomon White. And whatever the danger to himself, he'll be in London tomorrow as soon as this news is known."

Sir Stanley sat thinking, with his chin in his hand, his forehead wrinkled.

"There's some other reason, too. Now, what is it?"

Stafford guessed, but did not say.

"That girl will take some recovering before harm comes to her," said Sir Stanley softly, "your only hope is that friend Jack comes to your rescue."

"Jack o' Judgment?"

Sir Stanley nodded and the other smiled sadly.

"That's unlikely," he said; "indeed, it is impossible. I think I might as well tell you my own theory as to why she was taken and why Boundary took so much trouble to capture her."

"What is your theory?" asked Sir Stanley curiously.

"My theory, sir, is that she is Jack o' Judgment," said Stafford King.

"She – Jack o' Judgment?"

Sir Stanley was on his feet staring at him.

"Impossible! It is a man –"

"You seem to forget, sir," said Stafford, "that Miss White is a wonderful mimic."

"But why?"

"She wants to clear her father. She told me that only a week ago. And then I've been making inquiries on my own. I found that she was seen coming out of the Albemarle mansion, the night that Jack made his last visit to Boundary's flat."

Sir Stanley rose.

"Wait," he said and left the room.

Presently he came back with something in his hand.

"If Miss White is Jack o' Judgment, and if she were captured tonight, how do you account for this? it was under my pillow when I woke up."

He laid on the table the familiar Jack of Clubs.

Chapter XVI

IN THE TURKISH BATHS

Colonel Boundary had a breakfast party of three. Though he had been up the whole of the night, he showed no signs of weariness. Not so Pinto or Crewe, who looked fagged out and all the more tired because they were both conspicuously unshaven.

"Half the game's won," said the colonel. "We'll get rid of this girl and Solly White by the same stroke. I'm afraid of Solly, he knows too much. By the way, Raoul is coming over."

"Raoul!" said Crewe, sitting up suddenly, "why, colonel, you're mad! Didn't the Scotland Yard man tell you –"

"That he suspected a French hand in the case of 'Snow' Gregory? All the more reason why Raoul should come," said the colonel calmly; "he ought to report this morning."

"You're taking a risk," growled Pinto.

"Nothing unusual," replied the colonel, shelling a plover's egg. "It is the last thing in the world they would suspect at Scotland Yard after their warning, that I should bring Raoul over again. Besides, they don't know him anyway. He's just a harmless young French cabinet-maker. He doesn't talk and I will get him out of the silly habit of leaving his visiting-card."

There was a silence, which Crewe broke.

"You want him for –"

He did not finish the sentence.

"For work," replied the colonel. "It is a thousand pities, but it would be a thousand times more so if you and I were jugged, and waiting in the condemned cell for the arrival of Mr. Ellis, the eminent hangman. Raoul's a workman. We can trust him. He doesn't try any funny business. He lives out of this country and I can cover his tracks. Besides," the colonel went on, "I shall give him enough to live in comfort for the next two years. Raoul is a grateful little beast, and thank God! he can neither read nor write."

"I don't like it," said Crewe. "I hate that kind of thing. Why not give Solly a chance? Why not get up a fight – a duel, anything but cold-blooded murder?"

The colonel turned his cold eyes upon the other, and his lips parted in a mirthless smile.

"You're speaking up to your character now, aren't you, Crewe?" he said unpleasantly. "You're 'Gentleman Crewe' once again, eh? Want to do everything in the public school fashion? Well, you can cut out all that stuff and feed it to the pigs. I'm Dan Boundary, looking forward to a pleasant old age. There's nothing of the Knights of the Round Table about me."

Crewe flushed.

"All right," he said, "have it your own way."

"You bet your life I'm going to have it my own way," said the colonel. "Have you seen the girl this morning, Pinto?"

Pinto shook his head.

"You'll keep away from there for a couple of days. I've got Boyton on the spot and he'll be feeding her with bromide till she won't care whether she's in hell or Wigan. Besides, we'll all be shadowed for the next day or two, make no mistake about that. Stafford King won't let the grass grow under his feet. And now, you chaps, go home and try to look as though you've had a night's rest."

After their departure the colonel made his own preparations. There were Turkish baths in Westminster and it was to the Turkish baths he went. Clad in a towel, he passed from hot room to hot room, and finally came to the big, vaulted saloon, tiled from floor to roof, where in canvas-backed chairs the bathers doze and read. The colonel lay back in his chair, his eyes closed, apparently oblivious to his surroundings. Nor was it to be observed that he saw the thin little man who came and sat beside him. The newcomer was sallow-skinned and lantern-jawed, and his long arms were tattooed from shoulder to wrist.

"Here!" said a soft voice in French.

The colonel did not open his eyes. He merely dropped the palm fan which he was idly waving to and fro so that it hid his mouth.

"Do you remember a Monsieur White?" he said in the same tone.

"Perfectly," replied the other. "He was the man who would not have your little 'coco' friend – disposed of."

"That is the man," said the other. "You have a good memory, Raoul."

"Monsieur, my memory is wonderful, but alas! one cannot live on memory," he added sententiously.

"Then remember this: there is a place near London called Putney Heath."

"Putney Heath," repeated the other.

"There is a house called Bishopsholme."

"Bishopsholme," repeated the other.

"It is empty – to let, *à louer,* you understand. It is in a sad state of desolation. The garden, the house – you know the kind of place?"

"Perfectly, monsieur."

"At nine o'clock tonight and at nine o'clock tomorrow night you will be near the door. There is a large clump of bushes, behind which you will stand. You will stay there until ten. Between those hours M. White will approach and go into the house. You understand?"

"Perfectly, monsieur," said the voice again.

"You will shoot him so that he dies immediately."

"He is a dead man," said the other.

There was a long pause.

"I will pay you sixty thousand francs, and I will have a motorcar to take you direct to Dover. You will catch the night boat for Ostend. Your passport will be in order, and you can make your way to Paris at your leisure. The payment you will receive in Paris. Is that satisfactory?"

"Eminently so, monsieur," said the other. "I need a little for expenses for the moment. Also I wish information as to where the motorcar will meet me."

"It will be waiting for you at the corner of the first road past the house, on the way from London. You will not speak to the chauffeur and he will not speak to you. In the car you will find sufficient money for your immediate needs. Is there any necessity to explain further?"

"None whatever, monsieur," said the soft voice, and Raoul dropped his head on one side as though he were sleeping.

As for the colonel, he did not simulate slumber, but passed into dreamland, sleeping quietly and calmly, with a look of benevolence upon his big face.

The only other occupant of the cooling room, a big-framed man who was reading a newspaper, closed his eyes too – but he did not sleep.

Chapter XVII

SOLOMON COMES BACK

At nine o'clock that night the colonel, in immaculate evening-dress, sat playing double-dummy bridge with his two companions. In the light of the big shaded lamp overhead there was something particularly peaceful and innocent in their occupation. No word was spoken save of the game.

It was a quarter to nine, noted the colonel, looking at the little French clock on the mantelpiece. He rose, walked to the window and looked out. It was a stormy night and the wind was howling down the street, sending the rain in noisy splashes against the windowpanes. He grumbled his satisfaction and returned to the table.

"Did you see the paper?" asked Pinto presently.

"I saw the paper," said the colonel, not looking up from his hand. "I make a point of reading the newspapers."

"You see they've made a feature of –"

"Mention no names," said the colonel. "I know they've made a feature about it. So much the better. Everything depends –"

It was as he spoke that Solomon White came into the room. Boundary knew it was he before the door handle turned, before the hum of voices in the hall outside had ceased, but it was with a great pretence of surprise that he looked up.

"Why, if it isn't Solomon White!" he said.

The man was haggard and sick-looking. He had evidently dressed in a hurry, for his cravat was ill-tied and the collar gaped. He strode slowly up to the table and Boundary's manservant, with a little grin, closed the door.

"Where have you been all this time, Solomon?" asked Boundary genially. "Sit you down and play a hand."

"You know why I've come," breathed Solomon White.

"Surely I know why you've come. You've come to explain where you've been, old boy. Sit down," said Boundary.

"Where is my daughter?" asked White.

"Where is your daughter?" repeated the colonel. "Well, that's a queer question to ask us. *We've* been saying where is Solomon White all this time."

"I've been to Brighton," said the man, "but that's nothing to do with it."

"Been at Brighton? A very pleasant place, too," said Boundary. "And what were you doing at Brighton?"

"Keeping out of your way, damn you!" said White fiercely. "Trying to cure the fear of you which has made a rank coward of me. If you wanted to find a method for curing me, colonel, you've found it. I've come back for my daughter – where is she?"

The colonel pushed his chair back from the table and looked up with a quizzical smile.

"Now you're not going to take it hard, Solomon," he said. "We had to have you back and that was the only scheme we could think of. You see, there are lots of little bits of business that have to be cleared up, bits of business in which you had a hand the same as my other business associates."

"Where is the girl?" asked the man steadily.

"Well, I'm going to admit to you," said the colonel, with a fine show of frankness, "that I've put her away – no harm has come to her, you understand. She's at a little place at Putney Heath, a house I took specially for her, surrounded by loving guardians –"

"Like Pinto?" asked the man, looking down at the silent Silva.

"Like Lollie. Now you can't deny that Lollie's a very nice girl," said the colonel. "Sit down, Solomon, and talk things over."

"When I've got my girl I'll talk things over with you. Where is this place?"

"It is on Putney Heath," said the colonel. "Now aren't I being straightforward with you? If I had any bad designs against the girl, should I tell you where she is? If you go there, Solomon, take some of your copper friends."

"I have no copper friends," said the man angrily. "You know that well enough. What am I that I should go to the police? Can I go to them with clean hands?"

"Well, that's a question I've often asked myself," said the colonel. "I've often said –"

"What is the name of the house?" interrupted White. "I want to see whether you're playing square with me, Boundary, and if you're not, by –"

"Don't threaten me, don't threaten me, Solomon," said the colonel with a good-humored gesture. "I'm a nervous man and I suffer from heart disease. You ought to know better than that. Bishopsholme is the place. It is the fourth big house after passing Tredennis Road – a fine villa standing in its own grounds. It looks a bit deserted because it was empty until a few days ago, when I put a scrap or two of furniture into it. Why not wait –"

"First I'll find out whether you're speaking the truth, and if you're not –"

"Gently, gently," growled Crewe. "What's the good of kicking up a row, White? The colonel's dealing straighter with you than you're dealing with us."

He was not in the colonel's secrets, and he himself was deceived, thinking that the girl had been removed to the house which he now heard about for the first time, and that the sole object of the abduction was to bring White back.

"Stay a while," said Boundary. "It is only just nine –"

But White was gone.

He pushed past the servant, one of the readiest and most dangerous of the colonel's instruments, and into the half-dark corridor. There was a light on the landing below, and as he ran down the stairs he thought he saw somebody standing there. It looked like a woman till the figure turned, and then Solomon White stood stock still. It was the first time he had seen Jack o' Judgment. The shimmer of the black silk coat, the curious suggestion of pallor which the white mask conveyed, the slouch hat, throwing a black bar of shadow diagonally across the face, lent the figure a peculiarly sinister aspect.

"Stand!"

The voice was commanding, the glittering revolver in the figure's hand more so.

"Who are you?" gasped Solomon White.

"Jack o' Judgment! Have you ever heard of little Jack?" chuckled the figure. "Oh, here's a new one – Solomon White, too, and never heard of Jack o' Judgment! Didn't you see me when they took me out of 'Snow' Gregory's pocket? Little Jack o' Judgment!"

Solomon White stepped back, his face twitching.

"I had nothing to do with that," he said hoarsely, "nothing to do with that, do you hear?"

"Where are you going? Won't you tell Jack something, give him a bit of news? Poor old Jack hears nothing these days," sighed the figure, laughter bubbling between the words.

"I'm going on private business. Get out of my way," said the other, remembering the urgency of his mission.

"But you'll tell Jack o' Judgment?" wheedled the figure, "you'll tell poor old Jack where you are going to find your beautiful daughter?"

"You know!" said the man.

He took a step forward, but the revolver waved him back.

"You'll speak, or you don't pass," said Jack o' Judgment. "You don't pass until you speak; do you hear, Solomon White?"

The man thought.

"It is a place called Bishopsholme," he said gruffly, "on Putney Heath. Now let me pass."

"Wait, wait!" said the figure eagerly, "wait for me – only five minutes! I won't keep you! But don't go, there's death there, Solomon White! It is waiting for you – don't you feel it in your bones?"

The voice sank to a whisper, and in spite of himself, a cold shiver passed down White's spine. He half-turned to go back.

"Wait!" said the figure again eagerly, fiercely. "I shall not keep you a minute – a second!"

Solomon White stood irresolutely, and the mask seemed to melt into the darkness. White strained his ears to catch the soft patter of its shoes as it mounted the stairs, but no sound came. Then with a start he seemed to awake as if from a bad dream, and without another word strode down the remaining stairs into the night.

On the landing above, the strange being who called himself "Jack o' Judgment" stood outside the door of Boundary's flat. He had taken a key from his pocket and had it poised, when he heard the clatter of the other's feet. He stood undecidedly, but only for a second, then the key slipped into the lock and the door opened. The butler from his little pantry saw the figure and slammed his own door, bolting it with trembling fingers.

In a second Jack o' Judgment was in the room facing the paralyzed trio.

He spoke no word, but suddenly his right arm was raised, some shining object flew from his hand, and there was a crash of glass and instantly a vile odor. On the opposite wall where the bottle had broken appeared a dark and irregular stain.

Then, without so much as a laugh, he stepped back through the door and raced down the stairs in pursuit of White. It was too late; the man had disappeared. Jack o' Judgment stood for a moment listening, then he slipped off the black coat and ripped off the mask. The coat was of the finest silk, for he rolled it into the space of a pocket-handkerchief and slipped it in his pocket. The handkerchief went the same way. If there had been observers, they would have caught a glimpse of a man in evening dress as he went swiftly down the half-lighted stairway.

He turned and walked in the shadow of the building and passed down a side street, where a big limousine was awaiting him. He gave a murmured direction to the driver, and the car sped on its way.

Chapter XVIII

THE JUDGMENT OF DEATH

Solomon White had a taxi waiting, and gave his directions. He was sufficiently loyal to the band to avoid calling especial attention to the house where the girl was imprisoned, and he told his cab to wait at the end of Putney Heath. The night was wild and boisterous and very dark, but he carried an electric torch, and presently he came to weather-stained gates bearing in letters which had half-faded the name he sought. He pushed open the gate with some trouble. There was a curving carriage-drive which led to the front door, which stood at the head of a flight of steps under a square and ugly portico.

He looked up at the building, but it was in darkness. Apparently it was empty, but he knew enough of the colonel's methods to know that Boundary would not advertise the presence of the girl to the outside world.

He stood hesitating, wondering. The whole thing might be a trap, but Solomon White was not easily scared. He took a revolver from his pocket, drew back the hammer and walked forward cautiously. There was no sign of life. The rustling of shrubs and trees was the only mournful sound which varied the roar of the storm.

He was opposite the door, and one foot was raised to surmount the first step, when there came a sound like the sharp tap of a drum.

"Rap-rap!"

Solomon White stood for fully a second before he crumbled and fell, and he was dead before he reached the ground.

Still there was no sign or sound of life. A church clock boomed out the quarter to ten. A motorcar went past, and then the laurel bushes by the side of the steps moved, and a man in a black mackintosh stepped out. He bent over the dead man, picked up the fallen torch and flashed the light on the dead man's face, then, with a grunt of satisfaction, Raoul Pontarlier unscrewed his Soubet silencer and slipped his automatic into the wet pocket of his mackintosh.

Feeling in an inside pocket for a cigarette, he found one and lit it from the smoldering end of a tinder-lighter. Then, carefully concealing the lighted cigarette in the palm of his hand, he walked softly and noiselessly down the drive, keeping to the shadow of the bushes and watching to left and right for signs of approaching pedestrians. At two points he could see the heath road, and nobody was in sight. There was plenty of time, and men had been ruined by haste. He reached the gate and carefully looked over. The road was deserted. His hand was on the gate, when something cold and hard was pushed against his ear and he turned round.

"Put up your hands!" said a mocking voice. "Put them up!"

The Frenchman's hands rose slowly.

"Now turn round and face the house. Quick!" said the voice. "*Marchez!* Halt!"

Raoul stopped. If he could only get his hands down and duck, one lightning dive. . . .

His captor evidently read his thoughts, for he felt a hand slip into his mackintosh pocket, and he was relieved of the weight of his automatic.

"Go forward, up the steps. Stop!"

The stranger had seen the huddled figure of White, and stooped over him. He made no comment. He knew the man was dead before his hands had touched him.

"Mount the steps, *canaille!*" said the voice, and Raoul walked slowly up the steps of the house and halted with his face against the door.

A hand came up under his uplifted arm and sought the keyhole. A few minutes' fumbling until the prongs of the skeleton key had found its corresponding wards, and then the door swung open, emitting a scent of mustiness and decay.

"*Marchez!*" said the stranger, and Raoul walked forward and heard the door slam behind him.

The house was not empty, in the sense that it was unfurnished. The unknown was using an electric torch of extraordinary brilliancy, and revealed a dilapidated hall-stand and a musty chair. He took a brief survey and then:

"Down those stairs!" he said, and the murderer obeyed.

They were in the kitchen now, and again the bright light gleamed about. The windows were heavily shuttered, the grate was rusty, and a few odd pieces of china on the sideboard were dirty. There was a gas bracket in the center over a large deal table, and this the stranger turned on. He heard the hiss of escaping gas, struck a match and lit it, and then for the first time Raoul gazed in fear and astonishment upon the man who held him.

"Monsieur," he stammered, "who are you?"

The masked figure slipped his hand into his pocket and flicked a card upon the table, and Raoul, looking down, saw the Jack of Clubs, and knew that his end was near.

For three hours the Frenchman had lain on the floor, tied hand and foot, a gag in his mouth, and the clocks were striking two when Jack o' Judgment came back. This time he wore neither mask nor coat but over his arm he carried a coil of fine rope. Raoul watched him, fascinated, as he walked about the kitchen, whistling softly to himself, and now and again breaking into scraps of song.

"Monsieur, monsieur," blubbered the terrified man, "I would make a confession. I will make a statement before the judge –"

Jack o' Judgment smiled.

"You shall make a statement before your judge, for I am he," he said, "and I think this is the place."

He glanced up at the high roof of the kitchen, for there was a stout hook, where in old times heavy sides of bacon hung. He drew the table under the place and put a chair on top. Then he mounted, and with a skillful cast of his rope caught the hook and drew the rope slowly through. He did not move the table or take any notice of the man on the floor, but stood as a workman might stand who was calculating distances, and all the time he whistled softly.

"Monsieur, monsieur, for God's sake spare me! I will make reparation!"

"You speak truly," said the other without taking his eyes from the rope, "for it is reparation you make this night for two dead men, and God knows how many besides."

"Two?"

The murderer twisted his head.

"For a man called Gregory particularly," said Jack o' Judgment, "shot down like a mad dog."

"I was paid to do it. I knew nothing against him, I had no malice in my heart," said the man eagerly.

"Nor have I," said Jack o' Judgment, "for behold! I shall kill you without passion, as a warning to all villains of all nationalities."

"This is against the law," whined the man, beads of sweat standing on his forehead. "Give me a knife and let me fight you. You coward!"

"Give Solomon White a pistol, and let him fight you," said the other. "It is against the law – well, I know it. But it is much more speedy than the law, my little cabbage!"

He was busy making a slip-knot at one end of the rope, and presently he had finished it to his satisfaction.

"Raoul Pontarlier," he said, "this is a moment for which I have waited."

The man screamed and twisted his head, but the noose was about his neck and tightening. Then with a wrench Jack o' Judgment jerked him to his feet.

"On to the table," he said sternly. "Mount! It is quicker so!"

"I will not, I will not!" yelled the Frenchman. His voice rose to a shrill scream. "I – help!. . . help!. . ."

Half an hour later Jack o' Judgment came down the dark path, stopping only for a second to look upon the figure of Solomon White.

"God have mercy on you all!" he said soberly, and passed into the night.

Chapter XIX

THE COLONEL IS SHOCKED

"The Putney mystery," said the *Daily Megaphone*, "surpasses any of recent years in its sensational character. There is a touch of the bizarre in this grim spectacle of the dead man at the door of the empty house, and the swaying figure of his murderer hanging in the kitchen, with no other mark of identification than a playing card pinned to his breast.

"The tragedy can be reconstructed up to a point. Mr. White was evidently killed in the garden by the Frenchman who was found hanging. The automatic pistol in his pocket, which had recently been discharged, might support this theory even if the police had not found tracks of his feet in the laurels. But who hanged the man Raoul with a hangman's rope? That is the supreme mystery of all. The Putney police can offer no information on the subject, and Scotland Yard is as reticent. The circumstances of the discovery are as follows. At three o'clock on the morning of the 4th, Police-Constable Robinson, who was patrolling his beat, entered the garden, as is customary when houses are empty, to see if any doors had been forced. There had been an epidemic of burglaries in the region of Putney Heath during the past two or three months, and the police are exercising unusual vigilance in relation to these houses. The constable might not have made his inspection that night but for the fact that the garden gate had been left wide open. . . ."

Here followed an account of how the body was found and how further investigation led the constable to the kitchen to make his second gruesome discovery.

Colonel Boundary folded up the paper slowly and put it down. He had bought a copy of an early edition of the evening newspaper as he was stepping into his car, and now he was driving slowly through the park. He lit a cigar and gazed stolidly from the window. But his face showed no sign of mental perturbation.

The car had made the circuit of the Park twice when, turning again by Marble Arch, he saw Crewe standing on the sidewalk. A word to his chauffeur, and the machine drew up.

"Come in," he said curtly, and the other obeyed.

The hand that he lifted to take his cigarette from his lips trembled, and the colonel eyed him with quiet amusement.

"They've got you rattled too, have they?" he said.

"My God! It's awful!" said Crewe. "Awful!"

"What's awful about it?" asked the colonel. "White's dead, ain't he? And Raoul's dead, ain't he? Two men who might talk and give a lot of trouble."

"What did he say before he died? That's what I've been thinking. What did he say?"

"Who? Raoul?" demanded the colonel. He had asked himself the same question before. "What could he say? Anyway, if he had a statement to make, and his statement was worth taking, why, he'd be alive today!

Raoul was the one witness that they wanted, if they only knew it. They've bungled pretty badly, whoever they are."

"This Jack o' Judgment," quavered Crewe, his mouth working. "Who is he? What is he?"

"How do I know?" snarled the colonel. "You ask me these fool questions – do you expect a reply? They're dead, and that's done with. I'd sooner he killed Raoul than made a mess of my room, anyway!"

"Why did he do it?" asked Crewe.

The colonel growled something about fools and their questions, but offered no explanation.

"It may have been a monkey trick to make us change, our quarters – the stuff was sulfuretted hydrogen and asafoetida. It may have been just bravado, but if he thinks he can scare me –"

He sucked viciously at his cigar end.

"I've got workmen in to strip the walls and re-paper the bit that's soiled," he said. "I'll be back there tonight."

The colonel threw the end of his cigar from the window and relapsed into moody reverie. When he spoke it was in a more cheerful tone.

"Crewe," he said, "that guy at Scotland Yard has given me an idea."

"Which guy?" asked Crewe, steadying his voice.

"The First Commissioner," said the colonel, lighting another cigar. "He particularly wanted to know if 'Snow' had any relations. Curse 'Snow'!" he said between his teeth, and dropping his mask of urbanity. "I wish he'd – well, it doesn't matter; he's dead, anyway – he's dead."

"Relations?" said Crewe. "Did you tell him anything?"

"I told him all I knew, and that was very little," said the colonel, "but it struck me that Sir Stanley knows much more about this fellow 'Snow' than we do. At any rate, somebody's been making inquiries, and I guess that somebody is the fellow who settled Raoul."

"Jack o' Judgment?"

"Jack o' Judgment," repeated the colonel grimly. "You showed 'Snow' Gregory into the gang – what do you know about him?"

Crewe shook his head.

"Very little," he said. "I met him in Monte Carlo. He was down and out. He seemed a likely fellow – educated, a gentleman and all that sort of thing – and when I found that he'd hit the dope, I thought he'd be the kind of man you might want."

The colonel nodded.

"He never talked about his relations. The only thing I know was that he had a father or an uncle, who was in India, and I gathered that he had forged his name to a bill. When I arrived in Monte Carlo he was spending the money as fast as he could. I guess that was why he called himself Gregory, for I'm sure it wasn't his name."

"You're sure he never spoke of a brother?"

"Never," said Crewe; "he never talked about himself at all. He was generally under the influence of dope or was recovering from it."

The colonel pushed back his hat and rubbed his forehead.

"There must be some way of identifying him," he said. "He came from Oxford, you say?"

"Yes, I know that," said Crewe; "he spoke of it once."

"What house in Oxford? There are several colleges, aren't there?"

"From Balliol," said Crewe. "I distinctly remember him talking about Balliol."

"What year would that be?"

Crewe reflected.

"He left college two years before I met him at Monte Carlo," he said; "that would be –" He gave the year.

"Well, it is pretty simple," said the colonel. "Send a man to Oxford and get the names of all the men that left Balliol in that year. Find out how many you can trace, and I dare say that will narrow the search down to two or three men. Now get after this at once, Crewe. Spare no expense. If it costs half a million I'm going to discover who Mr. Jack o' Judgment is when he's at home."

He dismissed Crewe and gave fresh instructions to his driver, and ten minutes later he was stepping out of his limousine at the entrance to Scotland Yard.

Stafford King was not in, or at any rate was not available. Greatly daring, the colonel sent his card to the First Commissioner. Sir Stanley Belcom read the name and raised his eyebrows.

"Show him in," he said, and for the second time the colonel was ushered into the presence of the chief.

"Well, colonel," said Sir Stanley, "this is rather a dreadful business."

"Terrible, terrible!" said the colonel, shaking his head. "Solomon White was one of my best friends. I've been searching for him for weeks."

"So I've heard," said Sir Stanley dryly. "Have you any theory?"

"None whatever."

"What about this man called Raoul? Is he unknown to you?" asked Sir Stanley.

"That's what I've come to see you about, sir," said the colonel in a confidential tone. "You remember the last time I was here, you suggested that possibly the murderer of poor Gregory might be a Frenchman. *You* remember how you told me that these French assassins have a trick of leaving some fantastic card or sign of their handiwork?"

Sir Stanley nodded.

"Well, here you have the same thing repeated," said the colonel triumphantly, "and the identical card. Do you think, sir, that the murderer of my poor friend Gregory and my poor friend White was the same man?"

"In fact, Raoul?" asked Sir Stanley.

The colonel nodded, and for a few moments Sir Stanley communed with his well-kept fingernails.

"I don't think it will do any harm if I tell you that that is my theory also, Colonel Boundary," he said, "and, giving confidence for confidence, would you have any objection to telling me whether Raoul is one of your – er – business associates?"

There was just the slightest shade of irony in the last two words, but the colonel preferred to ignore it.

"I'm very glad you asked me that question, sir," he said with a sigh, so palpably a sigh of relief that the recording angel might be excused if he were deceived. "I have never seen Raoul before. In fact, my knowledge of Frenchmen is a very small one. I do very little business in France, and I certainly do no business at all with men of that class."

"What class?" asked the other quickly.

The colonel shrugged his big shoulders.

"I am only going on what the newspapers say," he said. "They suggest that this man is an apache."

"You do not know him?" asked Sir Stanley after a pause.

"I have never seen him in my life," said the colonel.

Again Sir Stanley examined his fingernails as though searching for some flaw.

"Then you will be surprised to learn," he drawled at last, "that you sat next to him in the cooling-room of the Yildiz Turkish Baths."

The colonel's heart missed a beat, but he did not flinch.

"You surprise me," he said. "I have only been to the Turkish baths once during the past three months, and that was yesterday."

Sir Stanley nodded.

"According to my information, which was supplied to me by my very able assistant, Mr. Stafford King, that was also the morning when Raoul was seen to enter that building."

"And he sat next to me?" said the colonel incredulously.

"He sat next to you," said Sir Stanley, with evidence of enjoyment.

"Well, that is the most amazing coincidence," exclaimed the colonel, "I have ever met with in my life! To imagine that that scoundrel sat shoulder to shoulder with me – good heavens! It makes me hot to think about it."

"I was afraid it would," said the First Commissioner.

He pressed the bell and his secretary came in.

"See if Mr. Stafford King is in the building, and tell him to come to me, please," he said. "You see, colonel, we were hoping you would supply us with a great deal of very useful information. We naturally thought it was something more than a coincidence that this man and you should foregather at a Turkish bath – a most admirable rendezvous, by the way."

"You may accept my word of honor," said Colonel Boundary impressively, "that I had no more idea of that man's presence, or of his identity, or of his very existence, than you had."

Stafford King came in at that moment, and the colonel, noting the haggard face and the look of care in the dark-lined eyes, felt a certain amount of satisfaction.

"I've just been telling the colonel about his meeting in the Turkish baths," said Sir Stanley. "I suppose there is no doubt at all as to that happening?"

"None whatever, sir," said Stafford shortly. "Both the colonel and this man were seen by Sergeant Livingstone."

"The colonel suggests that it was a coincidence, and that he has never spoken to the man," said Sir Stanley. "What do you say to that, King?"

Stafford King's lips curled.

"If the colonel says so, of course, it must be true."

"Sarcasm never worries me," said the colonel. "I'm always getting into trouble, and I'm always getting out again. Give a dog a bad name and –"

He stopped. There arose in his mind a mental picture of a man swinging in an underground kitchen, and in spite of his self-control he shuddered.

"And hang him, eh?" said Sir Stanley. "Now, I'm going to put matters to you very plainly, colonel. There have been three or four very unpleasant happenings. There has been the death of the chief witness for the Crown against you; there has been the death of this unhappy man White, who was closely associated with you in your business deals, and who had recently broken away from you, unless our information is inaccurate; there is the death of Raoul, who was seen seated next to you and apparently carrying on a conversation behind a fan."

"He never spoke a word to me," protested the colonel.

"And we have the disappearance of Miss White, which is one of the most important of the happenings, because we have reason to believe that Miss White, at any rate, is still alive," said Sir Stanley, taking no notice of the interruption. "Now, colonel, you may or may not have the key to all these mysteries. You may or may not know who your mysterious friend, the Jack o' Judgment –"

"He's no friend of mine, by heaven!" said the colonel, and neither man doubted that he spoke the truth.

"As I say, you may know all these things. But principally at this moment we are anxious to secure authentic news concerning Miss White. Both I and Mr. Stafford King have particular reasons for desiring information on that subject. Can you help us?"

The colonel shook his head.

"If by spending a hundred thousand pounds I could help you, I would do it," he said fervently, "but as to Miss White and where she is, I am as much at sea as you. Do you believe that, sir?"

"No," said Sir Stanley truthfully; "I don't."

Chapter XX

"SWELL" CREWE BACKS OUT

The colonel left Scotland Yard with a sense that he had spent the morning not unprofitably. It was his way to beard the lion in his den, and after all, the police department was no more formidable than any other public department. He spent the morning quietly in Pinto's flat, making certain preparations. The workmen were making a thorough job of his damaged wall, as he found when he looked in, and the horrible odor had almost disappeared. It was to be a much longer job than he thought. It had been necessary to cut away and replace the plaster under the paper for the infernal mixture had soaked deep. Still the colonel had plenty to occupy his mind. What he called his legitimate business had been sadly neglected of late. Reports had come in from all sorts of agencies, reports which might by careful study be turned to the greatest advantage. There was the affair of Lady Glenmerrin. He had been months accumulating evidence of that lady's marital delinquencies, and now the iron was ready to strike – and he simply had no interest in a deal which might very easily transfer the famous Glenmerrin Farms to his charge at a nominal figure.

And there were other prospects as alluring. But for the moment the colonel was mainly interested in the stock value of Colonel Dan Boundary and the possibility of violent fluctuations. He was losing grip. The story of Jack o' Judgment had circulated with amazing rapidity, by all manner of underground channels, to people vitally concerned. Crewe, who had been a stand-by in almost every big coup he had pulled off, was as stable as pulp. White his right-hand man, was dead. Pinto – well, Pinto would go his own way just when it suited him. He had no doubt whatever as to Pinto's loyalty. Silva had big estates in Portugal, to which he would retire just when things were getting warm and interesting. Moreover, the British Government could not extradite Pinto from his native land.

The colonel found himself regretting that he had missed the opportunity of taking up American citizenship during the seven years he had spent in San Francisco. And what of Crewe? Crewe was to reveal himself most unmistakably. He came in in the late afternoon and found the colonel working through the litter on his desk.

"Have you started your search at Oxford?" asked the colonel.

"I've sent two men down there – the best men in London," replied Crewe.

He drew up a chair to the desk and flung his hat on a near-by couch.

"I want to have a little talk with you, colonel."

Boundary looked up sharply.

"That sounds bad," he said. "What do you want to talk about? The weather?"

"Hardly," said Crewe. A little pause, and then: "Colonel, I'm going to quit."

The colonel made no reply. He went on writing his letter, and not until he reached the end of the page and carefully blotted the epistle did he meet Crewe's eyes.

"So you're going to quit, are you?" said Boundary. "Cold feet?"

"Something like that," said Crewe. "Of course, I'm not going to leave you in the lurch."

"Oh, no," said the colonel with elaborate politeness, "nobody's going to leave me in the lurch. You're just going to quit, that's all, and I've got to face the music."

"Why don't you quit too, colonel?"

"Quit what?" asked Boundary. "And how? You might as well ask a tree to quit the earth, to uproot itself and go on living. What happens when I walk out of this office and take a first-class state-room to New

York? You think the Boundary Gang collapses, fades away, just dies off, eh? The moment I leave there's a squeal, and that squeal will be loud enough to reach me in whatever part of the world I may be. There are a dozen handy little combinations which will think that I am double-crossing them, and they'll be falling over one another to get in with the first tale."

Crewe licked his dry lips.

"Well that certainly may be in your case, colonel, but it doesn't happen to be in mine. I've covered all my tracks so that there's no evidence against me."

"That's true," said the colonel. "You've just managed to keep out of taking an important part. I congratulate you."

"There's no sense in getting riled about it," said Crewe; "it has just been my luck, that's all. Well, I want to take advantage of this luck."

"In what way?"

"I'm out of any bad trouble. The police, if they search for a million years, couldn't get a scrap of evidence to convict me," he said, "even if they'd had you when Hanson betrayed you, they couldn't have convicted me."

"That's true," said the colonel again. He shook his head impatiently. "Well, what does all this lead to, Crewe? Do you want to be demobilized?" he asked humorously.

"That's about the size of it," said Crewe. "I don't want to be in anything fresh, and I certainly don't want to be in this –"

"What?"

"In this Maisie White business," said Crewe doggedly. "Let Pinto do his own dirty work."

"My dirty work too," said the colonel. "But I reckon you've overlooked one important fact."

"What's that?" demanded Crewe suspiciously.

"You've overlooked a young gentleman called Jack o' Judgment," said the colonel, and enjoyed the look of consternation which came to the other's face. "There's a fellow that doesn't want any evidence. He hanged Raoul all right."

"Do you think he did it?" said Crewe in a hushed voice.

"Do I think he did it?" The colonel smiled. "Why, who else? And when he comes to judge you, I guess he's not going to worry very much about affidavits and sworn statements, and he's not going to take you before a magistrate before he hands you over to the coroner."

Crewe jumped to his feet.

"What have I done?" he asked harshly.

"What have you done? Well, you know that best," said the colonel with a wave of his hand. "You say the police haven't got you and haven't a case against you. Maybe you're right. That Greek was saying the same sort of thing to me. He was here this afternoon squealing about taking the girl to the Argentine, and wanted us to send the doctor, and he'll be waiting to meet us when we land. There's no evidence against him either. Maybe there's more evidence than you imagine. I wouldn't bank too much upon the police passing you by, if I were you, Crewe. There's something about Mr. Stafford King that I don't like. He's got more brains in his little finger than that dude commissioner has in the whole of his body. He doesn't say much, but I guess he thinks a lot, and I'd give something to know what he's thinking about me just now."

Chapter XXI

THE BRIDE OF DEATH

Time had long ceased to have any significance for Maisie White. There was daylight and nightlight. She seemed to remember that she had made a great fight on the day she arrived at this strange house when the hard-faced nurses had strapped her to the bed, and an old man, with trembling fingers, had pushed a needle into her arm. She remembered it hurt, and then she remembered very little else. She viewed life with a dull apathy and without much understanding. She ceased to resent the presence of the women who came and went, and even the uncleanly old doctor no longer filled her with a sense of revulsion. She just wanted to be left alone to sleep, to dream the strangest dreams that any girl had ever had. She did not know that this was the action of bromide of potassium, consistently administered in every drink she took, in every morsel of food she ate. Bromide in bread, in coffee, in mashed potatoes, in rice, in all the vehicles by which the drug could be administered.

Sometimes by reason of her sheer vitality she flung off the effects of the dope, and was keenly conscious of her surroundings. There was one girl who came and went, a pretty girl with fluffy golden hair, who looked at her dispassionately and made no reply to the questions with which Maisie plied her. And once she had seen Pinto and would have screamed, but they stopped her in time. One night the old doctor had come into the room very drunk. He was crying and moaning in a maudlin fashion about some mysterious position which he had lost, and he had sat on the bed and, cursed his passion for strong drink with such vehemence that she, in her half-dazed state of mind, had found herself interested against her will.

In one of her lucid intervals she had realized a vital fact, that she was under the influence of a drug, and instinctively knew that she was becoming more and more immune to its action. She formed a vague plan, which she had almost forgotten the next morning. She must always be sleepy, almost dazed; she must never show signs of returning consciousness. She had been a week in the "nursing home" before she made this plan. She could lie now with her eyes shut, picking up the threads. She heard somebody talk of a ship and of a passport, and learned that she was to be removed in another week. She could not find where, but it was somewhere on a ship. She tried once, when the nurses were out of the room, to get out of bed and walk to the window. Her legs gave way beneath her, and it was with the greatest difficulty that she managed to crawl back to bed.

There was no escape that way. There was no help either from the nurses who were not nurses at all, nor from the maudlin little doctor, nor from the pretty girl who came sometimes and looked down on her with undisguised contempt – or was it pity? Then one night she woke in a fright. Two people were talking. She half turned her head and saw that Pinto was in the room, and his face was a flaming fury. She had seen that look before, but now his rage was directed at somebody else, and with a start she recognized the pretty girl that the nurses called Lollie.

"You're not in this, Lollie," said the man, and she laughed.

"That's just where you're wrong, Silva," she replied. "I'm very much in it. What happens to this girl when she leaves here heaven only knows – I guess it's up to the colonel. But while she's here I'm looking after her."

"You are, are you?" he said between his teeth. "Well, now you can go and take a walk."

"I can also take a seat too," she said.

He walked over to her and glowered down at the girl, and she puffed a cloud of cigarette smoke in his face.

"I'm a crook because it pays me to be a crook," said the girl calmly. "If it's jollying along one of the colonel's blue-eyed innocents, or keeping a watchful eye upon Mr. King, or acting trustful maiden to some poor fool from the country – why, I'm ready and willing, because that's my job. But this is a different matter altogether. If the colonel says she's got to go abroad, why, I suppose she's got to go. But she's not going to be on my conscience, that's all," said Lollie.

They passed through the door into a smaller room where the night watchers sat. She made as though to sit at the table when he gripped her arm and swung her round. She put up her hands to defend herself, but was thrown against the wall, and his grip was on her throat.

"Do you know what I'll do for you?" he hissed.

"I don't care what you do," she said. She was on the verge of tears. "You're not going into that room – you're *not* going!"

She sprang at him, but with a snarl like a wild beast, he turned and struck her, and she fell against the wall.

"Now get out" – he pointed to the door – "get out and don't show your face here again. And if you've got any information, you can report it to the colonel and see what he's got to say to you!"

She slunk from the room. Pinto went back to the room where the girl lay.

"Cover your head with a blanket, my pretty?" he said. "Pinto must not see that pretty face, eh?"

He laid hold of the blanket's edge and pulled it gently down. But the blanket would not come away. It was being clutched tightly. With a jerk he wrenched it down, then stumbled backwards to the floor, a grotesque and ludicrous figure, for the white silk mask of Jack o' Judgment confronted him and the hateful voice of his enemy shrilled:

"I'm Death! Jack o' Judgment! Poor old Jack! Jack, the hangman! You'll meet him one day, Pinto – meet him now!"

Pinto collapsed – he had fainted.

Chapter XXII

MAISIE TELLS HER STORY

"There is one fact which I would impress upon you," said Sir Stanley Belcom, addressing the heads of his departments at the early morning conference at Scotland Yard, "and it is this, that the criminal has nine chances against the one which the law possesses. He has the initiative in the first place, and if he fails to evade detection, the law gives him certain opportunities of defense and imposes certain restrictions which prevent one taking a line which would bring the truth of his assertions or denials to light. It protects him; it will not admit evidence against him; it will not allow the jury to be influenced by the record of his previous crimes until they have delivered their verdict upon the one on which he stands charged; in fact, gentlemen, the criminal, if he were intelligent, would score all the time."

"That's true enough, sir," said Cole, of the Record Office. "I've never yet met a criminal who wasn't a fool."

"And you never will till you meet Colonel Boundary," said Sir Stanley with a good-natured smile, "and the reason you do not meet him is because he is not a fool. But, gentlemen, every criminal has one weak spot, and sooner or later he exposes the chink in his armor to the sword of justice – if you do not mind so theatrical an illustration. Here, again, I do not think that Boundary will make any such exposure. One of you gentlemen has again brought up the question as to the prosecution of the Boundary Gang, and particularly the colonel himself. Well, I am all in favor of it, though I doubt whether the Home Secretary or the Public Prosecutor would agree with my point of view. We have a great deal of evidence, but not sufficient evidence to convict. We know this man is a blackmailer and that he engages in terrorizing his unfortunate victims, but the mere fact that we know is not sufficient. We need the evidence, and that evidence we have not got. And that is where our mysterious Jack o' Judgment is going to score. He knows, and it is sufficient for him that he *does* know. He calls for no corroborative evidence, but convicts and executes his judgment without recourse to the law books. I do not think that the official police will ever capture Boundary, and if it is left to them, he will die sanctified by old age and ten years of comfortable repentance. He will probably end his life in a cathedral town, and may indeed become a member of the town council – hullo, King, what is the matter?"

Stafford King had rushed in. He was dusty and hot of face, and there was a light of excitement in his eyes.

"She's found, sir, she's found!"

"She's found?" Sir Stanley frowned. "To whom are you referring? Miss White?"

Stafford could only nod.

With a gesture the commissioner dismissed the conference. Then:

"Where was she found?" he asked.

"In her own flat, sir. That is the amazing thing about it."

"What! Did she come back herself?"

Stafford shook his head.

"It is an astonishing story, sir. She was, of course, detained and held prisoner somewhere, and last night – she will not give me any details – she was carried from the house where she had been kept prisoner. She had an awful experience, at which she only hints, poor girl! Apparently she fainted, and when she came to she was in a motorcar being carried along rapidly. And that is about all she'll tell me."

"But who brought her away?" asked the commissioner.

Again Stafford shook his head.

"For some reason or other she is reticent and will give no information at all. It is evident she has been drugged, for she looks wretchedly ill – of course, I haven't pressed her for particulars."

"It is a strange story," said the commissioner.

"I have a feeling," Stafford went on, "that she has given a promise to her unknown rescuer that she will not tell more than is necessary."

"But it is necessary to tell the police," said the commissioner, "and even more important for the young lady to tell her – fiancé, I hope, King?"

The young man reddened and smiled.

"I agree with you that this is not the moment when you can cross-examine the girl, but I want you to see her as soon as you possibly can and try to induce her to tell you all she knows."

Maisie White lay on the sofa in her own room. She was still weak, but oh! the relief of being back again and of ending that terrible nightmare which had oppressed her for – how long? Even the depressing effect of the drug could not quench the exaltation of finding herself free. She went over the details of the night one by one. She must do it, she thought. She must never lose grip of what happened or forget her promise.

First she recalled seeing the weird figure of Jack o' Judgment. He had lifted her from the bed and had laid her on the floor. She remembered seeing him slip beneath the blankets, and then Pinto had come. She recalled the cracked voice of her rescuer, his fantastic language.

She had awakened to consciousness to find herself in a big car which was passing quickly through the dark and deserted streets. She had no recollection of being carried from the room or of being handed to the thickset man who stood on a ladder outside the open window. All she recalled was her waking to consciousness and seeing in the half-light the gleam of a white silk handkerchief.

She was too dazed to be terrified, and the soft voice which spoke into her ear quelled any inclinations she might have had to struggle. For the man was holding her in his arms as tenderly as a brother might hold a sister, or a father a child.

"You're safe, Miss White," said the voice. "Do you understand? Are you awake?"

"Yes," she whispered.

"You know what I have saved you from?"

She nodded.

"I want you to do something for me now. Will you?" She nodded again. "Are you sure you understand?" said the voice anxiously.

"I quite understand," she replied.

She could have almost smiled at his consideration.

"I am taking you to your home, and tomorrow your friends will know that you have returned. But you're not to tell them about the house where they have kept you. You must not tell them about Silva or anybody that was in that house. Do you understand?"

"But why?" she began, and he laughed softly.

"I am not trying to shield them," he said, answering her unspoken thought, "but if you give information you can only tell a little, and the police can only discover a little, and the men can only be punished a little. And there's so much that they deserve, so many lives they have ruined, so much sorrow they have caused, that it would be a hideous injustice if they were only punished – a little. Will you leave them to me?"

She struggled to an erect position and stared at him.

"I know you," she whispered fearlessly; "you are Jack o' Judgment."

"Jack o' Judgment!" he laughed a little bitterly. "Yes, I am Jack o' Judgment."

"Who are you?" she asked.

"A living lie," he replied bitterly, "a masquerader, a mummer, a nobody."

She did not know what impelled her to do the thing, but she put out her hand and laid it on his. She felt the silky smoothness of the glove and then his other hand covered hers.

"Thank you," he said simply. "Do you think you can walk? We are just turning into Doughty Street. We've passed the policeman on his beat; he is going the other way. Can you walk upstairs by yourself?"

"I – I'll try," she said, but when he assisted her from the car she nearly fell, and he half carried, half supported her into her room.

He stood hesitating near the door.

"I shall be all right," she smiled. "How quickly you understand my thoughts!"

"Wouldn't it be well if I sent somebody to you – a nurse? Have you the key I gave you?"

"How did you get it?" she asked suddenly, and he laughed again.

"Jack o' Judgment," he mocked, "wise old Jack o' Judgment! He has everything and nothing! Suppose I send a nurse to you, a nice nurse. I could send the key to her by messenger. Would you like that?"

She looked doubtful.

"I think I would," she said with a weak smile. "I am not quite sure of myself."

He did not take off the soft felt hat which was drawn tightly over his ears, nor did he remove his mask or cloak. She was making up her mind to take a closer stock of him, when unexpectedly he backed towards the door, and with a little nod was gone. He had left her on the couch, and there she was, half dozing and half drugged when the matronly nurse from St. George's Institute arrived half an hour later.

Stafford called in the afternoon and was surprised and delighted to learn that he could speak to the girl. He found her looking better and more cheerful. He bent over and kissed her cheek, and her hand sought his.

"Now, I'm going to be awfully official," he laughed, "I want you to tell me all sorts of things. The chief is very anxious that we should lose no time in getting your story."

She shook her head.

"There's no story to tell, Stafford," she said.

"No story to tell?" he said incredulously. "But weren't you abducted?"

She nodded.

"There's that much you know," she said; "I was abducted and taken away. I have been detained and I think drugged."

"No harm has come to you?" he asked anxiously.

Again she shook her head.

"But where did they take you? Who was it? Who were the people?"

"I can't tell you," she said.

"You don't know?"

She hesitated.

"Yes, I think I know, but I can't tell you."

"But why?" he asked in astonishment.

"Because the man who rescued me begged me not to tell, and, Stafford, you don't know what he saved me from."

"He – he – who was it?" asked Stafford.

"The man called Jack o' Judgment," said the girl slowly, and Stafford jumped up with a cry.

"Jack o' Judgment!" he said. "I ought to have guessed! Did you see his face?" he demanded eagerly.

She shook her head again.

"Did he give you any clue as to his identity?"

"None whatever," she replied with a little gleam of amusement in her eyes. "What a detective you are, Stafford! And I thought you were coming down here to tell me" – the color went to her cheeks – "well, to tell me the news," she added hastily. "Is there any news?"

"None, except –"

Then he remembered that she knew nothing whatever of her father's death and its tragic sequel, and this was not the moment to tell her. Later, when she was stronger, perhaps.

She was watching him with trouble in her eyes. She had noted how quickly he had stopped and guessed that there was something to be told which he was withholding for fear of hurting her. Her father was uppermost in her mind and it was natural that she should think of him.

"Is there any news of my father?" she asked quietly.

"None," he lied.

"You're not speaking the truth, Stafford." She put her hand on his arm. "Stafford, is there any news of my father?"

He looked at her, and she saw the pain in his face.

"Why don't you wait a little while, and I'll tell you all the news," he said with an assumption of gaiety. "There have been several fashionable weddings –"

"Please tell me," she said, "Stafford. I've been for weeks under the influence of a drug, and somehow it has numbed pain, even mental pain, and perhaps you will never find me in a better condition to hear – the worst."

"The worst has happened, Maisie," he said gently.

"He has been arrested?" she asked.

He shook his head.

"No, dear, worse than that."

"Not – not suicide?" she said between her set teeth.

Again he shook his head. "He is dead," he said softly.

"Dead!"

There was a long silence which he did not break.

"Dead!" she said again. "How?"

"He was shot by – we think it was by a member of the Boundary Gang, a man named Raoul."

She looked up at him.

"I have never heard my father speak of him."

"He was a man imported from France, according to our theory."

"And was he captured?"

"He was killed too," said Stafford; "he was caught in the act and instantly executed."

"By whom?" she asked.

"By Jack o' Judgment," replied Stafford.

"Jack o' Judgment!" She breathed the words. "And I – I never thanked him! I never knew!"

He told her the story step by step of the discovery which the police had made and the theories they had formed.

"He was lured there," said the girl.

She did not cry. She seemed incapable of tears.

"He was lured there and murdered, and Jack o' Judgment slew his murderer? Poor father! Poor, dear daddy!"

And then the tears came.

Half an hour later he left her in charge of the nurse and went back to Scotland Yard to report.

Chapter XXIII

THE GANG FUND

The news of the girl's escape had been received in another quarter. Colonel Boundary had sat in his favorite chair and listened without comment to Pinto's halting explanation.

"Oh, they went out of the window and down a ladder, did they?" said the colonel sarcastically when the Portuguese had finished, "and you had a fit on the mat, I suppose? Well, that's a hell of a fine story! And what did you do? You who were plastered all over with guns? Couldn't you shoot?"

"Did you shoot when you saw Jack o' Judgment?" said the other sullenly. "It is no good your telling me what I ought to do."

"Maybe it isn't," said the colonel. "Well, there's nothing to do now, anyway. The girl's gone, and all your fine plans have come unstuck."

"They weren't my plans," said Pinto indignantly, "it was your scheme throughout."

The colonel bit off the end of his cigar and contemplated the ceiling reflectively.

"We can only wait and see what will happen," he said. "The odds are all in favor of our being raided."

Pinto went pale.

"Yes," said the colonel, talking to himself, "I guess this is our last day of freedom. Well, Pinto, I hope you can pick oakum."

"Oh, shut up about oakum," growled the other; "it isn't a joke."

"It is not a joke," said the colonel, "and if it is, it is one of those jokes that make people laugh the most. And do you know the kind of joke that makes people laugh the most, Pinto? It is when somebody gets hurt; and we are the people who are going to get hurt."

"Do you think she'll tell the police?"

"It is extremely likely," said the colonel; "in fact, it is extremely unlikely that she won't tell the police. I am rather glad I'm out of it."

Pinto leaped up.

"You're out of it!" he shouted. "You're in it up to the neck!"

The colonel shook his head.

"I'm absolutely out of it, Pinto," he said, flicking the ash of his cigar into the fireplace. "I cannot be identified with this unhappy affair by so much as a fingerprint."

The Portuguese scowled down at him.

"So that's the game, is it? You're going to double-cross us? You're going to be out of it and we're going to be in it."

"Sit down, you fool. Double-cross you! You are easily scared at a little leg-pulling. I'm merely pointing out that it is not a matter in which I am greatly interested. It is a good thing for you I'm not. Who are the police after? You and Crewe and the rest of the gang? Not on your life! They're after me. They get the trunk and all the branches come down with it. Do you see? There's no sense in lopping off a few branches even of deadwood. It won't be good enough if they connect you with the case, unless they connect me too. They're after the big horns, they're not shooting the little bucks. If she tells the police, they're going to nose around for two or three days, seeing how far they can connect me with it. And if there's any connection – the slightest, Pinto – why, they'll pinch you without a doubt, but they'll pinch me too."

The colonel blew a blue ring of smoke into the air and watched it float to the ceiling.

"The advantage of having a business associate like me is that I'm a sort of insurance to you little crooks. I am the big fish they're trying to hook, and their bait isn't the kind of bait that you'd swallow."

"I've burned all the papers I had," explained Pinto, "and covered my trail."

"When you burned your boats and came in with me," said the colonel, "you burned everything that was worth burning. I tell you it isn't you they're trailing. It is me or nothing. Maybe they'll scare you," he said reflectively, "hoping you'll turn King's evidence. I've got a feeling that you won't – if I had a feeling the other way about, Pinto, you wouldn't see the curtain rise at the Orpheum tonight. And now," said the colonel, "we'll go out."

He rose abruptly, walked into his bedroom, and came out wearing his broad felt hat. He found Pinto biting his fingernails nervously and looking out of the window.

"I don't want to go out," said Pinto.

"Come out," said the colonel. "What's the good of staying here, anyway? Besides, if they are going to pinch you, I don't want them to pinch you in my rooms. It would look bad."

They walked downstairs into the street, and a few minutes later were strolling across the Green Park, the colonel a picture of a contented bourgeoisie with his half-smoked cigar, and his hands clasped together under the tails of his alpaca coat.

"I don't see how you can say they've no evidence against you. Suppose Crotin squeals?"

"He ain't stopped squealing yet," said the colonel philosophically, "but I don't see what difference it makes. Pinto, you haven't got the hang of my methods, and I doubt if you ever will. You're a clever, useful fellow, but if you were allowed to run the gang, you'd have it in jail in a month. Take Crotin," he said. "I dare say he's feeling sore, and maybe this damned Jack o' Judgment person is standing behind him telling him –" He stopped. "No, he wouldn't either," he said after a moment's thought, "Jack o' Judgment knows as much about it as I do."

"What are you talking about?" asked the other impatiently.

"Crotin," said the colonel; "he hasn't any evidence against me. You see, I do not do any business by letters. You fellows have often wanted me to write to this person and that, but writing is evidence. Do you get me? And what evidence has Crotin? Absolutely none. I have never written a line to him in my life. Crewe brought him down to the flat. We gave him a dinner and put the proposal to him in plain language. There's nothing he could take before a judge and jury – absolutely nothing."

He took the cigar from his mouth and blew a cloud of smoke.

"That's the way I've built the business up – no letters, no documents, nothing that a lawyer can make head or tail of."

"What about the documents that Hanson talked about?"

The colonel frowned and then laughed.

"They're nothing but records of our transactions, and they're not evidence. Why, even the police have given up the search for them. By the way, I haven't done with Crotin," he said after a while.

"He's done with you, I should think," said Pinto grimly.

The colonel nodded.

"I guess so, but he hasn't done with the gang. You can take him on next."

"I?" said Pinto in affright. "Now look here, colonel, don't you think it's time we laid low –"

"Laid low!" said the colonel scornfully. "We're either going to get into trouble or we're not. If we're not going to get into trouble, we might as well go on. Besides, we want the money. The business has slackened off, and we haven't had a deal since the Spillsbury affair, and that won't last very long. We've got to split our loot six ways, Pinto, and that leaves very little for anybody."

"Where are you going now?" asked the other, as the colonel changed his direction.

"It just struck me that we might as well go over to the bank and see how our balance stands. Also, with the exchange going against us, I want to tell Ferguson to buy dollars."

The handsome premises of the Victoria and City Bank in Victoria Street were only a stone's throw from the park; and, whatever might be the views of Ferguson, the manager, as to the colonel's moral character, he had a considerable respect for him as a financier, and Dan Boundary was shown immediately into the manager's office.

He was gone some time, whilst Pinto waited impatiently outside. The colonel never invited other members, even of the inmost council, to share his knowledge of finances. They all knew roughly the condition of the exchequer, but really the balance at the Victoria and City was the colonel's own. It was the practice of the Boundary Gang (as was subsequently revealed) to share, after each coup, every man taking that to which he was entitled. The money was split between five, the sixth share going to what was known as the Gang Account, a common fund upon which all could draw in moments of necessity.

The Gang Fund was not so described in the books of the bank. It was known as "Account B." The expenses of operations were usually paid out of the colonel's private account, and credited to him when the share-out came. He was absolute master of his own balance, but it required three signatures to extract a check from Account B. One of the objects of the colonel's visit was to reduce this number to two, the death of Solomon White having removed one of the signatories.

He returned to Pinto, apparently not too well satisfied.

"There's quite a lot of money in the Gang Account," he said. "I've struck off Solly's name, and your signature and mine, or mine and Crewe's, is sufficient now."

"Or mine and Crewe's, I suppose?" suggested Pinto, and the colonel smiled.

"Oh, no," said he. "I'm not a great believer in the indispensability of any man, but I'm making the signature of Dan Boundary indispensable before that account is touched."

They walked back through the park, and the colonel expounded his philosophy of wrong living.

"The man who runs an honest business and mixes it with a little crooked work is bound to be caught," he said, "because his mind is concentrated on the unpaying side of the game. You've got to run a crook business in an honest way if you want to escape the law and pay big dividends. They call our system blackmail, but it ain't. A blackmailer asks for something for nothing, and he's bound to get caught sooner or later. We offer spot cash for all the things we steal, and that baffles the law. And we're not the only people in London, or in England, or in the world, who are pulling bargains by scaring the fellow we buy from. It is done every day in the City of London; it is done every day by the trusts that control the little shops in the suburbs; it is done even by the big proprietary companies that tell a miserable little tradesman that, if he doesn't stop selling one article, they won't supply him with theirs. Living, Pinto, is preying. The only mistake a crook ever makes is when he goes outside of his legitimate business and lets some other consideration than the piling up of money influence him."

"How do you mean?" asked Pinto wearily. He hated the colonel when he was in this communicative mood of his.

"Well," said the colonel slowly, "I shouldn't have been so keen to go after Maisie White if it hadn't been that you were fond of her and wanted her. That's what I call letting love interfere with business."

"But you said you were afraid of her blabbing. You don't put it on to me," said the indignant Pinto.

"I was and I wasn't," said the colonel. "I think I almost persuaded myself that the girl was a danger. Of course, she isn't. Even Solomon White wasn't a danger."

He stopped dead, and, speaking slowly and pointing his words with a huge forefinger on the other's chest, he said:

"Bear this fact in mind, Pinto, that I have no malice against Miss White, and I don't think that she can harm me. As far as I'm concerned, I will never hurt a hair of her head or do her the slightest harm. I believe that she has nothing against me, and I give orders to anybody who's connected with me – in fact, to all of my business associates – that that girl is not to be interfered with."

Slowly, emphatically, every word emphasized, the colonel spoke, but Pinto did not smile. He had seen the colonel in this gentle mood before, and he knew that Maisie White was doomed.

Chapter XXIV

PINTO GOES NORTH

Had Pinto been a psychologist, which he was not, he might have been struck by the unusual reference on the part of the colonel to the funds of the gang. It was a subject to which the colonel very seldom referred, and it was certainly one which he did not emphasize. The truth was that the colonel's investigations into his own private affairs had not been as satisfactory as he had hoped would be the case.

He was in the habit of advancing money, and the gang owed him a considerable sum, money which had been advanced for the pursuit of various enterprises. To draw that money would leave the Gang Fund sadly depleted, and he could not afford to draw upon it at a moment when they were all on edge. Not only were the two principal subordinates in the condition of mind which led them to jump at every knock and start at every shadow, but he had been receiving urgent messages from all parts of the country from the other men, and he had determined upon a step which he had not taken for three years – a meeting of the full "Board" of his lawless organization.

That night summonses went forth calling his "business associates" to an Extraordinary General Meeting of the North European Smelter Syndicate. This was one of the companies which he operated, and the existence of which was justified by a small smelting works in the North of England, and owed its international character to the fact that it had branch works in Sweden. Its turnover was small, its list of stockholders was select. A summons to a General Meeting of the North European Smelter Company meant that the affairs of the gang were critical, and in this spirit the call was obeyed.

The meeting was held in the banquet hall of a West End restaurant, and the twenty men who assembled differed very little in appearance from twenty other provincial business men who might have been gathered to discuss the affairs of any company.

Their coming excited no comment, and apparently did not even arouse the attention of vigilant Scotland Yard. Nor, had the colonel's speech been taken down by a shorthand writer and submitted to the police, could any suggestion be found of the significance of the meeting. He spoke of the difficulties of trading, of the "competition" with which the company was faced, and called upon all the shareholders to assist loyally the executive in a very critical and trying time. But those who listened knew very well that the "competition" was the competition of the police, and they had their own ideas as to what constituted the trying time to which the colonel made reference.

It was a very commonplace, ordinary company meeting, which ended in a conventional way by a vote of confidence in the directors. It was when that had been passed, and the meeting had been broken up, and members and officials were talking together, that the real business started.

Then it was that Selby, the stout little man whose special job was to act as intermediary between the company and its more criminal enterprises, received his instructions to speed up. Selby was the receiver of letters. A burglar or a pickpocket who acquired in the course of his activities documents and letters which had hitherto been worthless found a ready market through Selby. Eighty letters out of every hundred were absolutely valueless, but occasionally they would find a rich gem, a love letter discreetly cherished, on which a new "operation" would be based. Then would begin the torturing of a human soul, the opening of new vistas of despair, the stage be cleared for a new tragedy.

The colonel was to find that the chief anxiety of his "shareholders" was not as to the future of the company or as to the success of its trading. Again and again he was asked a question couched in identical words, and again and again he replied with a shrug of his big shoulders:

"What's the good of worrying about a thing like that? Jack o' Judgment is a crook! That's all he is, boys, a crook. He's not the sort of man who'll go to the police and give us away; he wouldn't dare put his nose inside a police station. You leave him to us, we'll fix him sooner or later."

"But," somebody asked uneasily, "what about Raoul, that fellow who was killed at Putney?"

The colonel lifted his eyebrows.

"Raoul," he said; "he was nothing to do with us. I never heard the fellow's name until I read it in the paper. As to White" – he shrugged his shoulders again – "we can't prevent people having private quarrels, and may be this Frenchman and White had one. My theory is," he said, elaborating an idea which had only at that moment occurred to him, "that Raoul, White and this Jack o' Judgment were working together. Maybe it isn't a bad thing that White was killed under the circumstances."

He dropped his hand on the other man's shoulder and oozed geniality.

"Now, back you go, my lads, and don't worry. Leave it to old Dan to fix Jack o' Judgment, or Bill o' Judgment, or Tom o' Judgment, whoever he may be, and that we'll fix him you can be certain."

Coming away from the meeting, he expressed himself as being perfectly satisfied with its results. He brought Pinto and Crewe back with him in his car, and dropped the latter at Piccadilly Circus. Pinto would have been glad to have joined the "Swell," but the colonel detained him.

"I want to talk to you, Pinto," he said.

"I've had enough business for today," said the Portuguese.

"So have I," said the colonel, "but that doesn't prevent my attending to pressing affairs. I was talking to you today – or was it yesterday? – about Crotin."

"The Yorkshire woolen merchant?" said Pinto.

"That's the fellow," replied the colonel. "I suggested you should go and see him."

"And I suggested that I shouldn't," said Pinto; "let him rest. You'll never get another chance like you had before."

"Rest nothing," said the colonel testily, "you're scared because you imagine Crotin is warned? What do you think?"

Pinto was silent.

"I suppose you think that, because Jack o' Judgment intervened at the right moment, he went back to Yorkshire feeling full of himself? Well, you're wrong. You don't understand one side of the psychology of this business. That little fellow is quaking in his shoes and wondering what his grand wife would say if the fact that he was a bigamist was revealed. And there's more reason for his fear today than ever there was. Look here!"

He took a newspaper out of his pocket and Pinto remembered that, even during the meeting, the colonel had twice made reference to its columns and had wondered why. He had suspected that there had been some reference to the Boundary Gang, but this was not the case. The paragraph which the colonel pointed out with his thick forefinger was this:

> "By the death of Sir George Tressillian Morgan an ancient baronetcy has become extinct. His estate, which has been sworn at over a million, passes to his niece, Lady Sybil Crotin, the daughter

of Lord Westsevern, Sir George's son and heir having been killed in the war. Lady Sybil is the wife of a well-known Yorkshire mill-owner."

"I didn't know that," said Pinto, interested in spite of himself.

"Nor did I till today," said the colonel. "The fact is, this damned Jack o' Judgment has put everything else out of our minds. And you can see for yourself, Pinto, that this business is important."

Pinto nodded.

"We are not only after the mill, but here's a chance of making a real big coup. Now I can't send anybody else to Yorkshire – Crewe is impossible. Crotin knows him, and the moment he puts in an appearance, as likely as not Crotin would lose his head and give the whole show away. It is you or nobody."

He rubbed his chin thoughtfully.

"You know, there are times when I'm sorry about Solomon White," he said, "he was the boy for this kind of business – that is to say in the old days – he got a bit above himself towards the end."

Pinto was to find that the colonel had made all arrangements, and that for the previous two days he had been planning a predatory raid on the Yorkshireman.

There was to be a bazaar in Huddersfield on behalf of a local hospital, in which Lady Sybil Crotin took a great interest. She was organizing the fête and had invited subscriptions.

"They're not coming in very fast, according to their local paper," said the colonel, "and that has given me an idea. You're a presentable sort of fellow, Pinto, and it is likely you'll be all the more successful because you're a foreigner. You'll go up to Yorkshire and you'll take a thousand pounds, and if necessary you'll subscribe pretty liberally to the fund, but it must be done through Lady Sybil. You can make yourself known to her and invite yourself to the house, where you can meet Crotin himself."

He made other suggestions, for he had worked out the whole scheme in detail for the other to carry into effect. Pinto's objections slowly dissipated. He was a vain man and had all the vices of his vanity. A desire to be thought well of, to be regarded as a rich man when he was in fact on the verge of ruin, had brought him into crooked practices and eventually into the circle of the colonel's acquaintances.

To appear amongst the fair as a giver of largesse on a magnificent scale suited him down to the ground. It was a part for which he was eminently fitted, as the colonel, a shrewd judge of humanity, knew quite well.

"I'll take it on," said Pinto, "but do you think he'll squeal?"

Boundary shook his head.

"I never knew a man who was caught on the rebound to squeal," he said. "No, no, you needn't worry about that. All you have to do is to use your discretion, choose the right moment, preparing him by a few hints for what is coming, and you'll find he'll sit down, like the hard-headed business man he is, and talk money."

Pinto pulled a little face.

"I know what you're thinking," said the colonel. "You hate the idea of the generous donor being unmasked and appearing to anybody as a blackmailer. Well, you needn't worry about that. Lady Sybil will not know, nor will anybody else that counts. And, believe me, Crotin doesn't count. Anyway, you can pretend that you're a perfectly innocent agent in the matter, that you know me slightly and that I've dropped hints which made you curious and which you are anxious to verify."

Pinto went off to make preparations for the journey. He had one of the top flats in the Albemarle building, a suite of rooms which, if they were not as expensively furnished as the colonel's, were more artistic. He had recently acquired the services of a new "daily valet" – a step he could take without fear that his secrets would be betrayed, since he had no secrets in his own rooms, kept no documents of any kind, and received no visitors.

The man opened the door to his ring.

"No, sir, nobody has been," said the servant in answer to his query, and Pinto was relieved.

For the past two days he had been living in a condition bordering on panic. It seemed unlikely that the colonel's confidence would be justified and that the police would take no action. And yet the incredible had happened. There had not been so much as an inquiry; and not once, though he had been on his guard, had he detected one shadow trailing him. His spirits rose, and he whistled cheerfully as he directed the packing of his trunk, for he was traveling North fully equipped for any social event which might await him.

"I am going to Yorkshire," he explained. "I'll give you my address before I leave, and you can let me know if there are any inquiries and who the inquirers were."

"Certainly, sir," said the man respectfully, and Pinto eyed him approvingly.

"I think you'll suit me, Cobalt," he said. "My last valet was rather a fool and inclined to stick his nose into business which did not concern him."

The man smiled.

"I shan't trouble you that way, sir," he said.

"Of course, there's nothing to hide," said Pinto with a shrug, "but you know what people are. They think that because you're associated in business with Colonel Boundary you're up to all sorts of tricks."

"That's what Mr. Snakit said, sir," remarked the man.

"Snakit?" said the puzzled Pinto. "Who the devil is Snakit?"

Then he remembered the little detective whom Maisie had employed and who had been bought over by the colonel.

"Oh, you see him, do you?" he asked carelessly.

"He comes up, sir, now and again. He's the colonel's valet, isn't he, sir?"

Pinto grinned.

"Not exactly," he said. "I shouldn't discuss things with Snakit. That man is quite reliable and –"

"Anyway, sir, I should not discuss your business," said the valet with dignity.

He finished packing and, after assisting his master to dress, was dismissed for the night.

"A useful fellow, that," thought Pinto, as the door closed behind the man. The "useful fellow" reached the street and, after walking a few hundred yards, found a disengaged taxi and gave an address. Maisie White was writing when her bell rang. It rang three times – two long and one short peals – and she went downstairs to admit her visitor. She did not speak until she was back in her room, and then she faced the polite little man whom Pinto had called Cobalt.

"Well, Mr. Grey," she said.

"I wish you'd call me Cobalt, miss," said the man with a smile. "I like to keep up the name, otherwise I'm inclined to give myself away."

"Have you found out anything?"

"Very little, miss," said the detective. "There's nothing to find in the apartment itself."

"You secured the situation as valet?"

He nodded.

"Thanks to the recommendations you got me, miss, there was no difficulty at all. Silva wanted a servant and accepted the testimonials without question."

"And you've discovered nothing?" she said in a disappointed tone.

"Not in Mr. Silva's room. The only thing I found out was that he's going to Yorkshire tomorrow."

"For long?" she asked.

"For some considerable time," said the detective.

"At least, I guess so, because he has packed half a dozen suits, top hats and all sorts of things which I should imagine he wouldn't take away unless he intended making a long stay."

"Have you any idea of the place he's going to?"

"I shall discover that tomorrow, miss," said Cobalt. "I thought I'd tell you as much as I know."

"And you have not been into the colonel's flat?"

The man shook his head.

"It is guarded inside and out, miss, now. He has not only his butler, who is a tough customer, to look after him, but he has Snakit, the man you employed, I understand."

"That's the gentleman," said the girl with a little smile. "Very good, Cobalt – you'll 'phone me if you make any other discoveries."

She was sitting at her solitary breakfast the next morning when the telephone bell rang. It was from a call office, and presently she heard Cobalt's voice. "Just a word, miss. He leaves by the ten-twenty-five train for Huddersfield," said the voice, "and the person he is going to see is Lady Sybil somebody, and there's money in it."

"How do you know?" she asked quickly.

"I heard him speaking to the colonel on the landing and I heard the words: 'He'll pay.'"

She thought a moment.

"Ten-twenty-five," she repeated; "thank you very much, Mr. Cobalt."

She hung up the receiver and sat for a moment in thought, then passed quickly to her bedroom and began to dress.

Chapter XXV

A PATRON OF CHARITY

Lady Sybil Crotin was not a popular woman. She was conscious that she had married beneath her – more conscious lately that there had been no necessity to make the marriage, and she had grown a little soured. She could never mix with the homely wives of local millionaires; she professed a horror of the vulgarities with which she was surrounded, hated and loathed her lord and master's flamboyant home, which she described as something between a feudal castle and a picture-palace; and openly despised her husband's friends and their feminine relatives.

She made a point of spending at least six months of the year away from Yorkshire, and came back with protest at her lot written visibly upon her face.

A thin, angular woman, with pale green eyes and straight, tight lips, she had never been beautiful, but five or six years in an uncongenial environment had hardened and wasted her. That her husband adored her and never spoke of her save in a tone of awe was common property and a favorite subject for local humor. That she regarded him with contempt and irritation was as well known.

In view of Lady Sybil Crotin's unpopularity, it was perhaps a great mistake that she should make herself responsible for the raising of funds for the local women's hospital. But she was under the impression that there was a magic in her name and station which would overcome what she described as shyness, but which was in point of fact the frank dislike of her neighbors. A subscription list that she had opened had a weak and unpromising appearance. She had with the greatest difficulty secured help for the bazaar, and knew, even though it had been opened by a duchess, that it was a failure, even from the very first day.

Had she herself made a generous contribution to the bazaar fund, there might have been a hope; but she was mean, and the big, bleak hall she had chosen as the venue because of its cheapness was unsuitable for the entertainment she sponsored.

On the afternoon of the second day, Lady Sybil was pulling on her gloves, eyeing her husband with an unfriendly gaze as he sat at lunch.

"It was no more than I expected," she said bitterly. "I was a fool ever to start the thing – this is the last time I ever attempt to help local charities."

Mr. Crotin rubbed his bald head in perplexity.

"They'll come," he said hopefully, referring to the patrons whose absence was the cause of Lady Sybil's annoyance. "They'll come when they hear what a fine show it is. And if they don't, Syb, I'll come along and spend a couple of hundred pounds myself."

"You'll do no such thing," she snapped; "and please get out of that ridiculous habit of reducing my name to one syllable. If the people of the town can't help to support their own hospital, then they don't deserve to have one, and I'm certainly not going to allow you to waste our money on that sort of nonsense."

"Have your own way, love," said Mr. Crotin meekly.

"Besides," she said, "it would be all over the town that it was your money which was coming in, and these horrid people would be laughing at me."

She finished buttoning her gloves and was looking at him curiously.

"What is the matter with you, John?" she asked suddenly, and he almost jumped.

"With me, love?" he said with a brave attempt at a smile. "Why, there's nothing the matter with me. What should there be?"

"You've been very strange lately," she said, "ever since you came back from London."

"I think I ate something that disagreed with my digestion," he said uneasily. "I didn't know that I'd been different."

"Are things well at your – factory?" she asked.

"At mills? Oh, aye, they're all right," he said. "I wish everything was as right as them."

"As they," she corrected.

"As they," said the humble Mr. Crotin.

"There's something wrong," she said, and shook her head, and Mr. Crotin found himself going white. "I'll have a talk with you when I've got this wretched bazaar business out of my head," she added, and with a little nod she left him.

He walked to the window of the long dining-hall and watched her car disappearing down the drive, and then with a sigh went back to his *entremets.*

When Colonel Dan Boundary surmised that this unfortunate victim of his blackmail would be worried, he was not far from the mark. Crotin had spent many sleepless nights since he came back from London, nights full of terror, that left him a wreck to meet the fears of the days which followed. He lived all the time in the shadow of vengeful justice and exaggerated his danger to an incredible degree; perhaps it was in anticipating what his wife would say that he experienced the most poignant misery.

He had taken to secret drinking too; little nips at odd intervals, both in his room and in his private office. Life had lost its savor, and now a new agony was added to the knowledge that his wife had detected the change. He went to his office and spent a gloomy afternoon wandering about the mills, and came back an hour before his usual time. He had not the heart to make a call at the bazaar, and speculated unhappily upon the proceeds of the afternoon session.

It was therefore with something like pleasure that he heard his wife on the telephone speaking more cheerfully than he had heard her for months.

"Is that you, John?" she was almost civil. "I'm bringing somebody home to dinner. Will you tell Phillips?"

"That's right, love," said Mr. Crotin eagerly.

He would be glad to see some new face, and that it was a new face he could guess by the interest in Lady Sybil's tone.

"It is a Mr. de Silva. Have you ever met him?"

"No, love, I've not. Is he a foreigner?"

"He's a Portuguese gentleman," said his wife's voice; "and he has been most helpful and most generous."

"Bring him along," said Crotin heartily. "I'll be glad to meet him. How has the sale been, love?"

"Very good indeed," she replied; "splendid, in fact – thanks to Mr. de Silva."

John Crotin was dressing when his wife returned, and it was not until half an hour later that he met Pinto Silva for the first time. Pinto was a man who dressed well and looked well. John Crotin thought he was the most impressive personality he had met, when he stalked into the drawing room and took the proffered hand of the mill-owner.

"This is Mr. de Silva," said his wife, who had been waiting for her guest. "As I told you, John, Mr. de Silva has been awfully kind. I don't know what you're going to do with all those perfectly useless things you've bought," she added to the polished Portuguese, and Pinto shrugged.

"Give them away," he said; "there must, for example, be a lot of poor women in the country who would be glad of the linen I have bought."

At this point dinner was announced and he took Lady Sybil in. The meal was approaching its end when she revived the question of the disposal of his purchases.

"Are you greatly interested in charities, Mr. de Silva?"

Pinto inclined his head.

"Both here and in Portugal I take a very deep interest in the welfare of the poor," he said solemnly.

"That's fine," said Mr. Crotin, nodding approvingly. "I know what these poor people have to suffer. I've been amongst them –"

His wife silenced him with a look.

"It frequently happens that cases are brought to my notice," Pinto went on, "and I have one or two cases of women in my mind where these purchases of mine would be most welcome. For example," he said,

"I heard the other day, quite by accident, of a poor woman in Wales whose husband deserted her."

Mr. Crotin had his fork halfway to his mouth, but put it down again.

"I don't know much about the case personally," said Pinto carelessly, "but the circumstances were brought to my notice by a friend. I think these people suffer more than we imagine; and I'll let you into a secret, Lady Sybil," he said, speaking impressively. He did not look at Crotin, but went on: "A few of my friends are thinking of buying a mill."

"A woolen mill?" she said, raising her eyebrows.

"A woolen mill!" he repeated.

"But why?" she asked.

"We wish to make garments and blankets for the benefit of the poor. We feel that, if we could run this sort of thing on a co-operative basis, we could manufacture the stuff cheaply, always providing, of course, that we could purchase a mill at a reasonable figure."

For the first time he looked at Crotin, and the man's face was ghastly white.

"What a queer idea!" said Lady Sybil. "A good mill will cost you a lot of money."

"We don't think so," said Pinto. "In fact, we expect to purchase a very excellent mill at a reasonable sum. That was my object in coming to Yorkshire, I may tell you, and it was only by accident that I saw the advertisement of your bazaar and called in."

"A fortunate accident for me," said Lady Sybil.

Crotin's eyes were on his plate, and he did not raise them.

"I think it is a great mistake to be too generous with the poor," said Lady Sybil, shaking her head. "These women are very seldom grateful."

"I realize that," said Pinto gravely. "But I am not seeking their gratitude. We find that many of these women are in terrible circumstances owing to no fault of their own. For example, this woman in Wales, whose husband is supposed to have deserted her – now, there is a bad case."

Lady Sybil was interested.

"We found on investigation," said Pinto, speaking slowly and impressively, "that the man who deserted her has since married and occupies a very important position in a town in the north of England."

Mr. Crotin dropped his knife with a crash and with a mumbled apology picked it up.

"But how terrible!" said Lady Sybil. "What a shocking thing! The man should be exposed. He is not fit to associate with human beings. Can't you do something to punish him?"

"That could be done," said Silva, "it could be done, but it would bring a great deal of unhappiness to his present wife, who is ignorant of her husband's treachery."

"Better she should know now than later," said the militant Lady Sybil. "I think you do very wrong to keep it from her."

Mr. Crotin rose unsteadily and his wife looked at him with suspicion.

"Aren't you feeling well, John?" she asked with asperity.

It was not the first time she had seen her husband's hand shaking and had diagnosed the cause more justly than she was doing at present, for John Crotin had scarcely taken a drink that evening.

"I'm going into the library, if you'll excuse me, love," he said. "Maybe, Mr. – Mr. de Silva will join me. I'd – I'd like to talk over the question of that mill with him."

Pinto nodded.

"Then run along now," said Lady Sybil, "and when you've finished talking, come back to me, Mr. de Silva. I want to know something about your charitable organizations in Portugal."

Pinto followed the other at a distance, saw him enter a big room and switch on the lights and followed, closing the door behind him.

Mr. Crotin's library was the most comfortable room in the house. It was lighted by French windows which opened on to a small terrace. Long red velvet curtains were drawn, and a little fire crackled on the hearth.

When the door closed Crotin turned upon his guest.

"Now, damn you," he said harshly, "what's thy proposition? Make it a reasonable sum and I'll pay thee."

Chapter XXVI

THE SOLDIER WHO FOLLOWED

In the train which had carried Pinto Silva to Huddersfield were one or two remarkable passengers, and it was not a coincidence that they did not meet. In a third-class carriage at the far end of the train was a soldier who carried a kit-bag and who whiled away the journey by reading a seemingly endless collection of magazines.

He got out at Huddersfield too, and Pinto might and probably did see him as he passed through the barrier. The soldier left his kit-bag at the cloak-room and eventually became one of the two dozen people who patronized Lady Sybil's bazaar on that afternoon. He passed Pinto twice, and once made a small purchase at the same stall where the Portuguese was buying lavishly. If Pinto saw him, then he did not remember the fact. One soldier looks very much like another, anyway.

Lady Sybil had reason to notice the representative of His Majesty's forces, and herself informed him severely that smoking was not allowed, and the man had put his cigarette under his heel with an apology and had walked out of the building. When Lady Sybil and her guest had entered her car and were driven away to Mill Hall, the soldier had been loitering near the entrance, and a few minutes later he was following the party in a taxi-cab which had been waiting at his order for the past two hours.

The taxi did not turn in at the stone-pillared gates of the Hall, but continued some distance beyond, when the soldier alighted and, turning back, walked boldly through the main entrance and passed up the drive. It was dusk by now, and nobody challenged him.

He made a reconnaissance of the house and found the dining room without any difficulty. The blinds were up and the servants were setting the table. Then he passed round to the wing of the building and discovered the library. He actually went into that room, because it was one of Lady Sybil's standing orders that the library should be "aired" and that the scent of Mr. Crotin's atrocious tobacco should be cleared.

He sniffed the stale fragrance and was satisfied that this was a room which was lived in.

If there was any real, confidential talk between the two men, it would be here, he thought, and looked round for a likely place of concealment. The room was innocent of cupboards. Only a big settee drawn diagonally across a corner of the room promised cover, and that looked too dangerous. If anybody sat there and by chance dropped something – a pipe or an ash-tray –

He walked back to the terrace to take his bearings in case he had to make a rapid exit. He looked round and then dropped suddenly to the cover of the balustrade, for he had seen a dark figure moving across the lawn, and it was coming straight for the terrace. He slipped back into the room and as he did so he heard a step in the passage without. He stepped lightly over to the settee and crouched down.

It was evidently a servant, for he heard the French windows closed and the clang of the shutters. They were evidently very ordinary folding-shutters, fastened with an old-fashioned steel bar – he made a mental note of this. Then he heard the swish of the curtain-rings upon the brass pole as the curtains were drawn. A dim light was switched on, somebody poked the fire, and then the light was put out and the door closed softly.

The intruder did some rapid thinking. He crossed to the nearest of the windows, noiselessly opened the shutters and pushed them back to the position in which they stood when not in use. Then he unlatched the window and left it, hoping that it would not blow open and betray him. This done, he again pulled the heavy curtains across and returned to his place of concealment. That was to be the way out for him if the necessity for a rapid retreat should arise.

There was no sound save the ticking of the clock and the noise of falling cinders for ten minutes, and then he heard something which brought him to the alert, all his senses awakened and concentrated. It was the sound of a light and stealthy footstep on the terrace outside. He wondered whether it was a servant and whether he would see that one of the windows was unshuttered. He had half a mind to investigate, when there came another sound – a lumbering foot in the passage. Suddenly the door was opened, the lights were flashed on, and the man behind the settee hugged the floor and held his breath.

"How much do I want?"

Pinto laughed and lit a cigarette.

"My dear Mr. Crotin, I really don't know what you mean."

"Let's have no more foolery," said the Yorkshireman roughly. "I know that you've come up from Colonel Boundary and I know what you've come for. You want to buy my mill, eh? Well, I'll make it worth your while not to buy my mill. You can take the money instead."

"I really am honest when I tell you that I don't understand what you are talking about. I have certainly come up to buy a mill – that is true. It is also true that I want to buy your mill."

"And what might you be thinking of paying for it?" asked Crotin between his teeth.

"Twenty thousand pounds," said Pinto nonchalantly.

"Twenty thousand, eh? It was thirty thousand the last time. You'll want me to give it to you soon. Nay, nay, my friend, I'll pay, but not in mills."

"Think of the poor," murmured Pinto.

"I'm thinking of them," said the other. "I'm thinking of the poor woman in Wales, too, and the poor woman in there." He jerked his head. Then, in a calmer tone: "I guessed at dinner where you came from. Colonel Boundary sent you."

Pinto shrugged.

"Let us mention no names," he said politely. "And who is Colonel Boundary, anyway?"

Crotin was at his desk now. He had taken out his checkbook and slapped it down upon the writing-pad.

"You've got me proper," he said, and his voice quavered. "I'll make an offer to you. I'll give you fifty thousand pounds if you write an agreement that you will not molest or bother me again."

There was a silence, and the soldier crouched behind the settee, listening intently. He heard Pinto laugh softly as one who is greatly amused.

"That, my good friend," said Pinto, "would be blackmail. You don't imagine that I would be guilty of such an iniquity? I know nothing about your past; I merely suggest that you should sell me one of your mills at a reasonable price."

"Twenty thousand pounds is reasonable for you, I suppose," said Crotin sarcastically.

"It is a lot of money," replied Pinto.

The Yorkshireman pulled open the drawer of his desk and slammed in the checkbook, closing it with a bang.

"Well, I'll give you nothing," he said, "neither mill nor money. You can clear out of here."

He crossed the room to the telephone.

"What are you going to do?" asked Pinto, secretly alarmed.

"I'm going to send for the police," said the other grimly. "I'm going to give myself up and I'm going to pinch thee too!"

If Crotin had turned the handle of the old-fashioned telephone, if he had continued in his resolution, if he had shown no sign of doubt, a different story might have been told. But with his hand raised, he hesitated, and Pinto clinched his argument.

"Why have all that trouble?" he said. "Your liberty and reputation are much more to you than a mill. You're a rich man. Your wife is wealthy in her own right. You have enough to live on for the rest of your life. Why make trouble?"

The little man dropped his head with a groan and walked wearily back to the desk.

"Suppose I sell this?" he said in a low voice. "How do I know you won't come again –"

"When a gentleman gives his word of honor," began Pinto with dignity, but was interrupted by a shrill laugh that made his blood run cold.

He swung round with an oath. Framed in an opening of the curtains which covered one of the windows was the Figure!

The black silk gown, the white masked face, the soft felt hat pulled down over the eyes – his teeth chattered at the sight of it, and he fell back against the wall.

"Who wouldn't trust Pinto?" squeaked the voice. "Who wouldn't take Pinto's word of honor? Jack o' Judgment wouldn't, poor old Jack o' Judgment!"

Jack o' Judgment! The soldier behind the settee heard the words and gasped. Without any thought of consequence he raised his head and looked. The Jack o' Judgment was standing where he expected him to be. He had come through the window which the soldier had left unbarred. This time he carried no weapon in his hand, and Pinto was quick to see the possibilities. The electric switch was within reach, and his hand shot out. There was a click and the room went dark.

But the figure of Jack o' Judgment was silhouetted against the night, and Pinto whipped out the long knife which never left him and sent it hurtling at his enemy. He saw the figure duck, heard the crash of broken glass, and then Jack o' Judgment vanished. In a rage which was three parts terror, he sprang through the open French windows on to the terrace in time to see a dark figure drop over the balustrade and fly across the park.

Chapter XXVII

THE CAPTURE OF "JACK"

Pinto leapt the parapet and was following swiftly in its wake. He guessed rather than knew that for once Jack o' Judgment had come unarmed, and a wild exultation filled him at the thought that it was left to him to unveil the mystery which was weighing even upon the iron nerve of the colonel.

The figure gained the shrubbery, and the pursuer heard the rustle of leaves as it plunged into the depths. In a second he was blundering after. He lost sight of his quarry and stopped to listen. There was no sound.

"Hiding," grunted Pinto. And then aloud: "Come out of it. I see you and I'll shoot you like a dog if you don't come to me!"

There was no reply. He dashed in the direction he thought Jack o' Judgment must have taken and again missed. With a curse he turned off in another direction and then suddenly glimpsed a shape before him and leapt at it. He was flung back with little or no effort, and stood bewildered, for the coat his hand had touched was rough and he had felt metal buttons.

"A soldier!" he gasped. "Who are you?"

"Steady," said the other; "don't get rattled, Pinto."

"Who are you?" asked Pinto again.

"My name is Stafford King," said the soldier, "and I think I shall want you."

Pinto half turned to go, but was gripped.

"You can go back to Huddersfield and pack your boxes," said Stafford King. "You won't leave the town except by my permission."

"What do you mean?" demanded Pinto, breathing heavily.

"I mean," said Stafford King, "that the unfortunate man you tried to blackmail must prosecute whatever be the consequence to himself. Now, Pinto, you've a grand chance of turning King's evidence."

Pinto made no reply. He was collecting his thoughts. Then, after a while, he said:

"I'll talk about that later, King. I'm staying at the Huddersfield Arms. I'll meet you there in an hour."

Stafford King did not move until the sound of Pinto's footsteps had died away. Then he began a systematic search, for he too was anxious to end the mystery of Jack o' Judgment. He had followed Pinto when he dashed from the room and had heard the Portuguese calling upon Jack o' Judgment to surrender. That mysterious individual, who was obviously lying low, could not be very far away.

He was in a shrubbery which proved later to be a clump of rhododendrons, in the center of which was a summer-house. To the heart of this shrubbery led three paths, one of which Stafford discovered quite close at hand. The sound of gravel under his feet gave him an idea, and he began walking backward till he came to the shadow of a tree, and then, simulating the sound of retreating footsteps, he waited.

After a while he heard a rustle, but did not move.

Somebody was coming cautiously through the bushes, and that somebody appeared as a shadowy, indistinct figure, not twenty yards away. Only the keenest eyesight could have detected it, and still Stafford waited. Presently he heard the soft crunch of gravel under its feet, and at that moment leapt towards it. The figure stood as though paralyzed for a second, and then, turning quickly, fled back to the heart of the bushes. Before it had gone a dozen paces Stafford had reached it, and his arm was about its neck.

"My friend," he breathed, "I don't know what I'm to do with you now I've got you, but I certainly am going to register your face for future reference."

"No, no," said a muffled voice from behind the mask. "No, no, don't; I beg of you!"

But the mask was plucked away, and, fumbling in his pocket, Stafford produced his electric lamp and flashed it on the face of his prisoner. Then, with a cry of amazement, he stepped back – for he had looked upon the face of Maisie White!

For a moment there was silence, neither speaking. Then Stafford found his voice.

"Maisie!" he said in bewilderment, "Maisie! You – Jack o' Judgment?"

She did not answer.

"Phew!" whistled Stafford.

Then sitting on a trunk, he laughed.

"It is Maisie, of all people in the world. And I suspected it, too!"

The girl had covered her face with her hands and was crying softly, and he moved towards her and put his arm about her shoulder.

"Darling, it is nothing very terrible. Please don't go on like that."

"Oh, you don't understand, you don't understand!" she wailed. "I wanted to catch Silva. I guessed that he was coming north on one of his blackmailing trips, and I followed him."

"Did you come up by the same train?"

He felt her nod.

"So did I," said Stafford with a little grin.

"I followed him to the bazaar," she said, "and then I watched him from a little eating-house on the opposite side of the road. Do you know, I wondered whether you were here too, and I looked everywhere for you, but apparently there was nobody in sight when Pinto came out with Lady Sybil, only a soldier."

"I was that soldier," said Stafford.

"I discovered where Mr. Crotin lived and came up later," she went on. "Of course, I had no very clear idea of what I was going to do, and it was only by the greatest luck that I found the window of the library open. It was the only window that was open," she said with a little laugh.

"It wasn't so much your luck as my forethought," smiled Stafford.

"Now I want to tell you about Jack o' Judgment," she began, but he stopped her.

"Let that explanation wait," he said; "the point is, that with your evidence and mine we have Pinto by the throat – what was that?"

There was the sound of a shot.

"Probably a poacher," said Stafford after a moment. "I can't imagine Pinto using a gun. Besides, I don't think he carries one. What did he throw at you?"

"A knife," she said, and he felt her shiver; "it just missed me. But tell me, how have we got Pinto?"

They had left the shrubbery and were walking towards the house. She stopped a little while to take off her long black cloak, and he saw that she was wearing a short-skirted dress beneath.

"We must compel Crotin to prosecute," said Stafford. "With our evidence nothing can save Pinto, and probably he will drag in the colonel, too. Even your evidence isn't necessary," he said after a moment's thought, "and if it's possible I will keep you out of it."

A woman's scream interrupted him.

"There's trouble there," he said, and raced for the house. Somebody was standing on the terrace as he approached, and hailed him excitedly.

"Is that you, Terence?"

It was a servant's voice.

"No," replied Stafford, "I am a police officer."

"Thank God!" said the man on the terrace. "Will you come up, sir? I thought it was the gamekeeper I was speaking to."

"What is the matter?" asked Stafford as he vaulted over the parapet.

"Mr. Crotin has shot himself, sir," said the butler in quavering tones.

Twelve hours later Stafford King reported to his chief, giving the details of the overnight tragedy.

"Poor fellow!" said Sir Stanley. "I was afraid of it ending that way."

"Did you know he was being blackmailed?" asked Stafford.

Sir Stanley nodded.

"We had a report, which apparently emanated from Jack o' Judgment, who of late has started sending his communications to me direct," said Sir Stanley. "You can, of course, do nothing with Pinto. Your evidence isn't sufficient. What a pity you hadn't a second witness." He thought for a moment. "Even then it wouldn't have been sufficient unless we had Crotin to support you."

Stafford cleared his throat.

"I have a second witness, sir," he said.

"The devil you have!" Sir Stanley raised his eyebrows. "Who was your second witness?"

"Jack o' Judgment," said Stafford, and Sir Stanley jumped to his feet.

"Jack o' Judgment!" he repeated. "What do you mean?"

"Jack o' Judgment was there," said Stafford, and told the story of the remarkable appearance of that mysterious figure.

He told everything, reserving the identification of Jack till the last.

"And then you flashed the lamp on his face," said Sir Stanley. "Well, who was it?"

"Maisie White," said Stafford.

"Good Lord!"

Sir Stanley walked to the window and stood looking out, his hands thrust into his pockets. Presently he turned.

"There's a bigger mystery here than I suspected," he said. "Have you asked Miss White for an explanation?"

Stafford shook his head.

"I thought it best to report the matter to you, sir, before I asked her to –"

"To incriminate herself, eh? Well, perhaps you did wisely, perhaps you did not. I should imagine that her explanation is a very simple one."

"What do you mean, sir?"

"I mean," said Sir Stanley, "that unless Jack o' Judgment has the gift of appearing in two places at once, she is not Jack."

"But I don't understand, sir?"

"I mean," said Sir Stanley, "that Jack o' Judgment was in the colonel's room last night, was in fact sitting by the colonel's bedside when that gentleman awoke, and according to the statement which Colonel Boundary has made to me about two hours ago in this room, warned him of his approaching end."

It was Stafford's turn to be astonished.

"Are you sure, sir?" he asked incredulously.

"Absolutely!" said Sir Stanley. "You don't imagine that the colonel would invent that sort of thing. For some reason or other, possibly to keep close to the trouble that's coming, the colonel insists upon bringing all his little chit-chat to me. He asked for an interview about ten o'clock this morning and reported to me that he had had this visitation. Moreover, the experience has had the effect of upsetting the colonel, and for the first time he seems to be thoroughly rattled. Where is Miss White?"

"She's here, sir."

"Here, eh?" said the commissioner. "So much the better. Can you bring her in?"

A few minutes later the girl sat facing the First Commissioner.

"Now, Miss White, we're going to ask you for a few facts about your masquerade," said Sir Stanley kindly. "I understand that you appeared wearing the costume, and giving a fairly good imitation of the voice of Jack o' Judgment. Now, I'm telling you before we go any further that I do not believe for one moment that you are Jack o' Judgment. Am I right?"

She nodded.

"Perfectly true, Sir Stanley," she said. "I don't know why I did such a mad thing, except that I knew Pinto was scared of him. I got the cloak from my dress-basket and made the mask myself. You see, I didn't know whether I might want it, but I thought that in a tight pinch, if I wished to terrify this man, that was the rôle to assume."

Sir Stanley nodded.

"And the voice, of course, was easy."

"But how could you imitate the voice if you have never seen Jack o' Judgment?"

"I saw him once." She shivered a little. "You seem to forget, Sir Stanley, that he rescued me from that dreadful house."

"Of course," said Sir Stanley, "and you imitated him, did you?" He turned to his subordinate. "I'm accepting Miss White's explanation, Stafford, and I advise you to do the same. She went up to watch Silva, as I understand, and took the costume with her as a sort of protection. Well, Miss White, are you satisfied with your detective work?"

She smiled ruefully.

"I'm afraid I'm a failure as a detective," she said.

"I'm afraid you are," laughed Sir Stanley, as he rose and offered his hand. "There is only one real detective in the world – and that is Jack o' Judgment!"

Chapter XXVIII

THE PASSING OF PHILLOPOLIS

If Pinto Silva had a hobby, it was the Orpheum Theater. The Orpheum had been in low water and had come into the market at a moment when theatrical managers and proprietors were singularly unenterprizing and money was short. Pinto had bought the property for a song, and had converted his purchase into a moderate success. The theater served a double purpose; it provided Pinto with a hobby, and offered an excuse for his wealth. Since it was a one-man show, and he produced no balance-sheet, his contemporaries could only make a guess as to the amount of money he made. If the truth be told, it was not very large, but small as it was, its dividends more or less justified his own leisure.

There had been one or two scandals about the Orpheum which had reached the public Press – scandals of a not particularly edifying character. But Pinto had managed to escape public opprobrium.

The Orpheum, at any rate, helped to baffle the police, who saw Silva living at the rate of twenty thousand a year, and were unable to trace the source of his income. That he had estates in Portugal was known; but they had been acquired, apparently, on the profits of the music hall. He was not a speculator, though he was a shareholder in a number of companies which were controlled by the colonel; and he was certainly not a gambler, in the generally accepted sense of the term.

Whilst he was suspected of being intimately connected with several shady transactions, he could boast truly that there was not a scrap of evidence to associate him with any breach of the law. He was less inclined to boast that evening, when he turned into the stage-box at the Orpheum, and pulling his chair into the shadow of the draperies, sat back and considered his position. He had returned from Yorkshire in a panic, and had met the fury of the colonel's reproaches. It was the worst quarter of an hour that Pinto had ever spent with his superior, and the memory made him shiver.

The stage-box at the Orpheum was never sold to any member of the public. It was Pinto's private possession, his sitting room and his office. He sat watching with gloomy interest the progress of the little revue which was a feature of the Orpheum program, and his mind was occupied by a very pressing problem. He was shaken, too, by the interview he had had with the Huddersfield police.

He had had to fake a story to explain why he left the library, and why, in his absence, Mr. Crotin had committed suicide. Fortunately, he had returned to the house by the front hall and was in the hall inventing a story of burglars to the agitated Lady Sybil when they heard the shot which ended the wretched life of the bigamist. That had saved him from being suspected of actual complicity in the crime. Suppose they had – he sweated at the thought.

There was a knock on the door of the box, and an attendant put in his head.

"There's a gentleman to see you, sir," he said; "he says he has an appointment."

"What is his name?"

"Mr. Cartwright."

Pinto nodded.

"Show him in, please," he said, and dismissed all unpleasant thoughts.

The newcomer proved to be a dapper little man, with a weather-beaten face. He was in evening dress, and spoke like a gentleman.

"I had your letter, Mr. Silva," he said. "You received my telephone message?"

"Yes," said Silva. "I wanted to see you particularly. You understand that what I say is wholly confidential."

"That I understand," said the man called Cartwright.

He took Pinto's proffered cigarette and lit it.

"I have been reading about you in the papers," said Pinto. "You're the man who did the non-stop flight for the Western Airplane Company?"

"That's right," smiled Cartwright. "I have done many long nights. I suppose you are referring to my San Sebastian trip?"

Pinto nodded.

"Now I want to ask you a few questions, and if they seem to be prying or personal, you must believe that I have no other wish than to secure information which is vital to myself. What position do you occupy with the Western Company?"

Cartwright shrugged his shoulders.

"I am a pilot," he said. "If you mean, am I a director of the firm or am I interested in the company financially, I regret that I must answer No. I wish I were," he added, "but I am merely an employee."

Pinto nodded.

"That is what I wanted to know," he said. "Now, here is another question. What does a first-class airplane cost?"

"It depends," said the other. "A long distance machine, such as I have been flying, would cost anything up to five thousand pounds."

"Could you buy one? Are they on the market?" asked Pinto quickly.

"I could buy a dozen tomorrow," said the other promptly. "The R.A.F. have been selling off their machines, and I know just where I could get one of the best in Britain."

Pinto was looking at the stage, biting his lips thoughtfully.

"I'll tell you what I want," he said. "I am not very keenly interested in aviation, but it may be necessary that I should return to Portugal in a great hurry. It is no news to you that we Portuguese are generally in the throes of some revolution or other."

"So I understand," said Cartwright, with a twinkle in his eye.

"In those circumstances," Pinto went on, "it may be necessary for me to leave this country without going through the formality of securing a passport. I want a machine which will carry me from London to, say, Cintra, without a stop, and I want a pilot who can take me across the sea by the direct route."

"Across the Bay of Biscay?" asked the aviator in surprise, and Pinto nodded.

"I should not want to touch any other country en route, for reasons which, I tell you frankly, are political."

Cartwright thought a moment.

"Yes, I think I can get you the machine, and I'm certain I can find you the pilot," he said.

"To put it bluntly," said Pinto, "would you take on an engagement for twelve months, secure the machine, house it and have it ready for me? I will pay you liberally." He mentioned a sum which satisfied the airman. "It must not be known that the machine is mine. You must buy it and keep it in your own name."

"There's no difficulty about that," said Cartwright. "Am I to understand that I must go ahead with the purchase of the airplane?"

"You can start right away," said Pinto. "The sooner you have the machine ready for a flight the better. I am here almost every night, and I will give orders to the collectors on the barrier that you are to come to me just whenever you want. If you will meet me here tomorrow morning, say at eleven o'clock, I can give you cash for the purchase of the machine, and I shall be happy to pay you half a year's salary in advance."

"It will take some time to clear my old job," said Cartwright thoughtfully, "but I think I can do it for you. At any rate, I can get time off to buy the machine. You say that you do not want anybody to know that it is yours?"

Pinto nodded.

"Well, that's easy," said the other. "I've been thinking about buying a machine of my own for some time and have made inquiries in several quarters."

He rose to leave and shook hands.

"Remember," said Pinto as a final warning, "not a word about this to any human soul."

"You can trust me," said the man.

Pinto watched the rest of the play with a lighter heart. After all, there could be nothing very much to fear. What had thrown him off his balance for the moment was the presence of Stafford King in Yorkshire, and when that detective chief did not make his appearance at the police inquiry nor had sought him in his hotel, it looked as though the colonel's words were true, and that Scotland Yard were after Boundary himself and none other.

He sat the performance through and then went to his club – an institution off Pall Mall which had been quite satisfied to accept Pinto to membership without making any too close inquiries as to his antecedents.

He spent some time before the tape machine, watching the news tick forth, then strolled into the smoking-room and read the evening papers for the second time. Only one item of news really interested him – it had interested the colonel too. The diamondsmiths' premises in Regent Street had been burgled the night before and the contents of the safe cleared. The colonel had arrested his flow of vituperation, to speculate as to the "artist" who had carried out this neat job.

Pinto read for a little, then threw the paper down. He wondered what made him so restive and why he was so anxious to find something to occupy his attention, and then he realized with a start that he did not want to go back to face Colonel Boundary. It was the first time he had ever experienced this sensation, and he did not like it. He had held his place in the gang by the assurance, which was also an assumption, that he was at least the colonel's equal. This irritated him. He put on his overcoat and turned into the street. It was a chilly night and a thin drizzle of rain was falling. He pulled up his coat-collar and looked about for a taxi-cab. Neither outside the club nor in Pall Mall was one visible.

He started to walk home, but still felt that disinclination to face the colonel. Then a thought struck him; he would go and see Phillopolis, the little Greek.

Phillopolis patronized a night-club in Soho, where he was usually to be found between midnight and two in the morning. Having an objective, Pinto felt in a happier frame of mine and walked briskly the intervening distance. He found his man sitting at a little marble-topped table by himself, contemplating a half-bottle of sweet champagne and a half-filled glass. He was evidently deep in thought, and started violently when Pinto addressed him.

"Sit down," he said with evident relief. "I thought it was –"

"Who did you think it was? You thought it was the police, I suppose?" said Pinto with heavy jocularity, and to his amazement he saw the little man wince.

"What has happened to Colonel Boundary?" asked the Greek irritably. "There used to be a time when anybody he spoke for was safe. I'm getting out of this country and I'm getting out quick," he added.

"Why?" asked Pinto, who was vitally interested.

The Greek threw out his hands with a little grimace.

"Nerves," he said. "I haven't got over that affair with the White girl."

"Pooh!" said the other. "If the police were moving in that matter, they'd have moved long ago. You are worrying yourself unnecessarily, Phillopolis."

Pinto's words slipped glibly from his tongue, but Phillopolis was unimpressed.

"I know when I've had enough," he said. "I've got my passport and I'm clearing out at the end of this week."

"Does the colonel know this?"

The Greek raised his shoulders indifferently.

"I don't know whether he does or whether he doesn't," he said. "Anyway, Boundary and I are only remotely connected in business, and my movements are no affair of his."

He looked curiously at the other.

"I wonder that a man like you, who is in the heart of things, stays on when the net is drawing round the old man."

"Loyalty is a vice with me," said Pinto virtuously. "Besides, there's no reason to bolt – as yet."

"I'm going whilst I'm safe," said Phillopolis, sipping his champagne. "At present the police have nothing against me and I'm going to take good care they have nothing. That's where I've the advantage of people like you."

Pinto smiled.

"They've nothing on me," he said easily. "I have an absolutely clean record."

It disturbed him, however, to discover that even so minor a member of the gang as Phillopolis was preparing to desert what he evidently regarded as a sinking ship. More than this, it confirmed him in the wisdom of his own precautions, and he was rather glad that he had taken it into his head to visit Phillopolis on that night.

"When do you leave?" he asked.

"The day after tomorrow," said Phillopolis. "I think I'll go down into Italy for a year. I've made enough money now to live without worrying about work, and I mean to enjoy myself."

Pinto looked at the man with interest. Here, at any rate, was one without a conscience. The knowledge that he had accumulated his fortune through the miseries of innocent girls shipped to foreign dance halls did not weigh greatly upon his mind.

"Lucky you!" said Pinto, as they walked out of the club together. "Where do you live, by the way?"

"In Somers Street, Soho. It is just round the corner," said Phillopolis. "Will you walk there with me?"

Pinto hesitated.

"Yes, I will," he said.

He wanted to see the sort of establishment which Phillopolis maintained. They chatted together till they came to the street, and then Phillopolis stopped.

"Do you mind if I go ahead?" he said. "I have a – friend there who might be worried by your coming."

Pinto smiled to himself.

"Certainly," he said. "I'll wait on the opposite side of the road until you are ready."

The man lived above a big furniture shop, and admission was gained by a side door. Pinto watched him pass through the portals and heard the door close. He was a long time gone, and evidently his "friend" was unprepared to receive visitors at that hour, or else Phillopolis himself had some reason for postponing the invitation.

The reason for the delay was explained in a sensational manner. Suddenly the door opened and a man came out. He was followed by two others and between them was Phillopolis, and the street-lamp shone upon the steel handcuffs on his wrists. Pinto drew back into a doorway and watched. Phillopolis was talking – it would perhaps be more accurate to say that he was raving at the top of his voice, cursing and sobbing in a frenzy.

"You planted them – it is a plant!" he yelled. "You devils!"

"Are you coming quietly?" said a voice. "Or are you going to make trouble? Take him, Dempsey!"

Phillopolis seemed to have forgotten Pinto's presence, for he went out of the street without once calling upon him to testify to his character and innocence. Pinto waited till he was gone, and then strolled across the road to the detective who stood before the door lighting his pipe.

"Good evening," he said, "has there been some trouble?"

The officer looked at him suspiciously. But Pinto was in evening dress and talked like a gentleman, and the policeman thawed.

"Nothing very serious, sir," he said, "except for the man. He's a fence."

"A what?" said Pinto with well-feigned innocence.

"A receiver of stolen property. We found his lodgings full of stuff."

"Good Heavens!" gasped Pinto.

"Yes, sir," said the man, delighted that he had created a sensation. "I never saw so much valuable property in one room in my life. There was a big burglary in Regent Street last night. A jeweler's shop was cleared out of about twenty thousand pounds' worth of necklaces, and we found every bit of it here tonight. We've always suspected this man," he went on confidentially. "Nobody knew how he got his living, but from information we received today we were able to catch him red-handed."

"Thank you," said Pinto faintly, and walked slowly home, for now he no longer feared to meet the colonel. He had something to tell him, something that would inspire even Boundary with apprehension.

Chapter XXIX

THE VOICE IN THE ROOM

As Silva anticipated, the colonel was up and waiting for him. He was playing Patience on his desk and looked up with a scowl as the Portuguese entered.

"So you've been skulking, have you, Pinto?" he began, but the other interrupted him.

"You can keep all that talk for another time," he said. "They've taken Phillopolis!"

The colonel swept his cards aside with a quick, nervous gesture.

"Taken Phillopolis?" he repeated slowly. "On what charge?"

"For being the receiver of stolen property," said the other. "They found the proceeds of the Regent Street burglary in his apartments."

The colonel opened his mouth to speak, then shut it again, and there was silence for two or three minutes.

"I see. They have planted the stuff on him, have they?"

"What do you mean?" asked Pinto.

"You don't suppose that Phillopolis is a fence, do you?" said the colonel scornfully. "Why, it is a business that a man must spend the whole of his life at before he can be successful. No, Phillopolis knows no more about that burglary or the jewels than you or I. The stuff has been planted in his rooms."

"But the police don't do that sort of thing."

"Who said the police did it?" snarled the colonel. "Of course they didn't. They haven't the sense. That's Mr. Jack o' Judgment once more, and this time, Pinto, he's real dangerous."

"Jack o' Judgment!" gasped Pinto. "But would he commit a burglary?"

The colonel laughed scornfully.

"Would he commit murder? Would he hang Raoul? Would he shoot you? Don't ask such damn-fool questions, Silva! Of course it was Jack o' Judgment. I tell you, the night you were in Yorkshire making a mess of that Crotin business, Jack o' Judgment came here, to this very room, and told me that he would ruin us one by one, and that he would leave me to the last. He mentioned us all – you, Crewe, Selby –"

He stopped suddenly and scratched his chin.

"But not Lollie Marsh," he said. "That's queer, he never mentioned Lollie Marsh!"

He was deep in thought for a few moments, then he went on:

"So he's worked off Phillopolis, has he? Well, Phillopolis has got to take his medicine. I can do nothing for him."

"But surely he can prove –" began Pinto.

"What can he prove?" asked the other. "Can he prove how he earns his money? He's been taken with the goods; he hasn't that chance," he snapped his fingers. "I'll make a prophecy," he said: "Phillopolis will get five years' penal servitude, and nothing in the world can save him from that."

"An innocent man!" said Pinto in amazement. "Impossible!"

"But is he innocent?" asked the colonel sourly. "That's the point you've got to keep in your mind. He may be innocent of one kind of crookedness, and be so mixed up in another that he cannot prove he is innocent of either. That's where they've got this fellow. He dare not appeal to the people who know him best, because they'd give him away. He can't tell the police who are his agents in Greece or Armenia, or they'll find out just the kind of agency he was running."

He squatted back in his chair, pulling at his long moustache.

"Phillopolis, Crewe, Pinto, Selby, and then me," said he, speaking to himself, "and he never mentioned Lollie Marsh. And Lollie has been the decoy duck that has been in every hunt we've had. This wants looking into, Pinto."

As he finished speaking there was a little buzz from the corner of the room and Pinto looked up startled. The colonel looked up too and a slow smile dawned on his face.

"A visitor," he said softly. "Not our old friend Jack o' Judgment, surely!"

"What is it?" asked Pinto.

"A little alarm I've had fixed under one of the treads of the stairs," said the other. "I don't like to be taken unawares."

"Perhaps it is Crewe," suggested the other.

"Crewe's gone home an hour ago," said the colonel. "No, this is a genuine visitor."

They waited for some time and then there was a knock at the outer door.

"Open it, Pinto," and as the other did not instantly move, "open it, damn you! What are you afraid of?"

"I'm not afraid of anything," growled the Portuguese and flung out of the room.

Yet he hesitated again before he turned the handle of the outer door. He flung it open and stepped back. He would have gone farther, but the wall was at his back and he could only stand with open mouth staring at the visitor. It was Maisie White.

She returned his gaze steadily.

"I want to see Colonel Boundary," she said.

"Certainly, certainly," said Pinto huskily.

He shut the door and ushered her into the colonel's presence. Boundary's eyes narrowed as he saw the girl. He suspected a trap and looked past her as though expecting to see an escort behind her.

"This is an unexpected honor, Miss White," he said suavely, and he looked meaningly at the clock on the mantelpiece. "We do not usually receive visitors so late, and especially charming lady visitors."

She was carrying a thick package, and this she laid on the table.

"I'm sorry it is so late," she said calmly, "but I have been all the evening checking my father's accounts. This is yours."

She handed the package to the colonel.

"That parcel contains banknotes to the value of twenty-seven thousand three hundred pounds," said the girl quietly; "it represents what remains of the money which my father drew from your gang."

"Tainted money, eh?" said the colonel humorously. "I think you're very foolish, Miss White. Your father earned this money by legitimate business enterprises."

"I know all about them," she said. "I won't ask you to count the notes, because it is only a question of getting the money off my own conscience, and the amount really doesn't matter."

"So you came here alone to make this act of reparation?" sneered the colonel.

"I came here to make this act of reparation," she replied steadily.

"Not alone, eh? Surrounded entirely by police. Mr. Stafford King in the offing, waiting outside in a taxi, or probably waiting on the mat," said the colonel in the same tone. "Well, well, you're quite safe with us, Miss White."

He took up the package and tore off the wrapping, revealing two wads of banknotes, and ran his finger along the edges.

"And how are you going to live?" he asked.

"By working," said the girl; "that's a strange way of earning a living, don't you think, colonel?"

"You'll never work harder than I have worked," said Colonel Dan Boundary good-humoredly. And, looking down at the money: "So that's

Solly White's share, is it? And I suppose it doesn't include the house he bought, or the car?"

"I've sold everything," said the girl quietly; "every piece of property he owned has been realized, and that is the proceeds."

With a little nod she was withdrawing, but Pinto barred her way.

"One moment, Miss White," he said, and there was a dangerous glint in his eye, "if you choose to come here alone in the middle of the night –"

The colonel stepped between them, and he swept the Portuguese backwards. Without a word he opened the door.

"Good night, Miss White," he said. "My kind regards to Mr. Stafford King, who I suppose is somewhere on the premises, and to all the bright lads of the Criminal Intelligence Department who are at this moment watching the house."

She smiled, but did not take his proffered hand.

"Good-bye," she said.

The colonel accompanied her to the outer door and switched on all the stair lights, as he could from the master-switch near the entrance to his flat, and waited until the echo of her footsteps had passed away before he came back to the man.

"You're a clever fellow, you are, Pinto," he said quietly; "you have one of the brightest minds in the gang."

"If she comes here alone –" began Pinto.

"Alone!" snarled the colonel. "I hinted a dozen times, if I hinted once, that she'd come with a young army of police. The first shout she made would have been the signal for your arrest and mine. Haven't you had your lesson tonight? How long do you think it would take Stafford King to trump up a charge against you and put you where the dogs wouldn't bite, eh?"

He walked to the window and watched the girl. There was a taxi-cab waiting at the entrance, and as he had suspected, a man was standing by the door and followed the girl into the cab before it drove away.

"She timed her visit. I suppose she gave herself five minutes. If she'd been here any longer, they would have been up for her, make no mistake about that, Pinto."

The colonel drew down the blinds with a crash and began pacing the room. He stopped at the farther end and looked at the wall.

"Do you know, I've often wondered why Jack o' Judgment damaged that wall?" he said. "He's got me guessing, and I've been guessing ever since."

"You thought it was a freak?" said Pinto, glad to keep his master off the subject of his Huddersfield blunder.

The colonel shook his head.

"I shouldn't think it was that," he said. "It was not like Jack o' Judgment to do freakish things. He has an object in everything he does."

"Perhaps it was to get you out of the room for the morning and make a search for your papers," suggested Pinto.

Again the colonel shook his head.

"He knows me better than that. He knew very well that I would shift every document from the room and that there was nothing for his bloodhounds to discover." He thought a moment, pulling at his long, yellow moustache. "Maybe," he said to himself, "maybe –"

"Maybe what?" asked Pinto.

"The workmen may have been up to some kind of dodge. They might have been policemen for all I know." He shrugged his shoulders. "Anyway, that's long ago, and if he'd made a discovery, why, I think we should have heard about it. Now, Pinto," – his tone changed – "I'm not going to talk to you about Crotin. You've made a proper mess of it, and I ought never to have sent you. We have two matters to settle. Crewe wants to get out, and I think you're getting ready to bolt."

"Me?" said Pinto with virtuous indignation. "Do you imagine I should leave you, colonel, if you were in for a bad time?"

"Do I imagine it?" The colonel laughed. "Don't be a fool. Sit down. When did you see Lollie Marsh last?"

Pinto considered.

"I haven't seen her for weeks."

"Neither have I," said the colonel. "Of course she has an excuse for staying away. She never comes unless she's sent for. If we've got a mug we want to lead down the easy path, why, there's nobody in London who can do it like Lollie. And I understand you had some disagreement with the young lady over Maisie White?"

"She interfered –" began Pinto.

"And probably saved your life," remarked the colonel meaningly. "No, you have no kick against Lollie for that."

He pulled open the drawer of his desk, took out a card and wrote rapidly.

"I'll put Snakit on her trail," he said.

"Snakit!" said the other contemptuously.

"He's all right for this kind of work," said the colonel, alluding to the little detective whom he had bought over from Maisie White's service. "Snakit can trail her. He does nothing for his keep, and Lollie doesn't know him, does she?"

"I don't think so," said Pinto absently. "If you believe that Lollie is double-crossing you, why don't you –"

"I'll write to you when I want any suggestions as to how to run my business," said the colonel unpleasantly. "Where does Lollie live?"

"Tavistock Avenue," said Pinto. "I wish you'd be a little more decent to me, colonel. I'm trying to play the game by you."

"And you'll soon get tired of trying," said the colonel. "Don't worry, Pinto. I know just how much I can depend upon you and just what your loyalty is worth. You'll sell me at the first opportunity, and you'll be dead about the same day. I only hope for your sake that the opportunity never arises. That's that," he said, as he finished the card and put it on one side. "Now what is the next thing?" He looked up at the ceiling for inspiration. "Crewe," he said, "Crewe is getting out of hand too. I put him on a job to trace 'Snow' Gregory's past. I haven't seen or heard of him for two days, either."

Somebody laughed. It was a queer, little faraway laugh, but Pinto recognized it and his hair almost stood on end. He looked across at the colonel with ashen face, and then swung round apprehensively toward the door.

"Did you hear that?" he whispered.

"I heard it – thank the lord!" said the colonel, and fetched a long sigh.

Pinto gazed at him in amazement.

"Why," he said in a low voice, "that was Jack o' Judgment!"

"I know," said the colonel nodding; "but I still thank the lord!"

He got up slowly and walked round the room, opened the door that led to his bedroom, and put on the light. The room was empty, and the only cupboard which might have concealed an intruder was wide open. He came back, walked into the entrance hall, and opened the door softly. The landing was empty too. He returned after fastening the door and slipping the bolts – bolts which he had had fixed during the previous week.

"You wonder why I held a thanksgiving service?" said the colonel slowly. "Well, I've heard that laugh before, and I thought my brain was going – that's all. I'd rather it were Jack o' Judgment in the flesh than Jack o' Judgment wandering loose around my hut."

"You heard it before?" said Pinto. "Here?"

"Here in this room," said the colonel. "I thought I was going daft. You're the first person who has heard it besides myself." He looked at Pinto. "A hell of a prospect, isn't it?" he said gloomily. "Let's talk about the weather!"

Chapter XXX

DIAMONDS FOR THE BANK

There was no hope for Phillopolis from the first. The case against him was so clear and so damning that the magistrate, before whom the preliminary inquiry was heard, had no hesitation in committing him to take his trial at the Old Bailey on a charge of receiving, and that at the first hearing. Every article which had been stolen from the diamondsmiths' company had been recovered in his flat. The police experts gave evidence to the effect that he had been a suspected man for years, that his method of earning a living had on several occasions been the subject of police inquiry. He was known to be, so the evidence ran, the associate of criminal characters, and on two occasions his flat had been privately raided.

The woman who passed as his wife had nothing good to say of him. It was not she who had admitted the police. Indeed, they found her in an upper room, locked in. Phillopolis was something of a tyrant, and on the day of his arrest he had had a quarrel with the woman, who had threatened to expose him to the police for some breach of the law. He had beaten her and locked her into an upper bedroom, and this act of tyranny had proved his downfall, if it were true, as he swore so vehemently that the articles which were found in his room had been planted there.

The colonel was not present, nor were any other members of the gang, save little Selby, who had been summoned to the colonel's presence and had arrived in the early morning.

"He hasn't a ghost of a chance," reported Selby, who had a lifelong acquaintance with criminals of the meaner sort, and had spent no small amount of his time in police courts, securing evidence as to the virtue of his protégés. "If he doesn't get ten years I'm a Dutchman."

"What does Phillopolis say?"

"He swears that the goods were not in his flat when he went out that night," he said, "but if they were planted, the work was done thoroughly.

The detectives found jewel cases under cushions, hidden in cupboards, on the tops of shelves, and one of the best bits of swag – a wonderful diamond necklace – was discovered in his boot, at the bottom of his trunk."

The conversation took place in the Green Park, which was a favorite haunt of the colonel's. He loved to sit on a chair by the side of the lake, watching the children sailing their boats and the ducks mothering their broods. He was silent. His eyes were bent upon the efforts of a small boy to bring a little waterlogged boat to a level keel and apparently he had no other interest.

"Have a cigar, Selby," he said at last. "What is the news in your part of the world?"

Selby was carefully biting off the end of his gift.

"Nothing much," he said. "We got some letters the other day from Mrs. Crombie-Brail. Her son has got into trouble at the Cape. Lew Litchfield got them. He was doing a job in Manchester."

Lew Litchfield was a bright young burglar of whom the colonel had heard, and he knew the kind of "job" on which Lew was engaged.

"You bought 'em?" he asked.

"I gave a tenner for them," said Selby. "I don't think they're much use."

The colonel shook his head.

"That's not the kind of letter that brings in money," he said. "You can't bleed a mother because her son got into trouble – at least, not for more than a hundred."

"Letters have been scarce lately," said his agent disconsolately; "I think people have either given up keeping or writing them."

"Maybe," said the colonel. "Anyway, I didn't bring you down to talk about letters. I've work for you."

Selby looked uneasy, and that in itself was a discouraging sign. Usually the little crook from the north hailed a job of any kind with enthusiasm.

It was an unmistakable proof to the colonel that he was losing grip, that the magic of his name and all that it implied in the way of protection from punishment, was less than it had been.

"You don't seem very pleased," he said.

Selby forced a smile.

"Well, colonel," he said, "I've a feeling they're after us, and I don't want to take any risks."

"You'll take this one," said the colonel. "There's somebody to be put away."

The man licked his lips.

"Well, I'm not in it," he said. "I had enough with that Hanson business."

"By 'put away' I don't mean murdered or ill-treated in any sense," said the colonel, "and besides, it is one of our own people."

But even this assurance did not satisfy the man.

"I don't like it," he said; "they tell me that this Jack o' Judgment –"

"Just forget Jack o' Judgment for a minute and think of yourself," snapped the colonel. "You've made your pile, and you find England's getting a bit too hot for you, don't you?"

"I do indeed," said the man fervently. "You know, colonel, I was thinking that a trip to America wouldn't be a bad idea."

"There are plenty of places to go to without going to Amcrica," said the colonel. "I tell you that I mean Lollie no harm."

"Lollie?" Selby was surprised, and showed it. "She hasn't –"

"I don't know what she's done yet, but I think it is time she went away," said the colonel, "and so far as I can judge, it is time you went too, Selby. I don't know whether Lollie is betraying us, and maybe I'm doing her an injustice," he went on, "but if I put up to her a suggestion that she should leave the country, maybe she'd probably turn me down. You know how suspicious these women are. The only idea I can think of is to scare her and make her bolt quick and sudden, and I want you to provide the means."

Selby was waiting.

"I bought a motor-boat, one of those swift motor-boats that the Government used during the war. I have it ready at Twickenham, and you can get all your goods on board and go to –"

"Where?"

"Anywhere you like," said the colonel, "Holland, Denmark – one place is as good as another, and it'll be a good sea-going boat. You see, my idea is this. If I think Lollie is negotiating to put us away, I can give her a fright which will make her jump at the means of getting out of England by the quickest and shortest route. You can go with her and keep her under your eye until the trouble blows over."

He saw a look in the man's face and correctly interpreted it.

"I'm not worried about *you* double-crossing me," he said, "even if you are abroad. I've enough evidence against you to bring you back under an extradition warrant." He laughed as Selby's face fell. "You see Selby, there's nothing in it that you can take exception to. I don't even know that Lollie will refuse to go in the ordinary way, but I must make preparations."

"It is a reasonable suggestion," said Selby, after considering the matter for a few minutes. "I'll do it, colonel."

"You'd better bring a couple of men to London who can handle Lollie if she gives any trouble – no, no," said the colonel, raising his hand in dignified protest, "there's going to be nothing rough. How can there be? You'll be in charge of it all, and it is up to you as to how Lollie is treated."

It did not occur to Selby until an hour later to ask the colonel how he knew that his hobby was motor-boating, but by that time the colonel had gone.

It was true, as Boundary said, that the gang was scared – and badly scared. It was equally true that they needed only one jar before it became a case of every man for himself. Already even the minor members were making their preparations to break away. The red light was burning clear before all eyes. But none knew how readily the colonel had recognized the signs, and how, in spite of his apparent philosophy and his contempt of danger, he, more than any of the others, was preparing for the inevitable crash.

Jack o' Judgment, he told himself, was playing his game better than he could play it himself. The arrest of Phillopolis had removed one of the men who might have been an inconvenient witness against him. White was gone, Raoul was gone. He had planned the disappearance of Selby, a most dangerous man, and Lollie Marsh, an even more dangerous woman and there remained only Pinto and Crewe.

When he had taken leave of his agent, the colonel walked to Westminster and boarded a car which carried him along the Embankment to Blackfriars. He might have been followed, and probably was, but this possibility did not worry him. He walked across Ludgate Circus, up St. Bride Street to Hatton Garden, and turned into the office of Myglebergs'. Mr. Mygleberg, a very suave and polite gentleman, received him and ushered him into a private room. This shrewd Dutchman had no illusions as to the colonel's probity, but he had no doubt either that the big man could pay handsomely for everything he bought.

"I'm glad you've come, colonel," he said; "I have been expecting you for a couple of days. We have just had a wonderful parcel of stones from Amsterdam, and I think some of them would suit you."

He disappeared and came back with a tray covered with the most beautiful diamonds that had ever left the cutter's hands. The colonel went over them slowly, examining them and putting a selected number aside.

"I'll take those," he said, and Mr. Mygleberg laughed.

"They're the best," he chuckled. "Trust you to know a good thing when you see it, colonel!"

"What have I to pay for these?"

Mygleberg made a rapid calculation and put the figures before Colonel Boundary.

"It is a big price," said the colonel, "but I don't think you have overcharged. Besides, I could always sell them again for that much."

Mr. Mygleberg nodded.

"I think you are wise to put your money into stones, colonel," he said; "they always go up and never go down in value. You can lose other things. They're easy and they're always convertible. I always tell my partner that if I ever become a millionaire I shall invest every penny in stones."

The colonel paid for the gems from a thick wad of notes he took from his hip-pocket. They were, in point of fact, the identical notes which Maisie White had handed to him the night previous. He waited whilst the jewels were made up into a little oblong package, heavily sealed and inscribed with the colonel's name and address, and then, shaking hands with Mygleberg and fixing a further appointment, he came out into Hatton Garden, whistling a little song and apparently the picture of contentment.

He was getting ready for flight too. This, the first of many packages which he intended depositing in the private safe of his bank, would go with the ever-increasing pile of American gold bonds of high denomination which filled that steel repository. For months the colonel had been converting his property into paper dollars. They were more easily negotiated and less traceable than English banknotes, and they were more get-at-able. A big balance in the books of the bank might be creditable and, given time, convertible into cash. Then nobody knew but himself the amount standing to his credit. He was not at the mercy of prying bank clerks or a manager who might be got at by the police. At a minute's notice, and without anybody being the wiser, he could demand the contents of his safe and walk from the bank premises without a soul being aware that he was carrying the bulk of his fortune away.

He took a cab and drove now to the bank premises. Ferguson, the manager, received him.

"Good morning, colonel," he said. "I was just writing you a note. You know your account is getting very low."

"Is that so?" said the colonel in surprise.

"I thought you wouldn't realize the fact," said Ferguson, "but you've been drawing very heavily of late."

"I'll put it right," said the colonel. "It is not overdrawn?" he asked jocularly, and Ferguson smiled.

"You've eighty thousand pounds in Account B," he said. "I suppose you don't want to touch that?"

Account B was the euphonious name for the fund which was the common property of all the leaders of the Boundary Gang.

"Unless you're anxious that I should get penal servitude for fraudulently converting the company's funds?" said the colonel in the same strain. "No, I'll fix my account some time today. In the meantime" – he produced a package from his hip-pocket – "I want this to go into my safe."

"Certainly," said Ferguson, and struck a bell. A clerk answered the call. "Take Colonel Boundary to the vaults. He wants to deposit something in his safe," he said, "or would you like me to do it, colonel?"

"I'll do it myself," said the colonel.

He followed the clerk down the spiral staircase to the well-lit vault, and with the key which the man handed him opened Safe No. 20. It was divided into two compartments, that on the left consisting of a deep drawer, which he pulled out. It was half filled with American paper currency, as he knew – currency neatly parceled and carefully packed by his own hands.

"I often wonder, Colonel Boundary," said the interested clerk, "why you don't use the bank safe. When a customer has his own, you know, we are not responsible for any of his losses."

"I know that," said the colonel genially. "Still one must take a risk."

He placed the package on the top of the money, pushed back the drawer, locked the safe and handed the key to the young man.

"I think the bank takes enough risks without asking them to accept anymore," he said, "and besides, I like to take a little risk myself sometimes."

"So I've heard," said the clerk innocently, and the colonel shot a questioning look at the young man.

Chapter XXXI

THE VOICE AGAIN

He left the bank with the sense of having done his duty by himself. He had not planned the route by which he was leaving the country, or the hour. Much was to happen before he shook the dust of England from his feet, and as he had arranged matters he would have plenty of time to think things over before he made his departure.

A great deal happened in the next few days to make him believe that the necessity for getting away was not very urgent. He met Stafford King in the Park one morning, and Stafford had been unusually communicative and friendly. Then the whispering voices in the flat had temporarily ceased, and Jack o' Judgment had given him no sign of his existence. It was five days after he had made his deposit in the bank that the first shock came to him. He found Snakit waiting on returning from a matinée, and the little detective was so important and mysterious that the colonel knew something had been discovered.

"Well," he asked, closing the door, "what have you found?"

"She is in communication with the police," said Snakit, "that's what I've found."

"Lollie?"

"Miss Marsh is the lady. In communication with the police," said the other impressively.

"Now just tell me what you mean," said the colonel. "Do you mean she's on speaking terms with the policeman on point duty at Piccadilly Circus?"

"I mean, sir," said Snakit with dignity, "that she's in the habit of meeting Mr. Stafford King, who is a well-known man at Scotland Yard –"

"He's well-known here too," interrupted the colonel. "Where does she meet him?"

"In all sorts of queer places – that's the suspicious part of it," said Snakit, who had joyously entered into the work which had been given to him, without realizing its unlawful character.

He had accepted without question the colonel's story that he was the victim of police persecution, and as this was the first news of any importance he had been able to bring to his employer, he was naturally inclined to make the most of it.

"He has met her twice at eleven o clock at night, at the bottom of St. James's Street, and walked up with her, very deeply engaged in conversation," said Snakit, consulting his notebook. "He met her once at the foot of the steps leading down from Waterloo Place, and they were together for an hour. This morning," he went on, speaking slowly, and evidently this was his tit-bit, "this morning Mr. Stafford King went to the Cunard office in Cockspur Street and booked cabin seventeen on the shelter deck of the *Lapland* for New York."

"In what name?"

"In the name of Miss Isabel Trenton."

The colonel nodded. It was a name that Lollie had used before, and the story rang true.

"When does the *Lapland* sail?" he asked, and again the detective consulted his book.

"Next Saturday," he said, "from Liverpool."

"Very good," said the colonel; "thank you, Snakit, you've done very well. See if you can pick them up tonight, or, stay –" He thought a moment. "No, don't shadow her tonight. I'll have a talk with her."

The news disturbed him. Lollie was getting ready to bolt – that was unimportant. But she was bolting with the assistance of the police, who had booked her passage. That meant that they had got as much out of her as she had to tell, and were clearing her out of the country before the blow fell. That was not only important, but it was grave. Either the police were going to strike at once or –

An idea struck him, and he telephoned through to Pinto. Another got him into touch with Crewe, and these three were in consultation when Selby came that afternoon.

He arrived at an unpropitious moment, for the colonel was in a cold fury, and the object of his wrath was Crewe, who sat with folded arms and tense face, looking down at the table.

"That gentleman business is played out, Crewe," stormed the colonel, "and I'm just about tired of hearing what you won't do and what you will do! If Lollie's put us away, she has got to go through it."

"What use will it be, supposing she has?" said the other doggedly. "I don't for a moment believe she has done anything of the sort. But suppose she has given you away, what are you going to do? Add to the indictment? She's sick of the game and wants to get away somewhere where she can live a decent life."

"Oh, you've been discussing it with her, have you?" said the colonel with dangerous calm. "And maybe you also are sick of the game and want to get away and live a decent life? I remember hearing you say something of that sort a few weeks ago."

"We're all sick of it," said Crewe. "Look at Pinto. Do you think he's keen?"

Pinto started.

"Why do you bring me into it?" he complained. "I'm standing by the colonel to the last. And I agree with him that we ought to know what Lollie told the police."

"She's told them nothing," said Crewe. "She isn't that kind of girl. Besides, what does she know?"

"She knows a lot," said the colonel. "I'll put a supposition to you. Suppose she's Jack o' Judgment?"

Crewe looked at him in astonishment.

"That's an absurd suggestion," he said. "How could she be?"

"I'll tell you how she could be," said the colonel; "she has never been with us when Jack made his appearance – you'll grant that?"

Crewe thought for a moment.

"There you're wrong," he said; "she was with us the night Jack first came."

The colonel was taken aback. A theory which he had formed was destroyed by that recollection.

"So she was. That's right, she was there! I remember he insulted her. But I'm certain she's seen him since; I am certain she's been working hand-in-glove with him since. Who was the Jack who went to Yorkshire?"

It was Crewe's turn to be nonplussed.

"Jack o' Judgment must be working with a pal," the colonel went on triumphantly, "and I suggest that that pal is Lollie Marsh."

"That's a lie!"

The colonel looked up quickly.

"Who said that?" he demanded harshly.

Crewe shook his head.

"It was not me," he said.

"Was it you, Selby?"

"Me?" said the astonished Selby. "No, I thought it was you who said it. It came from your end of the table, colonel."

The colonel got up.

"There's something wrong here," he said.

"I've got it!" It was Pinto who spoke. "Did you notice anything peculiar about the voice, colonel?" he asked eagerly. "I did, the first time I heard it, and I've been wondering how I'd heard it before, and just now it has struck me. It was a gramophone voice!"

"A gramophone voice?"

"It sounded like a voice on a speaking machine."

The colonel nodded slowly.

"Now you come to mention it, I think you're right," he said; "it sounded familiar to me. Of course, it was a gramophone voice."

They made a careful search of the apartment, taking down every book from the big shelf in one of the alcoves, and turning the leaves to discover the hidden machine. With this idea to guide them the search was more complete than it had been before. Every drawer in the desk was taken out, every scrap of furniture was minutely examined, even the massive legs of the colonel's writing table were tapped.

Crewe took no part in the search, but watched it with a slight smile of amusement, and the colonel turning, detected this.

"What the devil are you grinning about?" he said. "Why aren't you helping, Crewe? You've got an interest in this business."

"Not such an interest that I'm going to fool around looking for a gramophone voice that goes off at appropriate intervals," said Crewe. "Doesn't it strike you that it would have to be a pretty smart gramophone to chip in at the right moment?"

The colonel pondered this a minute and then went back to his place at the table, mopping his forehead.

"Pinto's right," he said; "the fellow has smuggled some fool machine into the flat, and we shall discover it sooner or later. I don't know how he controls it, or who controls it" – he looked suspiciously at Crewe – "or who controls it," he repeated.

"You said that before," said Crewe coolly.

The colonel had something on his lips to say, but swallowed it.

"We'll meet here tonight at eleven. I told Lollie to come. Now, Crewe," he said in a more gentle tone, "you're in this up to the neck, and you've got to go through with it. After all, your life and liberty are at stake as much as ours. If Lollie's played us false, we've got to be –"

"Lollie has not played you false, colonel," said Crewe. His face was very pale, the colonel noticed. "I like that girl, and –"

"So that's it," said the colonel, "a little love romance introduced into our sordid commercial lives! Maybe you know what she's been talking to Stafford King about?"

Crewe did not immediately reply.

"Do you?" asked the colonel.

"I know she has been trying to get out of the country, to break with the gang, but that she has given you or any of us away is a lie. Lollie's had a rotten life, and she's just sick of it, that's all. Do you blame her?"

"There's no question of blaming her or praising her," said the colonel patiently; "the question is whether we condemn her or whether she still has our confidence, and that we shall know tonight. You will be present, Crewe."

"I shall be present, you may be sure," said Crewe, and there was a look on his face which Pinto, for one, did not like.

Chapter XXXII

LOLLIE GOES AWAY

It seemed to "Swell" Crewe that the scene was curiously reminiscent of a trial in which he had once participated. The colonel, at the end of the long table, sat aloof and apparently noncommittal, a veritable judge and a merciless judge at that. Pinto sat at his right, Selby on his left, and Crewe himself sat halfway between the girl at the farther end of the table and Pinto.

Lollie Marsh had no doubt as to why she had been summoned. Her pretty face was drawn, the hands which were clasped on the table before her were restless, but what Crewe noticed more particularly was a certain untidiness both in her costume and in her usually well-coiffured hair. As though wearying of the part she had been playing, she was already discarding her makeup.

"I hate to bring you here, Lollie, and ask you these questions," the colonel was saying, "but we are all in some danger and we want to know just where we stand with you."

She made no reply.

"The charge against you is that you've been in communication with the police. Is that true?"

"If you mean that I've been in communication with Mr. Stafford King, that's true," she said. "You told me to get into touch with him. Haven't I been for weeks –"

"That's a pretty good excuse," interrupted the colonel, "but it won't work, Lollie. You don't touch with a man like Stafford King and meet him secretly in St. James's Street. And you don't touch by seeing him for half an hour at a time, and I haven't heard of you ever getting off with a fellow to the extent of his paying for your passage to America."

She started.

"You know the way it is done. You did it before, Lollie," the colonel went on. "Now, you've got to be a good girl and tell us how far you've gone."

She hesitated.

"I'll tell you the truth," she said. "I'm sick of this life, colonel. I want to go straight. I want to get away out of it all and – and – he's going to help me."

"A social reformer, eh?" said the colonel. "I didn't know the police went in for that sort of stunt. And when did he take this sudden liking for you, Lollie?"

"It wasn't a sudden liking at all," she said, "but I think it was because – well, because I stopped Pinto in the nursing home – and Miss White told him – I think that's all."

The colonel looked down on his pad.

"There's something in that," he said. "It sounds feasible. Didn't he question you?" he said, raising his eyes.

"About you?" she said.

"About us," corrected the colonel.

"He asked me nothing about you, nothing about your habits or your methods or about any of our funny business. I'll swear it," she said.

"You're not going to believe that, are you, colonel?" demanded Pinto. "You can see that she is lying and that she's double-crossing you?"

"She's neither lying nor double-crossing us." It was Crewe who spoke. "I don't know what you think about it, colonel, but I am convinced that Lollie is speaking the truth."

"You!" Pinto laughed loudly. "I think you're in a state of mind when you'd believe anything Lollie said. And anyway you're probably in with her."

"You're a liar," said Crewe, so quietly that none suspected the surprising thing that would follow, for of a sudden his fist shot out and caught Pinto under the jaw, sending him sprawling to the floor.

The colonel was instantly on his feet, his hand outspread.

"That's enough, Crewe," he said harshly. "I'll have none of that!"

Pinto picked himself up, his face livid.

"You'll pay for that," he said breathlessly, but "Swell" Crewe had walked to the girl and had laid his hand on her shoulder.

"Lollie," he said, "I'm believing you and I think the colonel is, too. If you're going out of the country, why I'll say good luck to you. You've made a very wise decision and one which we shall all make – some of us perhaps too late."

"Wait a moment," said the colonel. He exchanged a glance with Selby and the man slipped quietly from the room. "Before we do any of that fare-thee-well stuff, I've got a few words to say to you, Lollie. I'm with Crewe. I think it is time you went out of the country, but you're going out my way."

"What do you mean?" she asked.

Her hand clutched "Swell" Crewe's sleeve.

"You're going out my way," said the colonel, "and I swear no harm will come to you. You're leaving tonight."

"But how?" she asked, affrighted.

"Selby will tell you. You'll meet him downstairs. Now be a sensible girl and do as I tell you. Selby will go with you and see you safe. We made all preparations for your departure tonight."

"What's this, colonel?" asked Crewe.

"You're out of it," said the colonel savagely. "I'm running this show myself. If you want to join Lollie later, why you can. For the present, she's going just where I want her to go and in the way I have planned."

He held out his hand to the girl and she took it.

"Good-bye and good luck, Lollie!" he said.

"But can't I go back to my rooms?" she asked.

He shook his head.

"Do as I tell you," he said shortly.

She stood at the door and for a moment her eyes met Crewe's and he moved toward her.

"Wait."

The colonel gripped his arm.

"Good-bye, Lollie," and the door shut on the girl.

"Let me go," said Crewe between his teeth. "If she trusts you, I don't. This is some trick of that dirty half-breed!"

With a snarl of rage Pinto whipped his ever-ready knife from his hip pocket and flung it. It was the colonel who drew Crewe aside, or that moment was his last. The knife whizzed past and was buried almost to the hilt in the wall. The colonel broke the tense silence which followed.

"Pinto," he said in his silkiest voice, "if you ever want to know what it feels like to be a dead man, just repeat that performance, will you?"

Then his rage burst forth. "By God! I'll shoot either of you if you play the fool in front of me again. You dirty little pickpockets that I've taken from the gutter! You miserable little sneak-thieves!"

He let loose a flood of abuse that made even Crewe wince.

"Now sit down, both of you," he finished up, out of breath.

He went to the window and looked out. The car which he had hired for the occasion was still standing at the door and he distinguished Selby talking to the chauffeur.

"Listen you," he said, "and especially you, Crewe. You're too trusting with these females. Maybe Lollie's speaking the truth, but it is just as likely she's lying. I'm not going to take your corroboration, you know, Crewe," he said. "We've got to depend on her word. There's nobody else can speak for her, is there?"

Before Crewe could speak the colonel was answered:

"Jack o' Judgment! Poor old Jack o' Judgment! He'll speak for Lollie!"

The colonel looked up with a curse. There was nobody in the room, but the voice had been louder than ever he had heard it before. It seemed as though it emanated from a disembodied spirit that was floating through the air. There was a knock at the outer door.

Chapter XXXIII

WHERE THE VOICE LIVED

"Open it," said the colonel in a low voice; "open it, Crewe" – he pulled open the drawer and took out something – "and if it is Jack o' Judgment –"

Crewe opened the door, his heart beating at a furious rate, but it was Selby who came into the room and faced the half-leveled gun of the colonel.

"What do you want?" asked Boundary quickly. "You fool, I told you not to lose sight of her –"

"But when is she coming down?" asked Selby. "I've been waiting there all this time and there's a policeman at the corner of the street – I wondered whether you had seen him too."

"Not come down?" said the colonel. "She left here five minutes ago!"

"She hasn't come down," he said, "and I've certainly not passed her on the stairs. Is there any other way out?"

"No way that she could use," said the colonel shaking his head. "I've had new locks put on all the doors." He thought a moment. "If she hasn't come down she's gone up."

They went up the stairs together and searched, first Pinto's flat, and then the store-rooms and empty apartments on the floor higher up.

"Go down to the door and wait, in case she tries to get out," said the colonel.

He returned to the room with the two men and they looked at one another in frank astonishment.

"Have you any idea what's happened, Crewe?" asked the colonel suspiciously.

"No idea in the world," said Crewe.

"But she went downstairs," said the colonel. "I heard the alarm click."

"The alarm?" questioned Crewe.

"I've got a buzzer under one of the treads of the stairs," said the colonel. "It is useful to know when people are coming up."

Ten minutes passed and Selby returned to say that the policeman had been making inquiries as to whom the car belonged.

"You'd better get it away," said the colonel, "and send away your men."

"They've gone," said the other. "I wasn't taking any risks."

He disappeared to carry out the colonel's instructions, and they heard the whine of the moving car.

Boundary unlocked his tantalus and took out a full decanter of whisky. Without a word he poured three stiff doses into as many glasses and filled them with soda. Each man was thinking, and thinking after his own interests.

"Well, gentlemen," said the colonel at last. "I incline to give this business best."

He looked up and saw the dagger which Pinto had thrown. It was still embedded in the wall.

"It isn't enough that I should have Jack o' Judgment messing my room about," he growled, "but you must do something to the same wall! Pull it out and don't let me see it again, Pinto."

The Portuguese smiled sheepishly, walked to the wall and gripped the handle. Evidently the point had embedded in a lath, for the knife did not move. He pulled again, exerting all his strength and this time succeeded in extracting not only the knife but a large portion of the plaster and a strip of the wallpaper.

"You fool!" said the colonel angrily, "see what you have done – Jumping Moses!"

He walked to the wall and stared, for the dislodgment of plaster and paper had revealed three round black discs, set flush with the plaster and only separated from the room by the wallpaper, which had been stripped.

"Jumping Moses!" said the colonel softly. "Detectaphones!"

He took Pinto's knife from his hand and prised one of the discs loose. It was attached to a wire which was embedded in the plaster and this the colonel severed with a stroke of the knife.

"This is the business end of a microphone," he said.

"The voice!" gasped Pinto, and the colonel nodded.

"Of course. I was mad not to guess that," he said. "That's how he heard and that's how he spoke. Now, we're going to get to the bottom of this."

With a knife he slashed the plaster and exposed three wires that led straight downward and apparently through the floor. The colonel rested and eyed the debris thoughtfully.

"What is under this flat? Lee's office, isn't it? Of course, Lee's!" he said. "I'm the fool!"

He handed the knife back to Pinto, took an electric torch from his pocket and led the way from the flat. They passed down the half-darkened stairs to the floor beneath, on which was situated the three sets of offices. The colonel took a bunch of keys and tried them on the door of the surveyor's office. Presently he found one that fitted, and the door opened. He fumbled about for the electric switch, found it and flooded the room with light. It was a very ordinary clerk's office, with a small counter, the flap of which was raised. Inside the flap he saw something white on the floor, and, stooping, picked it up. It was a lady's handkerchief.

"L," he read. "That sounds like Lollie. Do you know this, Crewe?"

Crewe took the handkerchief and nodded.

"That is Lollie's," he said shortly.

"I thought so. This is where she was when we were looking for her. Here with Jack o' Judgment, eh? Let's try the inner office."

The inner office was locked, but he had no difficulty in gaining admission. Inside this was a private office which was simply furnished and had in one corner what appeared to be a telephone box. He opened the glass door and flashed his lamp inside. There was a little desk, a pair of receivers fastened to a headpiece, and a small vulcanite transmitter.

"This is where he sat," said the colonel meditatively, pointing to a stool, "and this –" he lifted up the earpieces – "is how he heard all our very interesting conversations. Go upstairs, Pinto, I want to try this transmitter."

He fixed the receiver to his ears and waited, and presently he heard distinctly the sound of Pinto closing the door of the room upstairs. Then he spoke through the receiver.

"Do you hear me, Pinto?"

"I hear you distinctly," said Pinto's voice.

"Speak a little lower. Carry on a conversation with yourself and let me try to hear you."

Pinto obeyed. He recited something from the Orpheum revue, a line or two of a song, and the colonel heard distinctly every syllable. He replaced the earpieces where he had found them, closed the door of the box and that of the outer office, and led the way upstairs. The whisky still stood upon the table and he lifted a glass and drained it at a draft.

"If you're a linguist, Crewe, you'll have heard of the phrase: *Sauve qui peut.* It means 'Git!' And that's the advice I'm giving and taking. Tomorrow we'll meet to liquidate the Boundary Gang and split the Gang Fund."

He turned his companions out to get what sleep they could. For him there was little sleep that night. Before the dawn came, he was at Twickenham, examining a big motor-launch that lay in a boat-house. It was the launch which should have carried Lollie Marsh and Selby on their river and sea journey. It was provisioned and ready for the trip. But first the colonel had to take from a locker in the stern of the boat a small black box and disconnect the wires from certain terminals before he stopped a little clock which ticked noisily. He had tuned his bomb to go off at four in the morning, by which time, he calculated, Lollie Marsh and her escort would be well out to sea. For the colonel regarded no evidence that might be brought against him as unimportant.

Chapter XXXIV

CONSCIENCE MONEY

The colonel was sleeping peacefully when Pinto rushed into his bedroom with the news. He was awake in a second and sat up in bed.

"What!" he said incredulously.

"Selby's pinched," said Pinto, his voice shaking. "My God! It's awful! It's dreadful! Colonel, we've got to get away today. I tell you they'll have us –"

"Just shut up for a minute, will you?" growled the colonel, swinging out of bed and searching for his slippers with the detached interest of one who was hearing a little gossip from the morning papers. "What is the charge against him?"

"Loitering with intention to commit a felony," said Pinto. "They took him to the station and searched his bag. He had brought a bag with him in preparation for the journey. And what do you think they found?"

"I know what they found," said the colonel; "a complete kit of burglar's tools. The fool must have left his bag in the hall and of course Jack o' Judgment planted the stuff. It is simple!"

"What can we do?" wailed Pinto. "What can we do?"

"Engage the best lawyer you can. Do it through one of your pals," said the colonel. "It will go hard with Selby. He's had a previous conviction."

"Do you think he'll split?" asked Pinto.

He looked yellow and haggard and he had much to do to keep his teeth from chattering.

"Not for a day or two," said the colonel, "and we shall be away by then. Does Crewe know?"

Pinto shook his head.

"I haven't any time to run about after that swine," he said impatiently.

"Well, you'd better do a little running now then," said the colonel. "We may want his signature for the bank."

"What are you going to do?"

"I'm going to draw what we've got and I advise you to do the same. I suppose you haven't made any preparations to get away, have you?"

"No," lied Pinto, remembering with thankfulness that he had received a letter that morning from the aviator Cartwright, telling him that the machine was in good order and ready to start at any moment. "No, I have never thought of getting away, colonel. I've always said I'll stick to the colonel –"

"H'm!" said the colonel, and there was no very great faith in Pinto revealed in his grunt.

Crewe came along an hour later and seemed the least perturbed of the lot.

"Here's the checkbook," said the colonel, taking it from a drawer. "Now the balance we have," he consulted a little waistcoat-pocket notebook, "is £81,317. I suggest we draw £80,000, split it three ways and part tonight."

"What about your own private account?" asked Pinto.

"That's my business," said the colonel sharply. He filled in the check, signed his name with a flourish and handed the pen to Crewe.

Crewe put his name beneath, saw that the check was made payable to bearer, and handed the book to the colonel.

"Here, Pinto." The colonel detached the form and blotted it. "Take a taxi-cab, see Ferguson, bring the money straight back here. Or, better still, go on to the City to the New York Guaranty and change it into American money."

"Do you trust Pinto?" asked Crewe bluntly after the other had gone.

"No," said the colonel, "I don't trust Pinto or you. And if Pinto had plenty of time I shouldn't expect to see that money again. But he's got to be back here in a couple of hours, and I don't think he can get away before. Besides, at the present juncture," he reflected, "he wouldn't bolt because he doesn't know how serious the position is."

"Where are you going, colonel?" asked Crewe curiously. "I mean, when you get away from here?"

Boundary's broad face creased with smiles.

"What a foolish question to ask," he said. "Timbuktu, Tangier, America, Buenos Ayres, Madrid, China –"

"Which means you're not going to tell, and I don't blame you," said Crewe.

"Where are you going?" asked the colonel. "If you're a fool you'll tell me."

Crewe shrugged his shoulders.

"To jail, I guess," he said bitterly, and the colonel chuckled.

"Maybe you've answered the question you put to me," he said, "but I'm going to make a fight of it. Dan Boundary is too old in the bones and hates exercise too much to survive the keen air and the bracing employment of Dartmoor – if we ever got there," he said ominously.

"What do you mean?" demanded Crewe.

"I mean that, when they've photographed Selby and circulated his picture, somebody is certain to recognize him as the man who handed the glass of water over the heads of the crowd when Hanson was killed –"

"Was it Selby?" gasped Crewe. "I wasn't in it. I knew nothing about it –"

The colonel laughed again.

"Of course you're not in anything," he bantered. "Yes, it was Selby, and it is ten chances to one that the usher would recognize him again if he saw him. That would mean – well, they don't hang folks at Dartmoor." He looked at his watch again. "I expect Pinto will be about an hour and a half," he said. "You will excuse me," he added with elaborate politeness "I have a lot of work to do."

He cleared the drawers of his writing-table by the simple process of pulling them out and emptying their contents upon the top. He went through these with remarkable rapidity, throwing the papers one by one into the fire, and he was engaged in this occupation when Pinto returned.

"Back already?" said the colonel in surprise, and then, after a glance at the other's face, he demanded: "What's wrong?"

Pinto was incapable of speech. He just put the check down upon the table.

"Haven't they cashed it?" asked the colonel with a frown.

"They can't cash it," said Pinto in a hollow voice. "There's no money there."

The colonel picked up the check.

"So there's no money there to meet it?" he said softly. "And why is there no money there to meet it?"

"Because it was drawn out three days ago. I thought –" said Pinto incoherently. "I saw Ferguson, and he told me that a check for the full amount came through from the Bank of England."

"In whose favor was it drawn?"

Pinto cleared his throat.

"In favor of the Chancellor of the Exchequer," he said. "That's why Ferguson passed it without question. He said that otherwise he would have sent a note to you."

"The Chancellor of the Exchequer!" snarled the colonel. "What does it mean?"

"Look here! Ferguson showed it me himself." He took a copy of *The Times* from his pocket and laid it on the table, pointing out the paragraph with trembling fingers.

It was in the advertisement column and it was brief:

> "The Chancellor of the Exchequer desires to acknowledge the receipt of £81,000 Conscience Money from Colonel D. B."

"Conscience money!"

The colonel sat back in his chair and laughed softly. He was genuinely amused.

"Of course, we can get this back," he said at last. "We can explain to the Chancellor of the Exchequer the trick that has been played upon us, but that means delay, and at the moment delay is really dangerous. I suppose both you fellows have money of your own? I know Pinto has. How do you stand, Crewe?"

"I have a little," said Crewe, "but honestly, I was depending upon my share of the Gang Fund."

"What about you, colonel?" asked Pinto meaningly. "If I may suggest it, we should pool our money and divide."

The colonel smiled.

"Don't be silly," he said tersely. "I doubt whether my balance at the bank is more than a couple of thousand pounds."

"But what about your private safe?" persisted Pinto. "A-ha! You didn't know I knew that, did you? As a matter of fact, Ferguson told me –"

"What the devil does Ferguson mean by discussing my business?" said the colonel wrathfully. "What did he tell you?"

"He told me that the package was received and that he had put it with the other in your safe."

"Package!" The colonel's voice was quiet, almost inaudible. "The package was received! When was the package received?"

"Yesterday," said Pinto. "He said it came along and he put it with the other. Now what have you got in –"

But the colonel was walking towards his bedroom with rapid strides. Presently he reappeared with his hat and coat on.

"Come with me, Crewe. We'll go down to the bank," he said. "You stay here, Pinto, and report anything that happens."

When they were on their way he confided to the other:

"I have a little money put aside," he said, "and I'm willing to finance you. You haven't been a bad fellow, Crewe. The only rotten turn you've ever done us is introducing that damned fellow, 'Snow' Gregory, and you didn't even do that, for I had met him before you brought him from Monte – which reminds me. Have you found out anything about him?"

"I have a letter here from Oxford," said Crewe, putting his hand in his pocket. "I hadn't opened my letters when Pinto came. You'll find all the news there, if there is any news."

He handed the envelope to the other and the colonel transferred it to his pocket.

"That'll keep," he said. "What was I talking about? Oh, yes, Gregory. The whole of this business has come about through Gregory. Gregory made Jack o' Judgment, and Jack o' Judgment has ruined us."

He sprang from the taxi at the door of the bank with an agile step, and went straight to the manager's office. Without any preliminary he began:

"What is this package that came for me yesterday, Ferguson?"

The manager looked surprised.

"It was an ordinary package, similar to that which you put in the safe the other day. It was sealed and wrapped and had your name on it. I rather wondered you hadn't brought it yourself, but it was put into your safe in the presence of two clerks."

"I'd like to see it," said the colonel.

Ferguson led the way down the stairs to the vaults and snapped back the lock of Safe 20. As he did so Crewe was conscious of a faint, musty odor.

"I smell something," said the colonel suspiciously.

He reached his hand into the safe and pulled open the long drawer, and as he did so a cloud of sickly-smelling vapor rose from its interior. For the first time Crewe heard Boundary groan. He pulled the drawer out under the light and looked in. There was nothing but a black mass of pulp, out of which glinted and gleamed a dozen pin-points of light.

With a howl of rage the colonel turned the contents upon the stone floor of the vault and raked it over with the end of his walking-stick. The diamonds were intact, and they at least were something; but the greater part of eight hundred thousand dollars was indistinguishable from any other kind of paper that had been treated with one of the most destructive acids known to chemical science.

Chapter XXXV

IN A BOX AT THE ORPHEUM

The colonel wiped his burned and discolored hands after he had dropped the last diamond into a medicine bottle which the bank manager happened to have in the room.

"That's something saved from the wreck, at any rate," he said.

He had gone suddenly old, and his mouth trembled, as many a younger mouth had trembled in despair that Colonel Boundary might become a rich man.

"Something saved from the wreck," he repeated slowly.

The manager's grave eyes were fixed on his.

"I'm not blaming you, Ferguson," said the colonel. "It was a plot to ruin me, and it succeeded."

"What do you think happened?" asked the troubled Ferguson.

"The second package was a box filled with a very strong acid," said the colonel. "Probably the box was made of soft metal, through which the acid would eat in a few hours. It was placed in the safe, and in time the corrosive worked through –"

He shrugged his shoulders and left the room without another word.

"Thirty-five years' work that represents, Crewe," he said as they were driving back to the flat; "thirty-five years of risk and thought and organization, and ended in pulp – stinking pulp – that burns your fingers when you touch it."

He began to whistle and Crewe noticed with curiosity that he chose the "Soldiers' Chorus" from "Faust" for the dirge to his lost fortune.

"Jack o' Judgment!" he said wonderingly. "Jack o' Judgment! Well, he's had his judgment all right, and I'm going to have mine. You needn't tell Pinto what happened this morning. Leave him guessing. He's got a pretty thick bank-roll, and I'll agree to that grand scheme of his for sharing out."

The thought seemed to cheer him, and by the time they reached the flat he was almost jovial.

"Well, what's the news?" asked Pinto eagerly.

"Fine," said the colonel. "Everything is as it should be."

"Stop rotting," growled the other. "What is the news?"

"The news, my lad," said the colonel, "is that I've decided to agree to your unselfish suggestion."

"What's that?" said the unsuspicious Pinto.

"That we should pool and divide."

"Jack o' Judgment's got your money, too!" said Pinto, who cherished no illusions about the colonel's generosity.

"How well he knows me!" said Boundary. "Now, come, Pinto, we're all in this, sink or swim. I told Crewe going down that I intended dividing; didn't I, Crewe?"

"You said something like that," said Crewe cautiously.

"Now we'll pool our money," said the colonel, "and split three ways. I'll make a fair proposition. We'll divide it into four and the man who puts in the most shall take two shares. Is it a bet?"

"I suppose so," said Pinto reluctantly. "What is the truth about your money? Did Jack o' Judgment get it?"

"I hadn't any money," said the colonel blandly. "I've about a thousand pounds hidden away in this room; that is all, if Jack hasn't been in."

He unlocked the safe and made an inspection.

"Yes, a little over a thousand, if anything. How much have you, Crewe?"

"Three thousand," said Crewe.

"That makes four thousand. Now what have you got, Pinto?"

"I've about five thousand," said Pinto, trying to appear unconcerned.

The colonel made a little whistling noise through his teeth.

"Bring fifty," he said. "I'm dead serious, Pinto. Bring fifty!"

"But how can I get it?" demanded the other frantically.

"Get it," said the colonel. "It is highly probable that it will be of no use to any of us. Let us at least have the illusion of being well off."

In greater leisure than either of her three companions in crime were exhibiting, Lollie Marsh was preparing to take her departure to New York. She was packing at leisure in her cozy flat on Tavistock Avenue, stopping now and again to consider the problem of the superfluous article of clothing – a problem which presents itself to all packers.

Between whiles she arrested her labors to think of something else. Kneeling down by the side of her trunk, she would give herself up to long reveries, which ended in a sigh and the resumption of her packing.

By the commonly accepted standards of civilization she was a wicked woman, but there are degrees of wickedness. She had searched her mind to recall all the qualms she had felt in her long association with the Boundary Gang, and took an unusual pleasure in her strange recollection. She remembered when she had refused to be drawn into the Crotin fraud; she recalled her stormy interview with the colonel when she declined to take a part in the ruining of young Debenham.

But mostly she was glad that she had never gone any farther to carry out the colonel's instructions in regard to Stafford King. Not that she would have succeeded, she told herself with a little smile, but she was glad she had never seriously tried. Her mind switched to Crewe and switched back again. Crewe's was the one face she did not wish to see, the one member of the gang that she put aside from the others and willfully veiled. Crewe had always been kind to her, always courteous, her champion in all bad times, and yet had never made love to her. She wondered what had brought him down to his present level, and why a man possessed of education, and who at one time, as she knew, had been an officer in a crack regiment, should have fallen so readily under Boundary's influence.

She made a little face and went on with her packing. She did not want to think about Crewe for obvious reasons. Yet, as he had said – But he hadn't said, she told herself. Very likely he was married, though that fact did not greatly trouble the girl. Such men as these have always a good as well as a bad past, pleasant as well as bitter memories, and possibly he included amongst the former the recollection of a girl whose shoelaces Lollie Marsh was not fit to tie.

She took a delight in torturing herself with pictures of her own humiliation, though she may have counted it to the good that she was capable of feeling humiliated at all. She finished her trunk, squeezed in the last article and locked down the lid. She looked at her wrist watch – it was half-past nine. Stafford King had not asked to see her, and she had the evening free.

She had only spoken the truth when she had told Boundary that the police chief had made no inquiries as to the gang. Stafford King knew human nature rather well, and he would not make the mistake of questioning her. Or perhaps it was because he did not wish to spoil the value of his gifts by fixing a price – the price of treachery.

She wondered what the colonel was doing, and Pinto – and Crewe. She impatiently stamped her foot. She was indulging in the kind of insanity of which hitherto she had shown no symptoms. She looked at her watch again and then remembered the Orpheum. It was a favorite house of hers. She could always get a free box if there was one vacant, and she had spent many of her lonely evenings in that way. She had always declined Pinto's offer to share his own, and of late he had got out of the habit of inviting her.

She dressed and took a taxi to the Orpheum. The booking office clerk knew her, and without asking her desires drew a slip from the ticket rack.

"I can give you Box C tonight, Miss Marsh," he said. "That is the one above the governor's."

The "governor" was Pinto.

"Have you a good house?"

The youth shook his head.

"We're not having the houses we had when Miss White was here," he said. "What's become of her, miss?"

"I don't know," said Lollie shortly.

She had to pass to the back of Pinto's box to reach the little staircase which led to the box above. She thought she heard voices, and stopping at the door, listened. Perhaps Crewe had come down or the colonel. But it was not Crewe's voice she heard. The door was slightly ajar, and the man who was talking was evidently on the point of departure, because she glimpsed his hand upon the handle and his voice was so distinct that he must have been quite near her.

"– three o'clock in the morning. You can't miss the aerodrome. It is a mile out of Bromley on the main road and on the right. You will see three red lamps burning in a triangle."

The aerodrome! She put her hand to her mouth to suppress an exclamation. Pinto was talking, but his voice was a mumble.

"Very good," said the strange voice. "I can carry three or four passengers if you like. There's plenty of room – of course, if you're by yourself, so much the better. I shall expect you at three o'clock. The weather's beautiful."

The door opened and she crouched against the wall so that the opening door hid her, and heard Pinto call the man back by name.

"Cartwright!" she repeated. "Cartwright. A mile out of Bromley on the main road. Three lamps in a red triangle!"

She was going to slip up the stairs, but the door had closed on Cartwright, and making a swift decision she passed the box and came again into the vestibule of the theater. Presently she saw the man appear. She guessed it was he by the smile on his face, and when he said "Good night" to the attendant at the barrier she recognized his voice. She followed him but let him get outside the theater before she spoke to him. Then suddenly she laid her hand on his arm: "Mr. Cartwright!"

He looked round into her smiling face in surprise, taking off his hat.

"That is my name," he said with a smile. "I don't remember –"

"Oh, I'm a friend of Mr. Silva," she said. "I've heard a lot about you."

"Oh, indeed?" said he.

He was a little puzzled because he thought that the projected flight was a dead secret; and she guessed his thoughts.

"You won't tell Mr. Silva I told you? He begged me not to repeat it to anybody, even to you. But he's leaving tomorrow morning, isn't he?"

He nodded.

"I know an awful lot," she said, and then: "Won't you come and have supper with me? I'm starving!"

Cartwright hesitated. He had not expected so charming a diversion, and really there was no reason why he should not accept the invitation. He was not due at Bromley until early in the morning, and the girl was young and pretty and a friend of his employer. It was she who hailed the taxi and they drove to a select little restaurant at the back of Shaftesbury Avenue.

"You're not seeing Pinto – I mean Mr. Silva – again tonight, are you?" she asked.

"No, I'm not seeing him until – well, until I see him," he smiled again.

"Well, I want to tell you something."

He thought she was charmingly embarrassed, and in truth she was, to invent the story she had to tell.

"You know why Mr. Silva is leaving England in such a hurry?"

He nodded. She wished she knew too, or had the slightest inkling of the yarn which Pinto had spun. And then the man enlightened her.

"Political," he said.

"Exactly; political," she said easily. "But you will realize that it is not necessarily he himself who is making this flight."

"I did understand that he was making the flight himself," said the aviator in surprise.

"But" – she was desperate now – "has he never told you of the other gentleman who was coming, the other political person who really must go to Portugal at once?"

"No, he certainly did not," said Cartwright; "he told me distinctly that he was going himself."

The girl leaned back in her chair, baffled, but thoughtful.

"Oh, of course, he told you that," she said with a knowing smile. "You see, there are some things he is not allowed to tell you. But do not be surprised if you have two passengers instead of one."

"I shan't be surprised, I shall be pleased. The machine will carry half a dozen," said Cartwright readily, "but I certainly thought –"

"Wait till you see him," said the girl, waving a warning finger with mock solemnity.

He found her a cheerful companion through the meal, but there were certain intervals of abstraction in her cheerfulness, intervals when she was thinking very rapidly and reconstructing the plan which Pinto had made. So he was one of the rats who were deserting the sinking ship and leaving the Colonel and Crewe to face the music. And Crewe – that was the thought uppermost in her mind.

When she parted from the pilot she had only one thought – to warn the colonel of Pinto's treachery – and Crewe. And somehow Crewe seemed to bulk most importantly at that moment.

Chapter XXXVI

LOLLIE PROPOSES

What should she do? It was her sense of loyalty which brought the colonel first to her mind. She must warn him. She went into a Tube station telephone box and rang through but received no answer. Her quest for Crewe had as little result. She drove off to the flat, thinking that possibly the telephone might be out of order or that they would have returned by the time she reached there, but there was no answer to her ring. She went out again into the street in despair and walked slowly towards Regent Street. Then she saw two people ahead of her, and recognized the swing of the colonel's shoulders. She broke into a run and overtook them. The colonel swung round as she uttered his name and peered at her.

"Lollie!" he said in surprise, and he looked past her as though seeking some police shadow.

"I have something important to tell you," she said. "Let us go up here."

They turned into a deserted side street, and rapidly she told her story.

"So Pinto's getting out, is he?" said the colonel thoughtfully. "Well, it is no more than I expected. An airplane, too? Well, that's enterprising. I thought of something of the sort, but there's nowhere I could go, except to America."

He dropped his head on to his chest and was considering something.

"Thank you, Lollie," he said simply. "I'm glad that you didn't go with Selby – you would never have got to the Continent alive."

He said this in an ordinary conversational tone, and the girl gasped. She did not ask him for an explanation and he offered none. Crewe, standing in the background, looked at the man with something like bewilderment.

"And now I think you'd better make a real getaway, and not trust to the police," said the colonel. "Maybe with the best intentions in the world, Stafford King can't save you if I happen to be jugged. And you too, Crewe," he turned to the other.

"So Pinto is going, eh?" he bit his nether lip, "and that is why he promised to bring the fifty thousand tomorrow morning. Well, somehow I don't think Pinto will go," he spoke deliberately. "I don't think Pinto will go."

"It is too dangerous for you to stop him –" began Crewe.

"I shall not try to stop him," said the other; "there's somebody besides myself on Pinto's track, and that somebody is going to pull him down."

"But why don't you escape, colonel?" she urged. "There is the airplane waiting at Bromley. We could easily persuade the man that Pinto had sent us."

He shook his head.

"You take your own advice," he said, "and clear out tonight. Get her away, Crewe. Don't worry about the police. You've got twenty-four hours in hand. This is Pinto's night," he said between his teeth. "Pinto – the dirty hound!"

Slowly they paced the street together in silence. When they came to the end the colonel turned.

"I want to shake hands with you, Lollie. I shook hands with you once before, intending to send you to a very quick decease. You're carrying your money with you, aren't you, Crewe?"

"Yes," said the other.

"Good!" responded the colonel. "Now get away."

He took no other farewell but turned abruptly and left them. Crewe was following him, but the girl caught his arm.

"Don't go," she said in a low voice. "Don't you know the colonel better?"

"I hate leaving him like this," he said.

"So do I," said the girl quietly. "I've still got some decent feeling left. We're all in this together. We're all crooks, as bad as we can possibly be, and if he's used us we've been willing tools. What is your Christian name?" she asked.

He looked at her in surprise.

"Jack," he said. "What a weird question to ask!"

"Isn't it?" she said with a laugh but a little catch in her throat. "Only we're to be comrades and stick to one another, and I hate calling you by your surname, so I'm going to call you Jack."

It was his turn to be amused. They walked in the opposite direction to that which the colonel had taken.

"You're very quiet," she said after a while.

"Aren't I?" he laughed.

"Have I offended you?" she asked quickly. "Was it wrong to call you Jack? Oh, yes, somebody else must have called you Jack."

"No, no, it isn't that," he said, "but I haven't been called by my Christian name for years and years," he said wearily, "and somehow it seems to span all the bad times and take me back to the – the –"

"The 'Jack' days?" she suggested, and he nodded.

Then after another period of silence.

"This is a queer ending to it all, isn't it?" he said, and her heart skipped a beat.

"Ending?" she whispered. "No, no, not ending! It may be the beginning of a new life. I haven't got religious," she added quickly, "and I'm not getting sentimental. All my past life doesn't come up in front of me as it does in the story-books. Only I've just faith that there's something better in life than I've ever found."

"I should think there is," said Crewe. "It couldn't be much worse, could it?"

"I haven't been bad," she said – "not bad like you probably think I have."

"I never thought you were bad," he said. "You were just a victim like the rest of them. You were only a kid when you started working for the colonel, weren't you?"

She nodded.

"Well, there's a chance for you, Lollie. Your passage is booked and all that sort of thing – have you sufficient money?"

"I've plenty of money," she said.

"Fine!" He dropped his hand lightly on her shoulder. "There's a big, big chance for you, my girl."

"And for you?" she asked.

He laughed.

"There is no chance for me at all," he said simply. "They'll take me and they'll take Pinto and last of all they'll take the colonel. It is written," he added philosophically. "Why – why, what is the matter?"

She stood stock-still and was holding on to his arm with both hands.

"You mustn't say that, you mustn't say that!" she said brokenly. "It isn't finished for you, Jack. There's a chance to get out, and the colonel has told you there's a chance. He meant it. He knows much more than we do. If you've got murder on your soul, or something worse; if you feel that you're altogether so bad that there isn't a chance for you, that there's no goodness in your life which can be expanded, why, just wait and take what's coming. But for God's sake know your mind, and if you feel that in another land, with – with someone who loves you by your side –"

Her voice broke.

"Why, Lollie," he said very gently. "You don't mean – ?"

"I'm just as shameless as I've ever been" she said, "but I'm not proposing to marry you, I'm not asking for anything save your friendship and your comradeship. I think people can love one another without – marrying and all that sort of thing; but do you – will you –"

"Will I go?" he asked.

She nodded.

"I'll go anywhere with that prospect in sight," and he slipped his arm round her shoulders, and, bending, kissed her on the cheek.

Chapter XXXVII

THE FALL OF PINTO

Whilst Pinto was putting the finishing touches to his scheme of flight, the colonel paced his room, whistling the "Soldiers' Chorus" jerkily. He was restless and nervous, and rendered all the more irritable by the disappearance of his servant, a minor member of the gang, who had been a participant in every act of villainy, and who had been in charge of the arrangements for the abduction of Maisie White. Twice in the course of the evening he wandered through the hall, opened the outer door, and looked out on to the landing.

On the first occasion there was nothing to see, but on the second it was only by the narrowest margin of time that he failed to detect a dark figure moving noiselessly up the stairs and disappearing on to the second landing. The man above heard the door open and close again, and stood watching. Then, when no sound reached him, he moved to the door of Pinto's flat, opened it, deposited the suit-case which he was carrying in the hall, and closed the door softly behind him.

He was within for about a quarter of an hour, then he reappeared, and still carrying his suit-case, passed swiftly down the stairs and out into the street. The clock struck half-past nine as he disappeared, and a quarter of an hour later Stafford King received by special messenger a communication which gave him something to think about. He read it through twice, then called up the First Commissioner and gave him the gist of the communication.

"That's the third time we've had this sort of message," he said.

"The others have proved right," said the Commissioner's voice, "why shouldn't this?"

"But it seems incredible," said Stafford in perplexity. "We've been watching these people for years and we've never found them with the goods."

"I should certainly act on it, King, if I were you," said the Commissioner. "Let me know what happens. Of course, you may make a mistake, but you must take a chance on that."

Pinto had a lot of business to do at the theater that night. For a week he had not banked the theater's takings, but had converted them into paper money, and now he took from his safe the last penny he could carry. It was half-past eleven when he came to his Club, where supper had been prepared for him. He paid the bill from notes he had taken from the bank that day. Presently the waiter came back.

"I beg your pardon, sir, but the cashier says that this note is a wrong 'un."

"A wrong 'un?" said Pinto in surprise, and took it in his hand.

There was no doubt whatever that the man was right. It was the most obvious forgery he had ever handled.

"Then I've been sold," he smiled; "here's another."

He took the second note and examined it. That also was bad, as he could tell at a glance. In the tail pocket of his dress-coat he had the money he had taken from the theater and was able to settle the bill. He was worried on the journey back to the flat. He had drawn a hundred pounds from the bank that morning in five-pound notes. He remembered putting them into his pocketbook and had no occasion to disturb them since. It was unlikely that the bank would have given him such obvious forgeries. He was stepping from the taxi when the awful truth dawned on him. The notes had been planted, the forgeries substituted for the good paper! He was putting his hand in his pocket, intending to take out the money and push it down the nearest drain, when he was gripped.

"Sorry and all that," said a voice.

He turned round shaking like an aspen.

"Stafford King," he said dully.

"Stafford King it is. I have a warrant for your arrest, Silva, on a charge of forging and uttering. Bring him up to his rooms."

The colonel heard the noise on the stairs and came to the door. He stood, a silent spectator, watching with unmoved face the procession as it passed up to the floor above.

"I want your key," said Stafford, and humbly the Portuguese handed it to him.

Stafford opened the door and snapped on the light.

"Bring him in," he said to the detective who held Pinto. "What room is this?"

"My dining room," said Pinto faintly.

Stafford entered the room, turning on the light as he did so.

"Hullo, Pinto," he said.

Pinto could only look.

The table was littered with copper-plates and ink rollers. There was a thick pad of counterfeit money on one corner of the table, held down by a paper weight; little bottles of acids were scattered about, and near the table was a small lever press, so small that a man might carry it in a corner of his handbag.

"I think I have got you, Pinto," said Stafford King, and Pinto Silva nodded before he fell limply into the arms of his captor.

Maisie White had gone to bed early and the bell rang three times before she awoke. She slipped into a dressing gown, and, going to the window, leaned out. She looked down upon the upturned face of a girl and in spite of the distance and the darkness of the night, recognized her. The man who stood in the background, however, she could not for the moment place. Nevertheless, she did not hesitate to go downstairs.

"Is that Miss White?" asked the girl.

"Yes. It is Lollie Marsh, isn't it? Won't you come in?"

Lollie was hesitant.

"Yes," she said after awhile and they went upstairs together. "I'm very sorry I disturbed you, Miss White, but it is a matter which can't very well wait. You know that Mr. Stafford King has been kind to me?"

Maisie nodded. She was looking at the girl with interest and was surprised to note how pretty she was. She could not forget what Lollie Marsh had done for her that dreadful night at the nursing home, and if the truth be told, she had inspired the assistance which Stafford had been giving the girl.

"Mr. King has booked my passage to America, as you probably know," Lollie went on, "but at the last moment I have been obliged to change my plans."

"I'm sorry to hear that," said the girl. "I was hoping that you'd get away before –"

"I am hoping to get away before," Lollie smiled faintly. "But you see, one has to be very quick, because things are moving at such a rapid rate. They arrested Pinto tonight – we only just heard of it."

"Arrested Silva?" said the girl in surprise. "That is news to me. What is the charge?"

"I didn't quite understand what the charge was. I know he's arrested," said Lollie. "The colonel has advised me to get out as quickly as I can. And there's a big chance for me, Miss White. I'm going to be married!"

She blurted the words out, and Maisie stared at her. Somehow she had never thought of Lollie Marsh as a person who would get married, and it was amazing to see the confusion and shyness in which her confession had thrown her.

"I congratulate you with all my heart," said Maisie. "Who is the fortunate man?"

"I can't tell you. Yes, I will," said the girl. "I'll trust you. I'm marrying Jack Crewe."

"Crewe? I remember. Mr. King spoke about him. But isn't he one of the – isn't he a friend of the colonel?"

Lollie nodded.

"Yes, but we're going away tonight. That is why I came to see you."

Maisie White clasped the girl's hands in hers.

"You yourself are facing a great happiness and a beautiful life," pleaded Lollie, her eyes filling with tears. "Can't you feel some sympathy with me? For I want love and happiness and security more even than you, because you have never known anything of the dreadful apprehensions and uncertainties such as I have passed through. And I want you to help me in this. I'm not going to ask you to influence Mr. King to do anything but his duty. But I want just a chance for Jack."

Maisie shook her head.

"I don't know that I can promise that," she said. "Mr. King has always spoken of your friend as one of the least dangerous of the gang. When are you leaving?"

"Tonight."

"Tonight? But how?"

"That's a secret."

"But it is a secret I won't reveal," smiled Maisie.

"By airplane," said Lollie after a moment's hesitation, and told the story of Pinto's preparation.

"You'd better not tell me where you're going," warned Maisie, but she didn't stop Lollie in time. "Well, I wish you luck and I'll do my best for you." She stopped and kissed the girl.

"There's one warning I want to give you, Miss White," said Lollie as she stood in the doorway. "The colonel is a desperate man and I don't think somehow that he's coming through this with his life. He's been a good friend of mine up to a point and according to his lights, but you've been good and Mr. King has been more than good. Beware of the colonel now that you have him at bay! That is all!"

Then she was gone.

Chapter XXXVIII

A USE FOR OLD FILMS

They brought Pinto Silva into the magistrate's court at Bow Street the following morning in a condition of collapse. The man was dazed by his misfortune, incapable of answering the questions which were put to him, or even of instructing the exasperated solicitor who had been with him for an hour.

By the solicitor's side was a grey-faced, shrunken man, whose clothes did not seem to fit him and who at the end of the proceedings whispered something into the lawyer's ear. But the application which was made for bail was rejected. The evidence was too damning, and the knowledge that the prisoner was not English and that it would be impossible to extradite him if he managed to make his escape to certain countries, all helped to influence the magistrate in his refusal.

Colonel Boundary did not speak to the man in the dock or as much as look at him. He got out of court after the proceedings had terminated, the cynosure of every policeman's eye, and drove back to his apartments. He had not heard from Crewe or Lollie that morning and he guessed that the two had left by airplane. So he was alone, he thought, and the very knowledge had the effect of stiffening him.

He could go through the remainder of his papers at his leisure, without fear of interruption. The lesser members of the gang had been controlled by Selby or Crewe, and they would not approach him directly, but he did not doubt that there were a score of little men waiting to jump into the witness box the moment he was caught, but he had by no means given up hope of escaping.

For days he had carried in his pocket the means of disguise, a safety razor, scissors and a small bottle of annatto solution to darken his face.

Despite his sixty-one years, he was a healthy and virile man, capable of undergoing hardships if the necessity arose, but, above all, he had a plan and an alternative plan.

He finished the destruction of his correspondence, and then began to search his pocket for any stray letters which he might have put away absent-mindedly. In making this search he came upon a long, white envelope addressed to Crewe, and wondered how it had come into his possession. Then he remembered that Crewe had handed him a letter.

He looked at the postmark.

From Oxford.

This was the report of the agents whom Crewe had sent down to discover the names of the men who had left Balliol in a certain year. "Snow" Gregory, who had been found shot in the streets of London, was a Balliol man who had left Oxford in that year. It was certain that it was a relative of "Snow" Gregory who was called Jack o' Judgment and who had taken upon himself the task of avenging the man's death.

What was "Snow" Gregory's real name? If he could find that, he might find Jack o' Judgment.

Slowly, as though with a sense that the great discovery was imminent, he tore open the letter and pulled out the three foolscap pages, which, with a covering note, constituted the contents. There were two lists of names of graduates who had passed out in the year which, if "Snow" Gregory spoke the truth in a moment of unusual confidence, was the year of his leaving.

The colonel's finger traced the lines one by one and he finished the first list without discovering a name which was familiar. He was halfway through the second list when he stopped and his finger jumped. For fully three minutes he sat glaring at the paper open-mouthed. Then:

"Merciful God!" he whispered.

He sat there for the greater part of an hour, his chin on his hand, his eyes glued to the name. And all the time his active mind was running back through the years, piecing together the evidence which enabled him to identify, without any shadow of doubt, Jack o' Judgment.

He rose and went to his bookcase and took down volume after volume. They were mostly reference books, and for some time he searched in vain. Then he found a Year Book which gave him the data he wanted, and he brought it back to the table and scribbled a few notes. These he read through and carefully burned.

He finished his labors with a bright look in his eye and strutted into his bedroom ten years younger in appearance than he had been that afternoon. He put out all the lights and sat for a little while in the shadow of the curtain, watching the street from the open window. At the corner of the block a Salvation Army meeting was in progress, and he was surprised that he had not noticed the fact, although this practice of the Salvationists holding meetings near his flat had before now driven him to utter distraction.

Very keenly he scrutinized the street for some sign of a lurking figure, and once saw a man walk past under the light of a street lamp and melt into the shadow of a doorway on the opposite side of the road. He went into his bedroom and brought back a pair of night glasses, and focused them upon the figure.

He chuckled and went out of the flat into the street, turning southward.

He did not go far, however, before he stopped and looked back, and his patience was rewarded by the sight of a figure crossing the road and entering the building he had just left. The colonel gave him time, and then retraced his steps. He took off his boots in the vestibule and went upstairs quietly. He was halfway up when he heard the soft thud of his own door closing, and grinned again. He gave the intruder time to get inside before he too inserted his key, and turning it without a sound, came into the darkened hall. There was a light in his room, and he heard the sound of a drawer being pulled open. Then he gripped the handle, and, flinging the door open, stepped in. The man who was looking through the desk sprang up in affright.

As Boundary had suspected, it was his former butler, the man who had deserted him the day before without a word. He was a big, heavy-jowled man of powerful build, and the momentary look of fright melted to a leer at the sight of the colonel's face.

"Well, Tom," said Boundary pleasantly, "come back for the pickings?"

"Something like that, guv'nor," said the other. "You don't blame me?"

"I've been pretty good to you, Tom," said the colonel.

"Ugh! I don't know that I've anything to thank you for."

Here was a man who a month before would have cringed at the colonel's upraised finger!

"Oh, don't you, Tom?" said Boundary softly. "Come, come, that's not very grateful."

"What have I got to be grateful to you for?" demanded the man.

"Grateful that you're alive, Tom," said the colonel, and the servant's face went hard.

"None of that, colonel," he snarled; "you can't afford to talk 'fresh' with me. I know a great deal more about you than you suppose. You think I've got no brains."

"I know you have brains, Tom," said the colonel, "but you can't use 'em."

"Can't I, eh? I haven't been looking after you for four or five years and doing your dirty work, colonel, without picking up a little intelligence – and a little information! You'd look comic if they put me in the witness box!"

He was gaining courage at the very mildness of the man of whom he once stood in terror.

"So you've come for the pickings?" said the colonel, ignoring his threat. "Well, help yourself."

He went to the sideboard, poured himself out a little whisky and sat down by the window to watch the man search. Tom pulled open another drawer and closed it again.

"Now look here, colonel," he said, "I haven't made so much money out of this business as you have. Things are pretty bad with me, and I think the least you can do is to give me something to remember you by."

The colonel did not answer. Apparently his thoughts were wandering.

"Tom," he said after awhile, "do you remember three months ago I bought a lot of old cinema films?"

"Yes, I remember," said the man, surprised at the change of subject. "What's that to do with it?"

"There were about ten boxes, weren't there?"

"A dozen, more likely," said the man impatiently. "Now look here, colonel –"

"Wait a moment, Tom. I'll discuss your share when you've given me a little help. Meeting you here – by the way, I saw you out of the window, skulking on the other side of the street – has given me an idea. Where did you put those films?"

The man grinned.

"Are you starting a cinema, colonel?"

"Something like that," replied Boundary; "it was the Salvation Army that gave me the idea really. Do you hear what an infernal noise that drum makes?"

The man made a gesture of impatience.

"What is it you want?" he asked. "If you want the films, I put them in my pantry, underneath the silver cupboard. I suppose, now that the partnership's broken up, you don't object to me taking the silver? I might be starting a little house on my own."

"Certainly, certainly, you can take the silver," said the colonel genially. "Bring me the films."

The man was halfway out of the room when he turned round.

"No tricks, mind you," he said, "no doing funny business when my back's turned."

"I shall not move from the chair, Tom. You don't seem to trust me."

The ex-valet made two journeys before he deposited a dozen shallow tin boxes on the desk.

"There they are," he said, "now tell me what's the game."

"First of all," said the colonel, "were you serious when you suggested that you knew something about me that would be worth a lot to the police? There goes that drum again, Tom. Do you know what use that drum is to me?"

"I don't know," growled the man. "Of course I meant what I said – and what's this stuff about the drum?"

"Why, the people in the street can hear nothing when that's going," said the colonel softly.

He put his hand in the inside of his coat, as though searching for a pocketbook, and so quick was he that the man, leaning over the table, did not see the weapon that killed him. Three times the colonel fired and the man slid in an inert heap to the ground.

"Might as well be hung for a sheep as a lamb, Tom," said the colonel, replacing the weapon; and turning the body over, he took the scarf-pin from his own tie and fastened it in that of the dead man. Then he took his watch and chain from his pocket and slipped it in the waistcoat of the other. He had a signet ring on his little finger and this he transferred to the finger of the limp figure.

Then he began opening the boxes of old films and twined their contents about the floor, pinning them to the curtains, twining them about the legs of the chairs, all the time whistling the "Soldiers' Chorus." He found a candle in the butler's pantry and planted it with a steady hand in the heap of celluloid coils. This he lighted with great care and went out, closing the door softly behind him. Half an hour later, Albemarle Place was blocked with fire engines and a dozen hoses were playing in vain upon the roaring furnace behind the gutted walls of Colonel Dan Boundary's residence.

Stafford King was an early caller at Doughty Street, and Maisie knew, both by the unusual hour of the visit and by the gravity of the visitor, that something extraordinary had happened.

"Well, Maisie," he said, "there's the end of the Boundary Gang – the colonel is dead."

"Dead?" she said, open-eyed.

"We don't know what happened, but the theory is that he shot himself and set light to the house. The body was found in the ruins, and I was able to identify some of the jewelry – you remember the police had it when he was arrested, and we kept a special note of it for future reference."

She heaved a long sigh.

"That's over, at last; it is the end of a nightmare," she said, "a horrible, horrible nightmare. I wonder –"

"What do you wonder?"

"I wonder if this is also the end of Jack o' Judgment?" she asked. "Or whether he will continue working to bring to justice those people whom the law cannot touch."

"Heaven only knows," said Stafford, "but I'll admit that Jack o' Judgment has been a most useful person so far as we are concerned. We should never have collected Pinto or Selby, or even the colonel, but for Jack. By the way, there is no news of Crewe and the girl."

"I suppose they've reached their destination by now?" she asked.

"Oh, rather," said Stafford; "hours and days ago. Where were they going, by the way?"

She shook her head.

"I'm not going to tell you that."

"You needn't," smiled Stafford. "They've gone to Portugal. It was Pinto's machine and I don't suppose he had any other idea in the world than to get back to his own beloved land. By the way, Pinto looks like getting ten years. To satisfy myself in regard to Crewe, I telegraphed to an Englishman at Finisterre, who is a good friend of mine and who lives in a wild and isolated spot somewhere near the lighthouse, and he sent me back a message to the effect that an airplane passed over Finisterre yesterday afternoon soon after lunch time. That must be friend Lollie."

She nodded.

"Do you know, I hope they get away. Is that rather dreadful of me?" she said.

He shook his head.

"No, I don't think so. I believe the chief shares your hope. He has queer views on things, and they irritate me sometimes. For example, he doesn't think that the colonel is dead."

"But I thought you had found the body?"

"He gets over that by saying that it isn't the body," said Stafford with a little laugh of annoyance. "It rather worries you after you have decided that you've rounded up the gang. I still believe that it is the colonel."

She thought a moment.

"I am inclined to agree with Sir Stanley," said she. "It isn't the sort of thing that the colonel would do. Men like Colonel Boundary are never without hope."

Stafford scratched his head.

"Well, if it isn't the colonel, he's gone; and please the pigs, we'll never see him again! There is only the question of rounding up the little people of the gang, and that won't be much trouble."

She put both her hands on his shoulders and looked at him smilingly.

"You're an optimist, dear," she said.

"Who wouldn't be?" he replied cheerfully. "You said that when the gang was wound up we would drop our sad and lonely lives apart and form a little gang of our own."

She laughed and kissed him, and he went back to his office to find that his chief had already arrived and had asked for him. Sir Stanley was reading the morning paper when Stafford came into his room, and his first words brought consternation to the younger man.

"Stafford," he said, "this is not the body of the colonel. I've just been to see it and I'm certain. Now, you've got to send a call out to all stations throughout the country, particularly the south of England, to look for a man, possibly clean-shaven, certainly without moustaches, who will be disguised as a tramp."

"Why a tramp, sir?" asked Stafford with an heroic attempt to preserve an open mind on a subject where he had reached a definite decision.

"Fifteen years ago," replied Sir Stanley, "when the colonel did most of his own dirty work, it was his favorite disguise. Search the casual wards, the common lodging-houses and the prisons. It is just likely that the colonel will commit a small offence, with the object of getting himself three months in jail – there's no hiding place like jail, you know, Stafford. The real danger is that he may not actually tramp or assume the guise of the real low-down loafer. He may have the sense to become a poor but honest workman, traveling third-class from town to town in search of work. Then he will present the greatest difficulty." He saw the look of doubt on the young man's face and laughed.

"You think he's dead, don't you?" he said.

"I'm perfectly sure he is, sir," replied Stafford frankly.

"An optimist to the last," smiled Sir Stanley and dismissed him with a nod.

Later he was to come to Stafford's little bureau and tell him things which he did not know before. Then for the first time Stafford King discovered how closely his lackadaisical chief had followed the developments of the past few months. He learnt for the first time of the big part which Jack o' Judgment had played in the detection of the gang.

"He had an office under the colonel's flat," said Sir Stanley. "Apparently it was bought with no other object than to provide our friend with an opportunity of spying on the colonel. He discolored the wall, brought in his own workmen and in the colonel's absence – he was driven from the occupation of the room by the smell – he installed microphones. With the aid of these he was able to listen to all the conversation downstairs and sometimes to chime in. It was Jack o' Judgment who – well, perhaps I'd better not tell you that, because officially, I am not supposed to know it. At any rate, Stafford," he said more seriously, "we have seen the smashing of one of the most iniquitous, villainous gangs that ever existed. God knows how many broken hearts there are in England today, how many poor souls who have been brought to a suicide's grave through the machinations of Colonel Boundary and his tools. I do not think there has been a more immoral force in existence in our time, and I hope we shall never see its like again. You sent out the message?" he asked at parting.

"Yes, sir. I warned all stations and all chief constables."

"Good!" said Sir Stanley, and his last words were: "Don't forget – Boundary is not dead!"

Chapter XXXIX

JACK O' JUDGMENT REVEALED

A stoutish, grey-haired man descended from a third-class carriage at Chatham Station and inquired of a porter the way to the dockyard. He carried a lot of carpenter's tools in a straw bag and smoked a short clay pipe. The porter looked at the man with his white, stubby beard critically.

"Trying to get a job, mate?" he asked.

"Why, yes," said the man.

"How old might you be?" demanded the porter.

"Sixty-four," said the other, and the porter shook his head.

"You won't get work easy. They're not very keen on us old 'uns," he said. "Why don't you try at Markham's, the builders in the High Street?

They're short of men. I saw a notice outside their yard only this morning."

The workman thanked the porter, shouldered his basket and tramped down the High Street. He was respectably dressed, and policemen on the look-out for suspicious tramps did not give him a second glance. He spent the greater part of the day walking from yard to yard, everywhere receiving the same answer. Late in the afternoon he had better luck. A small firm of ship repairers were in want of a jobbing carpenter and put him to work at once.

It was many years since Colonel Boundary had wielded a saw, but he made a good showing. After two hours' work, however, his back was aching and his hands were sore. He was glad when the yard bell announced the hour for knocking off. He had yet to find lodgings, but this did not worry him. He was careful to avoid the cheaper kind of lodging-house, and went to one which catered for the artisan, where he could get a room of his own and a clean bed. He paid a deposit, washed himself and left his tools, then went out in search of some refreshment.

At seven o'clock the next morning he was back at the yard. He thought several times during the day that he would have to throw the work up. His back ached furiously, his arms were like lead. But he persevered, and again another day drew to a close. By the third day he had got his muscles into play and found the work easy. He was asked by the foreman if he would care to go into the country to work at a house that the head of the firm was building, but he declined. He wanted to remain in the town where there were crowds. At the end of the week came his great chance. He had been sent down to the docks to do some repairs on a small steamer and had pleased the skipper, who was himself an elderly man, by the ability he had shown.

"You're worth twice as much as some of these darned young 'uns," grumbled the old man. "Are you married?"

"No," said the other.

"Got any kids?"

Boundary shook his head.

"Why don't you sign on with me?" asked the skipper. "I want a carpenter bad."

"Where are you going?" asked Boundary, breathing more quickly.

"We're going to Valparaiso first, then we're going to work down the coast, round the Horn to San Francisco and maybe we'll get a cargo across to China."

"I'll think it over," said the colonel.

That night he called on the captain and told him that he had made up his mind to go.

"Good!" said the skipper, "but you'll have to sign on tonight. I'm leaving tomorrow by the first tide."

The colonel nodded, not daring to speak. Here was luck, the greatest in the world. Nobody would suspect a carpenter, taken from a local firm and shipped with the captain's goodwill. At seven o'clock the next morning he was standing on the deck of the *Arabelle Sands,* watching the low coast-line slipping past. The ship was to make one call at Falmouth and two days later she reached that port. Boundary went ashore to buy some wood and a few tools that he found he needed, and pulled back to the ship in the afternoon. In the evening he accompanied the captain ashore.

"We shan't leave till tomorrow at twelve," said the captain. "You might as well spend a night on solid earth whilst you can. It will be a long time before you smell dirt again."

The captain's idea of a pleasant evening was to sit in the bar-parlor of the Sun Inn and drink interminable hot rums. He had fixed up a room for himself at the inn and offered Boundary a share, but the colonel preferred to sleep alone. He secured lodgings in the town, and making an excuse to the captain returned to his room early. He had purchased all the newspapers he could find and he wanted to study them quietly. It was with unusual relish that he read the account of an inquest on himself. There was no breath of suspicion that he was not dead.

"Old Dan Boundary has tricked them all. Clever old Dan Boundary!"

He chuckled at the thought. He had deceived all those clever men at Scotland Yard – Sir Stanley Belcom, Stafford King, Jack o' Judgment! Yes, he had deceived Jack o' Judgment and that seemed the least believable part of the affair. All the rest of the gang were captured or fugitives. He wondered whether Lollie Marsh and Crewe had reached Portugal and what they were doing there and how long their money would last and how they would earn more. He had his own money well secured. He had managed to get together quite a respectable sum, for there were other banks than the Victoria and City – odd accounts in assumed names which he had drawn upon on the very day of his supposed death.

There was a tap at the door.

"Come in," said Boundary, thinking it was the landlady.

He was in the middle of the room as he spoke, and he went back step by step as the visitor entered. His tongue clave to the roof of his mouth, his eyes were starting out of his head.

"You! You!" he croaked.

"Little Jack o' Judgment," said the mask mockingly. "Poor old Jack! Come to take farewell of the colonel before he goes to foreign parts!"

"Stop!" cried Boundary hoarsely. "I know you, damn you! I know you!"

He pulled back the curtains and glared out of the window. There was no need to ask any further questions. The house was surrounded. He swung round again at his tormentor and faced the white mask in a blind fury of rage.

"You're clever, aren't you?" he said. "Cleverer than all the police! But you weren't clever enough to save your son from death!"

The masked figure reeled back.

"Ah, that's got you! Little Jack o' Judgment!" mocked the colonel. "That's got you where it hurts you most, hasn't it? Your only son, too! And he went to the devil all the faster because of me – me – me!" He struck his breast with his clenched fist. "You can't bring him back to life, can you? That's one I've got against you."

"No," said Jack o' Judgment in a low voice. "I cannot bring him back to life, but I can destroy the man who destroyed him, who blighted his young life, who taught him vicious practices, who sapped his vitality with drugs –"

"That's a lie!" said the colonel. "Crewe picked him up at Monte Carlo, when he was on his beam-ends."

"Who sent him to Monte Carlo?" asked the other. "Who was the gambler who brought him down, and received the wreck he had made with the pretence that he had never met him before? It was you, Boundary?"

The colonel nodded.

"I was a fool to deny it. I pretended to Crewe that I hadn't met him before. Yes, it was I, and I glory in it. You think you're going to pinch me, now, and put me where I belong – on the scaffold maybe. But you can never wipe that memory out of your mind, that you had a son who died in the gutter, that you're a childless old man who has no son to follow you!"

"I can't wipe that out!" said Jack o' Judgment. "O, God! I can't wipe that out!"

He raised his hand to his masked face as though to hide the picture which Boundary conjured up.

"But I can wipe you out," he said fiercely, "and I've given my life, my career, my reputation, all that I hold dear to get you! I've smashed your schemes, I've ruined you, even if I've ruined myself. They're waiting for you downstairs, Boundary. I told them to be here at this very minute. Stafford King –"

"You'll never see me taken," said Boundary.

Two shots rang out together, and the colonel sprawled back over the bed – dead.

Propped against the wall was Jack o' Judgment, and the hand that gripped his breast dripped red. They heard the shots outside and Stafford King was the first to enter the room. One glance at the colonel was sufficient, and then he turned to the figure who had slipped to the floor and was sitting with his back propped against the wall.

"Good God!" said Stafford. "Jack o' Judgment!"

"Poor old Jack!" said the mocking voice.

Stafford's arm was about his shoulder, and he laid the head gently back upon his bent knee. He lifted the mask gently and the light of the oil lamp which swung from the ceiling fell upon the white face.

"Sir Stanley Belcom! Sir Stanley!" he softly whispered.

Sir Stanley turned his head and opened his eyes. The old look of good-humor shone.

"Poor old Jack o' Judgment!" he mimicked. "This is going to be a first-class scandal, Stafford. For the sake of the service you ought to hush it up."

"But nobody need know, sir," said Stafford. "You can explain to the Home Secretary –"

Sir Stanley shook his head.

"I'm going to see a greater Home Secretary than ever lived in Whitehall," he said slowly. "I'm finished, Stafford. Strip this mummery from me, if you can."

With shaking hands Stafford King tore off the black cloak and flung it under the bed.

"Now," said Sir Stanley weakly, "you can introduce me to the provincial police as the head of our department and you can keep my secret, Stafford – if you will."

Stafford laid his hand upon Sir Stanley's.

"I told my solicitor," Sir Stanley spoke with difficulty, "to give you a letter in case – in case anything happened. I know I haven't played the game by the department. I ought to have resigned years ago when I found what had happened to my poor boy. I was Chief of Police in one of the provinces of India at the time, but they wouldn't let me go. I came to Scotland Yard and was promoted – no, I haven't played the game with the department. And yet perhaps I have."

He did not speak for some time.

His breathing was growing fainter and fainter, and when Stafford asked him, he said he was in no pain.

"I had to deceive you," he said after awhile. "I had to pretend that Jack o' Judgment called on me too. That was to take suspicion from your – Miss White," he smiled. "No, I haven't played the game. I stood for the law, and yet – I broke that gang, which the law could not touch. Yes, I broke them! I broke them!" he whispered. "If Boundary hadn't known me I should have been gone before you came and resigned tomorrow," he said, "but he must have discovered the boy's name. I wonder he hadn't tried before. I smashed them, didn't I, Stafford? It cost me thousands. I have committed almost every kind of crime – I burgled the diamondsmiths', but you must give me your word you will never tell. Phillopolis must suffer. They must all be punished."

Stafford had sent the police from the room, but the police-surgeon would not be denied. He had the sense to see that nothing could be done for the dying man, however, and that a change of position would probably hasten the end. He, too, went and left them alone.

"Stafford, I have quite a lot of money," said the First Commissioner; "it is yours. There's a will . . . yours. . . ."

Then he ceased to speak and Stafford thought that the end had come but did not dare move in case he were mistaken. After five minutes the man in his arms stirred slightly and his voice sounded strangely clear and strong.

"Gregory, my boy, good old Gregory! Father's here, old man!"

His voice died away to a rumble and then to a murmur.

The tears were running down Stafford's face. He sensed all the tragedy, all the loneliness of this man who had offered so cheerful a face to the world. Then Sir Stanley struggled to draw himself to his feet, and Stafford held him.

"Gently, sir, gently," he said, "you're only hurting yourself."

The dying man laughed. It was a little shrill chuckle of merriment and Stafford's blood ran cold.

"Here I am, poor old Jack o' Judgment! Little old Jack o' Judgment! Give me the lives you took and the hopes you've blasted. Give them to Jack . . . Jack o' Judgment!"

They were his last words.

A year later First Commissioner Sir Stafford King received a letter from South America. It contained nothing but the photograph of a very good-looking man, and a singularly pretty woman, who held in her lap a very tiny baby.

"Here is the last of the Boundary Gang," said Sir Stafford to Maisie. "It is the one happy ending that has emerged from so much misery and evil."

"Why, it is Lollie Marsh!"

"Lollie Crewe, I think her name is now," said Stafford. "It was queer how Sir Stanley recognized the only human members of the gang."

"Then they got away after all?" said the girl. "I've often wondered what happened at that aerodrome."

Stafford laughed.

"Oh, yes," he said dryly, "they got away. They left at twenty minutes past three, after a long argument with the aviator, a man named Cartwright."

"How do you know?" she asked.

"Sir Stanley and I watched them go off," said Stafford.

He looked at the photograph again and shook his head.

"There were times when the Judgment of Jack was very merciful," he said soberly.

The End

www.ingramcontent.com/pod-product-compliance
Lightning Source LLC
Chambersburg PA
CBHW030418310726
48979CB00007B/1102

* 9 7 8 1 6 0 6 6 4 8 7 8 0 *